"My brother has spent the past year and a half trapped in your horrid country."

Frustration ground across the edges of his words. "When I came to rescue him, the French guide I paid quite handsomely betrayed us. Now Westerfield might well be dying, and he needs help. What must I do to convince you to help us?"

"That man is your brother? The sick one with the wretched cough?"

He probably raised that arrogant eyebrow at her, except she couldn't see it in the black. "Does it make a difference?"

It didn't. Or rather, it shouldn't. But could she blame him for wanting to protect his family? "When you learned he fell ill, you came over from England solely to get him?"

"Again, why does it matter?" His voice was hard, as though he hadn't a drop of mercy anywhere inside his tall, lanky form.

"Because…because…" *Because I had an older brother once, and if he'd been trapped in your country, I would have done anything to save him.*

But Laurent wasn't trapped in England. He was dead.

Because of England.

Books by Naomi Rawlings

Love Inspired Historical

Sanctuary for a Lady
The Wyoming Heir
The Soldier's Secrets
Falling for the Enemy

NAOMI RAWLINGS

A mother of two young boys, Naomi Rawlings spends her days picking up, cleaning, playing and, of course, writing. Her husband pastors a small church in Michigan's rugged Upper Peninsula, where her family shares its ten wooded acres with black bears, wolves, coyotes, deer and bald eagles. Naomi and her family live only three miles from Lake Superior, and while the scenery is beautiful, the area averages two hundred inches of snow per winter. Naomi writes bold, dramatic stories containing passionate words and powerful journeys. If you enjoyed the novel, she would love to hear from you. You can write Naomi at P.O. Box 134, Ontonagon, MI 49953, or contact her via her website and blog, at www.naomirawlings.com.

Falling for the Enemy

NAOMI RAWLINGS

[signature: Naomi Rawlings]

H **HARLEQUIN**® LOVE INSPIRED® HISTORICAL

Recycling programs
for this product may
not exist in your area.

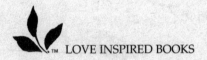 LOVE INSPIRED BOOKS

ISBN-13: 978-0-373-28296-8

Falling for the Enemy

www.Harlequin.com

Printed in U.S.A.

For there is neither Jew nor Greek, there is neither bond nor free, there is neither male nor female: for ye are all one in Christ Jesus.
—*Galatians* 3:28

Dedication

To my in-laws, George and Becky,
for raising a wonderful son and being awesome grandparents.

Acknowledgments

First and foremost, I'd like to thank my husband, Brian,
who loves and encourages me through each book I write.
Second, I'd like to thank my critique partner,
Melissa Jagears. My writing would suffer greatly without
your hard work and keen insights, and my heart would
suffer greatly without your friendship. Thank you for all the
hours of critiquing you poured into this story.

I also want to thank my agent, Natasha Kern,
for supporting me both professionally and personally.
Thank you to my editor, Elizabeth Mazer, for your helpful
suggestions and enthusiasm about my stories—and
especially for your love of all things French.

Beyond these people, numerous others
have given me support in one way or another:
Sally Chambers, Glenn Haggerty, Roseanna White
and Laurie Alice Eakes, to name a few.
Thank you all for your time and effort and
helping me to write the best books I possibly can.

Chapter One

Countryside of Ardennes, France
January 1805

Blackness pulsed around him, reaching its icy tentacles out to swirl about his feet and beneath his coat, up his torso until it nearly froze his skin. The tree branches clattered above, scrawny and bare of leaves as they scraped together like skeleton fingers. But Gregory Halston, third son of the sixth Marquess of Westerfield, remained still despite the foreboding sense that permeated the night, shrouding himself against a centuries-old oak as he stared at the fortified castle in the center of the field.

"Do you see them yet, Lord Gregory?"

"No."

But they had to be coming. Any moment now. Too much planning had gone into this night for something to go awry. The journey across the English Channel and a hostile country at war with his own, the exorbitant funds paid for a guide to lead them through a land that had been fighting for nearly a decade, an even larger sum paid to bribe a cook and a guard to sneak messages, ropes and a sack of supplies to a certain pair of prisoners inside.

The endeavor was worth every last guinea.

Or it would be, provided the plan worked.

"Shouldn't they have been here by now?" Farnsworth whispered. "And our guide has yet to arrive."

Gregory clamped his teeth together. While valets had their uses in London, bringing his on a trek across war-ravaged France wasn't one of his brightest ideas. "I realize that, thank you."

"Do you want me to check my timepiece?"

"As that would involve lighting a lantern and likely alerting the guards to our presence, no."

"I could always—"

"Farnsworth, stow it."

The man grunted, and Gregory blew a breath into the silence, keeping his eyes pinned on the shadowed castle. Four rectangular walls jutted toward the sky, with looming guard towers anchoring each corner and a moat surrounding the entire structure. As a fortress, it would have been impregnable. Now that it functioned as one of Napoleon's secret prisons, unauthorized entrance was utterly impossible.

What had his brother done to get himself jailed behind that massive stone edifice?

Gregory swallowed the lump forming in his throat. What Westerfield had done mattered little compared to getting him out. Unfortunately, Westerfield and his friend Kessler, the future Earl of Raleigh, had been imprisoned together, and rescuing one meant rescuing the other.

Gregory reached down and slid his palm slowly over the bullet scar in his thigh. He'd be happy to see his brother, yes. But as for the man who had faced him across a field at dawn nearly two years ago?

He would prefer to let him rot in prison.

"Do you think they had trouble deciphering the appointed time?" Farnsworth asked from beside him.

A trickle of apprehension started at the base of his neck and dripped down his spine. If only it was something so simple as a misread number. If only something hadn't gone wrong inside those castle walls.

"Perhaps they mistook your two for a three."

A dark blob, barely visible in the nighttime shadows, appeared through the opening of a second-story window, followed by a second blob.

The breath rushed from Gregory's lungs. They were coming. Everything was according to plan, just a bit late. In another moment their guide would arrive, and they could head across the hills and fields toward the coast, and then on to England.

He ran his eyes over the shadowed forms, now inching slowly down the wall with nothing but ropes to hold them. But there were only two. Where was the third? Had something happened to the guard who was supposed to escape with them, the one who had smuggled the black cloaks and ropes into the prison? The one that was supposed to "accidentally" drop a key when delivering food this night?

No, nothing could have happened to him. Westerfield and Kessler wouldn't be climbing down the castle wall if not for the guard, and the guard couldn't have changed his mind about the escape. Gregory had already paid the man half a fortune, and once he reached England, the information he could provide about Napoleon's police and secret prisons would net him another.

Perhaps the guard was one of the blobs and something had happened to Westerfield or Kessler.

Gregory tightened his hands into fists at his side. Just as long as his brother was one of the escaping forms. But with both men hidden beneath heavy cloaks as they inched down the dark castle wall, he couldn't distinguish which was Westerfield—if his brother was even there at all.

He slanted a glance at the nearest guard tower, where lanterns cast their narrow beams through the windows and into the field beyond. No call rang out from the guards. A few more moments, a silent swim across the little moat, and two men would be free.

Please, Father God, let Westerfield be one of them.

Just then a cough ricocheted against the quiet waters and one of the men slipped, dangling precariously from the rope.

A wave of ice swept through Gregory. He turned toward the tower. Had the guards heard? Surely they must have. A cough like that couldn't be ignored against such a silent night.

But no shout sounded from the tower, no extra lantern appeared at the window to better illuminate the out-of-doors. Nothing happened whatsoever.

Thank You, God.

The figure on the rope righted himself and climbed down the last few feet, slipping silently into the water. A moment later, the first escapee disappeared into the black depths.

"Stay here, Farnsworth." Wrapped in his own dark cloak, Gregory broke away from the line of trees and headed toward the moat. His breath puffed hot against the cool winter air as he stood exposed.

Half a minute passed, then another. He stared at the

calm surface of the water. How long did it take to swim a moat? Could something have happened underwater?

To both men, no less?

He wiped his damp palms on his thighs, though his gloves prevented the action from doing any good. This was something they hadn't taught him at Eton and Cambridge, how to enter a country he was at war with and effect a prison break. All those useless hours sitting in lectures, studying and writing essays, and for what? The two schools hadn't even taught him how to duel.

A head full of matted blond hair broke through the top of the water and heaved a gasp. Kessler.

Gregory's leg wound, though healed for over a year, smarted afresh. He crossed his arms over his chest. The rat could climb out of the moat on his own.

But Kessler didn't climb out, at least not immediately. Instead, he looked up, his face thin and drawn.

Gregory hardened his jaw. He'd known he'd see Kessler again, but it should have been in England surrounded by his family, not here on a field outside a prison in northern France. Not after he'd just helped the man who'd shot him to escape.

"Halston…" The world grew still around them, and even the lapping of the water seemed to cease, as though the air itself held its breath in anticipation of what Kessler might say.

Kessler stayed in the water, which had to be frigid given the cold January temperatures, and for a moment it seemed he decided to keep quiet. Then Kessler hefted himself onto the bank, the tendons in his emaciated hands and forearms stark even in the blackness. "I'm sorry."

The breath exploded from Gregory's lungs. His

wound had become so infected he'd almost died. What was he supposed to do with an apology?

A small splash rippled the water, and he tore his gaze away from Kessler to the dark head full of shaggy hair surfacing at his feet.

"Westerfield." The name felt odd on his tongue. His brother had been a mere heir to the Marquess of Westerfield when he'd entered France during a short-lived period of peace all those months ago. Now he was the marquess himself, and their father—the man the world had once called Westerfield—was dead.

Gregory held out a hand to pull Westerfield from the water.

The palm that reached up to wrap around him was naught but bones, with a grip so weak a child could break it. What had these despicable Frenchmen done to his once-strong brother?

Gregory hauled Westerfield out of the moat and wrapped his arms around him. Never mind that the embrace soaked his cloak and shirt. Never mind that they hadn't time for such things until they were at least shrouded in the shelter of the trees.

A horrid stench rose up around him, sour and reeking of urine and vermin. He nearly broke his hold, would have, except Westerfield's gaunt hand had only been the beginning of the horrid discovery. The man was so thin he might well be more corpse than human.

"Did they feed you?"

"On occasion." The rasp in his brother's words made the once-familiar voice barely recognizable. Westerfield sagged into him, as though too weak to stand on his own. Then a cough racked his chest, ringing out over the water and up the castle walls.

"Get him to the trees," Kessler murmured. "You can greet each other there."

Gregory wrapped his arms tighter around Westerfield, bracing him more than hugging him. Was his brother ill? That hadn't been reported. The guard had claimed Westerfield and Kessler were both in excellent health.

Gregory looked at Kessler. Though the man stood covered in a sopping black cloak, 'twas plain from his pronounced cheekbones and the drawn way his skin sank into his face that he'd fared little better than Westerfield. "There's only the two of you?"

Kessler frowned. "Yes. Were there supposed to be more?"

"I arranged for three escapes, the last was supposed to be the…"

A lantern appeared in one of the lower castle windows, voices carrying across the moat.

"Could there have been an escape?"

Despite Gregory's rather basic understanding of French, the meaning of the words was clear enough.

"*Non.* No escape, not here!"

"One of the cells below is empty."

"I know nothing of it."

"Wake the guards, and search the castle. The men couldn't have gotten outside these walls."

"What if they did?"

"We must hasten," Kessler growled quietly, then wrapped an arm beneath one of Westerfield's shoulders.

They scrambled toward the trees together, stopping only when they met Farnsworth. But the tree line could offer only momentary respite. They needed to get away, yet the guard hadn't made the escape, and their French guide was still missing.

Westerfield coughed again, the bone-deep sound jarring against the otherwise still night. "Slower next time."

A call rang out from somewhere inside the towering stone walls of the castle, followed by an echo in response. Gregory didn't look back to see whether more lanterns had appeared in the windows, but he could well guess the next cry before it left the mouth of a distant guard.

"Escape!"

The shout reverberated across the field and bounced against the trees.

A cold dread filled his chest. They'd been betrayed.

And stranded.

In the middle of France.

At the center of a war.

He glanced briefly around his group. Four men, all unmistakably English. Their clothing and coin might be French, but their tongues were English. They could manage to speak some French between them, yes, but not without accents.

By this time tomorrow night, they'd all be rotting inside a dark French dungeon, and something told him their new home was going to make the horrors his brother and Kessler had endured look trivial in comparison.

Danielle Belanger crouched beside the campfire and laid another stick on the licking flames, then sighed.

Another task failed.

Oh, she'd been sent to Reims to visit with her aunt, true. And the visit had gone rather well. Her mother's sister was kind, generous, well respected…

And had tried introducing her to every decent, un-married man in the city.

Those meetings had turned out about as well as all her introductions to men in her hometown of Abbeville.

Two and twenty years of age, and no one wanted to marry her.

Not that she wanted to marry any of them, but most girls four years her younger were happily married and bearing babes. Shouldn't she have had at least *one* marriage proposal by now?

Or rather, she'd had one, she supposed.

Well, more like a dozen. But none of them from men any sane woman would marry. Perhaps if she was blind and docile and preferred spending her days mucking stalls and spinning yarn, she could be happily married. But she certainly didn't take to mucking stalls—they stank too much. Or spinning yarn—one had to sit far too still to manage such a task. She wasn't blind, and as for the docile part, well…

"I could only get one." Serge, her younger brother by six years, emerged from the tangle of trees and shrubs lining the creek. A squirrel dangled from his hand by the tail.

She rolled her eyes. "Go back for another, then." He held out the squirrel for her to take. She merely crossed her arms. "*Papa* said you need to practice."

"Come on, Dani. You can have it skinned in half the time."

Which was likely why her younger brother had reached sixteen and was the slowest animal skinner in all of Abbeville.

"I caught and cleaned the rabbit last night. It's your turn." She eyed the bloodied animal, a large stab wound gaping in its chest. "And you've little choice about going back for more. Mayhap we could have shared just the one had your blade hit between the eyes. But knifing it in the chest like that, you lost too much meat."

Which her brother should have known.

Maybe he wasn't just the worst in Abbeville at handling a knife. He had to be the most inept in all of northern France.

She pushed up from her crouched position by the fire and stood, stretching her back before turning to head upstream.

"Where are you going?" Serge called after her.

"To look for berries."

"In January?"

She shrugged. So mayhap she wouldn't happen upon berries, but she might find some burdock or cattail root to dig. Anything to get her away from the fire. If she lingered there, she'd end up doing all Serge's work, and she could hardly sit still long enough for him to find another squirrel.

He likely wouldn't return until after dark, the dunce.

She made her way along the water, sluggish from the coolness of winter, but not frigid enough to turn to ice. Leafless brambles and shrubs sprang from soil still damp from yesterday's rain. She shivered inside her cloak and glanced up at the gray sky through the tree branches above. Home would be more temperate than this, near enough the channel's warm waters to drive winter's chill away.

Something rustled ahead, then a rabbit scampered out from beneath a bush and darted toward a little thicket. Within half a second, she had her blade in hand, her fingers gripping the familiar leather handle. One throw, quick as lightning and silent as a snake, and she'd have their supper.

Except *Papa* had all but commanded she let Serge do the hunting on their trip, saying he had to learn sometime. And she'd done most of the hunting on the way to Reims, then yesterday, on the first day of their journey, she'd killed a rabbit.

She was going to be good and obedient—for perhaps the third or fourth time in her life—and let Serge do tonight's hunting. She sighed, her grip loosening on the knife.

As though sensing the sudden lack of danger, the rabbit stopped and turned, sniffing the air before staring straight at her.

Too easy a kill to bother with now anyway. What was the fun of throwing a knife when her target was still rather than moving? She bent and slipped her blade back against her ankle and continued down the little stream, winding her way deeper into the woods.

She could almost see the resigned look in *Maman*'s eyes and hear her exasperated sigh when *Maman* realized her eldest daughter had returned to Abbeville husbandless. Two towns, with a suitable groom yet to be found. Two! *Papa* claimed God had a plan for her. That she only needed to wait on Him, and everything would fall into place.

Evidently *Papa* didn't understand how hard it was for her to wait for anything—let alone for God, Whom she couldn't see or touch.

As though waiting for the right man to happen along hadn't already taken long enough.

A rustling sounded from the trees behind her. Likely another rabbit. But no, the noise was too loud for such a small animal. A fox, perhaps?

She stilled until only the trickle of the creek over rocks and the tapping of tree branches in the wind filled her ears. Another sound, deep and rich, carried on the faint breeze.

A distant, undeniably male voice.

She reached for the knife strapped at her ankle once more, then straightened, stepping stealthily around twigs and through a tangle of saplings.

Probably not anyone to worry about. Just another traveling party stopped to make use of the stream.

Except they were settled awfully deep into the woods to be merely traveling.

Then again, she was nestled rather deeply into the woods, as well. But the trees provided ample opportunity to find game, and with only her and Serge, she didn't want to invite trouble. She could defend herself well enough, 'twas true, but she wasn't going to seek disquiet, either.

A different person would probably turn around and head back to the campsite, pack up and move another kilometer downstream before settling in for the night. That would certainly be the safe thing to do. The predictable, normal, safe thing.

But then she wouldn't know who the travelers were, whether they posed a threat.

She crept closer to the voices. The cadences were low, all male but slightly different. She slipped silently between two shrubs, years of moving quietly through the woods while hunting with *Papa* aiding her stealth. She only needed to creep a bit closer.

Something about the voices didn't sit right. The intonation seemed off, rough and coarse, without the gentle roll of French off one's tongue. Perhaps if she overheard a word or two, she could better understand why they were camped so obscurely. The men could be anyone from gendarmes to army deserters to thieves.

Or they could be normal travelers having just left Reims and heading toward the coast like her and Serge.

Either way, she needed to know.

She crouched lower and inched forward. Something moved ahead, a flash of cream on the other side of the brambles. Then a cough sounded, loud and harsh and from deep within the chest.

Whoever made up this party, one of their members seemed not much longer for this world.

A gruff voice filled the air. "I still say we're better to travel during the day."

The breath in her lungs turned to ice. She couldn't have heard right. No. Certainly not. It almost sounded as if they spoke…

"He's right," another man rasped, followed by a small cough. "We can't travel at night. We hardly know which way to go during the day. We'd be lost within a matter of hours."

English.

She swallowed against her suddenly dry throat. That vile country's navy had killed her older brother. If she never saw another Englishman or heard the language spoken again, she'd be happy, indeed.

But what were a band of Englishmen doing here?

She squeezed her eyes shut. No. Never mind. She didn't want to know.

Definitely didn't want to know.

Most assuredly didn't want to know.

She simply needed to get herself and her younger brother away from this place.

She began to back away as stealthily as she'd crept up. Except, with her hands shaking and her heartbeat thudding wildly in her ears, she wasn't stealthy at all. Clumsy, more like. Her foot cracked a dried twig, and her cloak brushed against the brambles. She paused for a moment. Had they heard?

"We're lost now." A third voice, higher pitched than the first two and with a hint of intelligence behind his words, spoke.

She let out a silent breath. They'd noticed nothing. Now she need only move quietly—because she could be quiet if she didn't let panic get the better of her—back through the brambles. Then she'd find Serge, and they'd pack up camp. Dinner could be some of the salt pork and bread they carried. No need for freshly roasted squirrel now, not when they had to find a gendarmerie post and report the Englishmen.

Because Englishmen traveling through France during the middle of a war could only be spies.

What secrets would these men impart to the British government if they reached the coast and no one stopped them? She was glad they were lost. They could walk around in circles for the next week.

Except by then, she'd have found that gendarmerie post and explained everything. A week hence, those British spies would be moldering in some nameless dungeon, likely being tortured and pouring forth whatever secrets they'd discovered about her country.

Which was exactly what they deserved.

But first she had to get away without anyone noticing.

"What do you want us to do? Stop and ask for directions?" The third, intelligent-sounding voice dripped with sarcasm. "Or perhaps a map? I'm sure there's a very welcoming gendarmerie station along the road to Saint-Quentin. We need only present ourselves and say, 'Good day, sirs. Could you tell me the quickest way from here to the channel? You see, I've two es—"

Something crashed in the woods behind her. Danielle whirled, the leather handle of her knife clamped tightly between her fingers. But too late. A male body slammed into her from the side and crashed her to the ground.

Shrubs scratched her arms and tore at her cloak as the man rolled himself over her. She fought as he struggled to sit up while holding her to the ground. He wasn't overlarge or terribly strong, but he plunked himself down directly atop her while trapping the forearm that held her knife beneath his knee. If she could only find some way to upend him...

"Come quickly! I've found a spy."

A spy? *Her?*

She wasn't a spy. She was just...well, spying, but not for the reason they thought. *They* were the spies, and she'd only wanted to make certain she and Serge were safe from the men camped so close to their own site.

Or rather, that's all she'd wanted to do until she'd discovered the mysterious men were English.

"What's that you say?" The English voices grew closer and footsteps thudded on the muddy ground.

"You found someone?"

If she was going to get free, she had to do so quickly. She'd not lie there docilely while men from the same country that had killed Laurent attempted to capture her. She brought her knee up, trying to uproot the oaf's bottom. The man only gripped her shoulders and pressed her harder against the damp earth. She twisted and turned, but his weight made it difficult to suck in air and his knee still pinned her knife hand.

"She was watching from the bushes," her captor explained. "I wouldn't have spotted her except she started moving as I was coming up from the stream with the water."

Danielle pressed her eyes shut and stifled a groan. She should have considered someone might be at the stream, should have thought to scout the area before she'd even started into the bushes. Instead, she'd turned into a complete and total idiot at the sound of one simple phrase in English.

"What's your name?" the intelligent voice asked in English.

She opened her eyes and stared at the tall form above her, with tousled dark brown hair, an arrogant, aristocratic nose, and eyes the color of fog over the ocean. Not quite gray but not quite blue, and just mysterious enough one might stare into them a bit too long, trying to understand—

"Her name matters not," a deeper voice snapped. "How much did she overhear?" Another man appeared above her, leaner and taller than the first, with a face so thin and wan the bones seemed to jut from it. His hands appeared just as bony, as though he hadn't had a good meal in the past half decade. But his emaciated body didn't stop his shrewd green eyes from narrowing at her.

She licked her lips. What should she tell them? She hadn't overheard much beyond that they were lost and debating when to travel. Could she pretend as though she didn't know English and hadn't understood a word? They had little reason to suspect a woman such as her would know their language.

And even if she wanted to answer their questions, she couldn't manage to speak more than a word or two with an English ignoramus sitting atop her stomach and squishing the air from her body.

"I daresay she didn't overhear anything," the raspy voice spoke from the other side of the brambles. Then that horrid coughing filled the air again.

"A woman like her isn't going to know English," the dunce atop her proclaimed. At least he was useful for something besides squishing the breath from her body. "Lord Westerfield is right."

Lord Westerfield? She nearly groaned, would have if she possessed the ability to breathe.

She moved her gaze between the two men standing above her, their patrician noses and arrogant bearings suddenly more than mere circumstance. As if finding regular Englishmen hiding in the woods wasn't trouble enough. She'd somehow stumbled into a nest of aristocrats.

Just her luck.

"Try in French, Halston." The thin blond man nudged the darker haired one—Halston, evidently.

Halston scowled at the other man. "You try in French. You're the one who's spent the past year and a half in this wretched country."

"The only French I found use for were curses. The rest of the language I'd like to forget as quickly as possible."

Danielle bit the side of her lip. This was probably supposed to be the moment she turned grateful for all those horrid English lessons her mother had forced upon her while growing up.

Except she still didn't feel all that grateful—though it was rather helpful to know what they were saying instead of being left to guess their intent.

And now that she had a moment to consider, she'd best not speak in English. She might lay pinned beneath a wiry man who felt far heavier than he looked, but she still had two things to her advantage. First, her captors didn't realize she understood their words, and second, they didn't know about Serge.

If she managed nothing else from this debacle, she would at least keep them from learning of her brother.

"Stand her up, Farnsworth. Let's have a look at her," the blond commanded.

"She's a person, Kessler, not some dog," Halston growled.

The two men stared at each other, the air between them igniting like the sudden spark of a flintlock. Then Kessler turned away and the man atop her began to rise.

She tightened the grip on her knife, waiting for the perfect moment...

Chapter Two

Gregory had never seen anything more astounding. One second the woman was lying docilely beneath Farnsworth's hold, and the next she'd reversed their positions, flipping his valet to the ground and sitting atop him, a knife pressed to his throat.

"Come any closer, and your servant dies." The woman spoke in a calm, controlled voice, and judging by the fierce look etched across her face, she wasn't bluffing. The French words fell comfortably off her tongue, only confirming what they'd already suspected. She knew not a lick of English.

Something sick rolled through his stomach. Why had he brought Farnsworth on this wretched journey in the first place? As though endangering himself, his brother and Kessler wasn't enough.

He took a step closer to the woman, but her grip on the knife only tightened and her lips pressed into a thin white line. How was he supposed to get her off Farnsworth if she wouldn't even let him approach?

"Lord Gregory," Farnsworth gasped, evidently not minding moving his throat to speak despite the wicked-looking blade pressed against it. "I could use a little help here, if you don't mind. Perhaps you might find my service to you worth a guinea or two and be willing to—"

"Silence!" the woman snapped.

Though the pronunciation in French was quite different from English, Gregory had no trouble recognizing the word.

He reached into his pocket and fished out two napoleons, speaking to Kessler without taking his eyes off the woman. "We can let her go." Once he convinced her to leave Farnsworth unharmed, that was. "She couldn't have understood what we were saying."

"No, but she likely understands we're English." Kessler tilted his nose down at the woman. "Where do you think she'll head the moment we free her?"

Of course Kessler would have to argue with him. Though he did agree on one point: the woman was trouble, plain as day, with all that thick black hair ready to tumble from beneath her mobcap, those sharp blue eyes, quick reflexes…

And the blade.

She'd lain meekly under Farnsworth the entire time they talked about her, and somehow they'd all missed she had a blade. "Ah, shouldn't we be more concerned about her freeing Farnsworth at the moment than us freeing her?"

Kessler waved his hand absently in the air. "She's only a wench. Surely she can't hold him for more than a minute or two, and then we'll need to know what to do with her."

True, they needed a plan for after she released Farnsworth, but first and foremost, they needed to get that knife away from her and his valet off the ground.

"Excusez moi." He stepped closer to the woman, the rusted French bumbling over his tongue. He cringed a

bit, and a trace of a smile curved the woman's lips. But at least she didn't press the knife closer to Farnsworth's throat. "I give you my word that we won't hurt you, but we have a few questions."

Kessler made a disapproving sound, but what did he expect the woman to be told? That they wouldn't let her go? They'd have to eventually. They could hardly cart another person all the way to the coast just to make certain she didn't run off and inform the gendarmes of their whereabouts. A napoleon or two would likely keep her silence for the next half century.

"Leave it be, Kessler," Westerfield said from where he lay on his blankets, his weak voice ten times more alarming than finding a woman spying on them through the bushes. Though if Gregory had to pick between some foul lung disease or a half-crazed Frenchwoman holding a knife to his neck, he might just pick the lung disease.

"You can't truly think the girl will keep quiet," Kessler protested, but he'd turned to face Westerfield, the rigidness leaving his shoulders like it did whenever the man was around his brother.

"Just watch." Gregory crouched down, meeting the woman's eyes. Eyes that were too blue in a face that was smooth and perfect as porcelain. She looked like some Celtic warrior sitting atop Farnsworth, the knife still gripped in her hand. She wasn't the typical English rose, but if a woman of her beauty entered a ballroom in London, she would have half-a-dozen suitors come morning.

Except first she needed the wealth and position that would place her in a London ballroom. Her presence in the woods, coupled with her rough brown coat, indicated she had neither.

He held up the two coins in his hand. "I'll give you two napoleons. One if you put that knife away, and another if you don't tell anyone we were here. We'll be gone in the morning and won't be back. Agreed?"

The woman's chin came up. "I don't want your filthy coin."

He slipped the French coins back into his pocket, took out two guineas and extended his hand. "Guineas, then."

She spit into the dirt at his feet. "As if filthy, English money will do more to change my mind."

He raised an eyebrow at that. His "filthy English money" was gold, like the napoleons, but the British currency was far more stable than the French, which was why he carried both with him.

"Are there any others in your traveling party?" Kessler snapped in a French accent not nearly as horrid as Gregory's. The liar.

The defiant look left the woman's face, and her eyes skittered wildly to the left then right. She drew her knife away from Farnsworth a fraction of an inch and sucked in a deep breath.

He sensed her plan an instant before she moved. She loosed a bloodcurdling scream and heaved herself off Farnsworth, bolting into the brush and vanishing even quicker than she'd first appeared.

Gregory instantly moved toward the creek. He lengthened his gait, one stride then two, nearly close enough to catch her. "Stop."

She sprang lithely through the brambles, then darted around a dead log and between two saplings, quick as a pickpocket running through London alleys. If not for his guessing her escape, she'd have been gone.

"Stop!" he tried again.

She didn't even look back, just kept running.

He pumped his legs harder. A thick stand of fir trees loomed ahead, its shadows black in the growing darkness. If she made it into the dense branches, he'd never find her. Yet she was only a few steps ahead of him. He couldn't reach her with his arms, but would likely fell her if he lunged.

He grimaced at the thought of crashing to the ground, as she'd just held a knife to his valet's throat. What else was he to do? He drew in a breath, readied his legs, braced himself for the pain of landing on the forest floor...

And dove.

His hands felt only the fabric of her skirts as he fell. He stretched farther as he collided with the dirt, finally gripping a limb beneath the layers of cloth. One hard yank, and the woman squealed. Then she crashed in front of him, landing in earth still soft from yesterday's rain.

She rolled quickly onto her back, but he kept hold of her ankle—which she attempted to kick furiously at his head.

"Be still," he gritted in English.

She only fought harder, as though his words, which she couldn't understand, had somehow incensed her.

He climbed closer, resting his weight on her legs until she was forced to stop kicking. Only then did he see why she struggled so hard. Her knife lay on the ground an arm's length in front of her.

"Farnsworth, Kessler," he called, then frowned. Was he really about to ask the man who'd shot him in the leg for help?

One way or another, this trip was going to be the death of him.

"Over here," he shouted a bit louder. "I need some... help."

It was galling to admit, both because Kessler would be involved in the helping, and because his opponent was a woman. Yet he couldn't keep her still enough to—

A sharp slice of pain seared his cheek, followed by a screeching, *"Non!"*

Teach him to not watch her wolfishly quick hands. He reached up to grasp the woman's wrist before she could withdraw it and stared down at her bloody nails while his cheek throbbed wildly. Blast, but that was going to leave a nice wound.

"Let me go. I know nothing," she spit out in French.

But she did know something. Otherwise, she wouldn't be struggling so hard to free herself. Otherwise, she would have taken his guineas.

Footfalls sounded, and a moment later Kessler's and Farnsworth's boots appeared on the ground beside him. "Someone get the knife."

Kessler headed toward the blade while Farnsworth hunkered down and grasped the woman's free arm.

"You're bleeding, Lord Gregory."

As though he hadn't noticed. He would have rolled his eyes if he wasn't so busy stilling the woman's legs as she tried to knee him in the stomach yet again. Instead, he wiped his bleeding cheek against the shoulder of his shirt.

Farnsworth clucked his tongue "And you're rather a mess."

That he was, covered in mud from ankles to shoulders. Even now cold dampness seeped through his clothing around his knees.

"Perhaps, but I have the girl." Which ought to count for something.

Kessler returned, knife in hand.

"Hold her other arm while I get up."

Kessler shoved the knife into a pocket of his great-coat and came near enough to take the woman's shoulder opposite Farnsworth. Gregory rolled away from her legs quickly enough so as not to get himself kicked—though she tried, the hoyden.

He stood while Kessler and Farnsworth hauled her up. Two men to hold one woman, and still she looked around as though planning another escape attempt. Then her gaze landed on the hilt of her knife peeking from Kessler's pocket.

Gregory sprang forward and wrenched the blade away an instant before the woman's hand touched the spot where the hilt had rested.

Her lips curled into a snarl.

He took a step back lest she attempt to swipe the blade from his hold. Instead she jerked hard on the shoulder Kessler held, forcing his hand to slip an inch.

"Hold still, wench, or we'll use that knife on you," Kessler snapped in French.

The woman stilled, panic flashing through her eyes for the briefest of instants before she masked it.

What was he going to do with her? Her hair had come completely free of her cap and hung wildly about her shoulders with thick clumps of mud matted in the riotous mess. More mud splattered her dress, starting at the hem and working up her body. And from how she'd lain on the ground earlier, the back of her dress was probably soaked through and caked with mud as well.

Yet somehow, despite her filth and bedraggled state, she was magnificent.

And here he'd thought Joan of Arc had been burned at the stake several centuries past. Surely the woman before him could lead an army into battle just as well as the legendary heroine.

"Before you ran, I asked who you traveled with." He spoke slowly in French, so she wouldn't mistake a single word of his statement

Her nose came up and her jaw hardened, yet she met his gaze with her icy, sky-blue eyes. Once again, she resembled the ancient woman warrior who had defied the English even when facing death.

"Answer me. Who else is with you?"

Silence permeated the forest, the faint trickle of the creek and the occasional tapping of tree branches in the breeze the only sounds surrounding them.

"Perhaps she travels alone, sir." Farnsworth shifted his weight beside the woman. "Or perhaps she doesn't understand your question."

Oh, she knew what he asked, all right. Knew more than she was willing to admit.

"Hold the knife to her throat," Kessler commanded. "She'll talk then."

Gregory ground his teeth together. The man had shot him in the leg, fled the country and then found himself in a French prison for sixteen months…and still failed to learn that violence seldom solved one's problems. "I promised not to harm her."

Though that had been before she'd fled into the woods, rolled around in the mud with him and scratched his cheek.

Kessler arched an eyebrow. "How else do you plan to force answers? She's not volunteering any."

He glanced at the woman's throat, slim and creamy beneath the mud that splattered it. Unfortunately, Kessler had a point.

And what kind of barbarian had this journey turned him into that he considered holding a knife on a woman?

"No. There's another way." He gestured in her direction, though she'd remained curiously still ever since Kessler had threatened to use the knife on her. "This is no fool lass. When she reached the creek, she headed upstream, which means her traveling party must be downstream. We only need to find them."

The woman jerked against Kessler's and Farnsworth's holds, forcing the two men to grapple for a better grip on her shoulders. Slight though she was, restraining a woman wasn't exactly an everyday task valets and future earls performed in England.

France, on the other hand, was proving to be quite different.

A torrent of French words poured from her mouth. Most of them came too fast for him to understand, though he caught something about how she'd sit down and talk with them now.

Finally.

"Do you remember those napoleons I showed you earlier?" He spoke haltingly as he approached her. "I have more, but you need to be silent first."

Her body grew still though her chest heaved from spent exertion. She tossed her head backward, likely trying to dislodge the mess of hair that had fallen over her face to hide her eyes.

Kessler and Farnsworth hardened their holds on her shoulders, but Gregory stepped forward and reached out a hand, smoothing the tangled hair away from her cheek and back over her shoulder. Frightened blue eyes came up to meet his, and he paused, his hand resting on her shoulder. He'd thought her beautiful before, but he'd underestimated. Her skin wasn't just creamy, but as soft as a daffodil's petals during spring. Her hair not merely long and wavy, but as rich as velvet. And those eyes…they appeared a light, icy-blue at first, but when standing this close, darker streaks flared through the lighter blue like little starbursts before they rimmed her irises. Irises that still held a muted look of fear.

Fear he'd put there.

"A comely thing, isn't she?" Kessler smirked.

Gregory dropped his hand, took an abrupt step back and blew out a breath. What was he thinking touching a woman's hair in such an intimate manner, letting his hand linger on her shoulder? He'd never behaved so forwardly in his life. Then again, save for his mother and sister, he'd never seen a grown woman's hair down, either.

"You're not to touch her, Kessler."

The man stared pointedly at where his hands gripped her shoulder and upper arm. "No?"

A sudden bout of memories flashed through his mind. Suzanna's hunched shoulders and tearstained face on that dark night. The quiet field outside their country estate at dawn. The searing pain in his leg as a bullet lodged itself beside the bone. As a simple serving girl on his family's estate, Suzanna had never shown this woman's fiery determination, nor was she as beautiful, but the situation was far too similar. He cleared his throat. "You know to what I refer."

All color had fled the lord's face, leaving it pale and drawn. Kessler's memories must have traveled to the same place as his own.

Good. Perchance those memories would help Kessler behave around the Frenchwoman.

"Then what do you propose we do with the wench? We certainly can't free her."

"The first thing we're going to do is check on Westerfield." Who'd been left untended for far too long. "Then we're going to find her traveling party."

Which would hopefully provide him with some answers. Because night was falling, and he still hadn't a clue what to do with her.

Danielle stumbled down onto the makeshift pallet where Farnsworth and Kessler thrust her. As if the English capturing the frigate where Laurent served and killing him hadn't been enough, now some English had captured her and were about to take Serge, as well.

Kessler knelt down to hold her in place then growled something unintelligible at Farnsworth. The servant walked stiffly away, back straight and posture perfect as he found a sack and rummaged through it. He started back for them, a length of thick rope in his hands.

"Non!" She attempted to pull away from Kessler, but the arrogant blond only clenched her arms harder.

"Quickly," he boomed at the servant.

"Please don't tie me. I promise I won't run." And she wouldn't, not when the men were planning to find Serge and bring him here. It would be easier to meet him in the English camp and then plan their escape. If she managed to free herself now, she'd not have time to find her brother and pack before the Englishmen were upon them. Better to wait and then run while everyone else slept.

But she wouldn't be able to escape if they tied her.

The servant knelt beside her and held the rope out to Kessler.

"You should have considered how we might deal with you before you held a knife to Farnsworth's neck." Kessler's cruel words bored into the back of her head.

"*Non.* Please…" She swallowed against the panic creeping into her voice, but that didn't stop the hot burn of tears from rising in her eyes.

"Stop." Halston's stern voice carried from the other side of the fire, where he sat watching her from beside the sick man's pallet. "Don't tie her."

"We haven't a choice." Kessler took the rope from Farnsworth, his grip leaving her for the barest of moments.

She used that instant to roll away. "I won't run. You have to believe me."

She sought Halston's eyes over the orange flicker of flames. He might be the one who had thwarted her escape, but he also seemed the most inclined to be merciful.

"You held a knife to my valet's throat, then ran through the woods like a madwoman." His gray-blue eyes locked with hers. "Why should I trust you?"

She bowed her head, letting the fight drain from her body. Why indeed? "I promise."

Halston stood and came around the fire, the small muscle along the side of his jaw working back and forth. "Fine. But run again and you *will* be tied."

Kessler stood. "You're a fool, Halston," he muttered in English, obviously still not comprehending that she could understand their conversation. "A pretty woman does naught but bat her eyes, and you believe anything she says."

"Just look at her. She's so frightened she's trembling."

Danielle glanced down at her hands, which unfortunately were shaking, and tucked them under her arms.

"Maybe leaving her unrestrained makes me a fool, but at least I'm not an ogre," Halston retorted.

The air between the two men sparked again, an angry exchange that she didn't begin to understand.

"Watch her closely." Kessler jutted his chin toward her. "If she flees, it's on you."

"Seeing how you're free at this moment because I rescued you, I don't think asking you to trust me is too big a request."

Free? Danielle looked between the two men. Free from what? The most obvious answer was prison. Had one of them been imprisoned for spying? Were they prison escapees as well as spies?

"How easily you forget." Kessler's eyes shot tiny sparks at Halston. "You started this entire mess nearly two years ago."

Halston looked away, rubbing a hand through his already tousled hair. "Farnsworth, go scout downstream and invite whoever's in charge of the woman's party back here. There's no need for threats or violence. We can likely pay them for their silence, and they should be able to convince the woman to cooperate."

"Yes, my lord." The servant started toward the creek, this time heading downstream rather than upstream.

Danielle stared at her hands, unbound—at least for now. A helplessly sick feeling rose in her chest. What if she was making the wrong choice? What if Halston let Kessler tie her and her brother tonight so they couldn't escape? What if the Englishmen were crueler to her younger brother than they had been to her?

She should have thought her actions through better from the beginning. Should have pretended she didn't care whether they searched the banks of the stream instead of panicking when they first asked who she traveled with.

But she'd always been a poor liar. She could fight to

defend herself, *oui*, but she gave herself away the moment she so much as thought about uttering a falsehood.

She glanced around the woods, surveying the brambles and saplings immediately surrounding them, the more stately trees rooted to the forest beyond. Better to not attempt any lies and stay quiet for the next few hours. Once darkness fell, she could lead her brother into the dense woods.

The sick man lying on the bedroll on the far side of the camp coughed—hadn't the servant called him Lord Westerfield? Not that she would utter the title "lord" to any man. Her captors might be English by birth, but they were in France now, and in France, everyone was a citizen. All of equal value and standing.

Halston gave her a hard look, then turned back toward the sick man. Kessler had moved to the opposite side of the fire where he rummaged through a sack, not nearly so trusting as Halston. His eyes didn't leave her for an instant.

Not that she could blame him.

So she tucked her knees up into her chest and waited.

And waited.

And waited. Soon the two hale Englishmen started arguing about which one of them would make tea for the sick one. Evidently neither knew the first thing about boiling water. And the British wondered why the French had overthrown their own aristocracy.

Halston sorted through a sack until he found some salt pork and offered it to Kessler, who wrinkled his nose but took of the offering.

Halston turned to her, the dried meat extended in his hand. She raised her chin and looked away. She'd rather starve than take food from those who shared the same nationality as the men who'd killed her brother.

The brambles near the creek rustled, and she tensed, watching, waiting. If any harm had come to Serge, she'd find some way to punish them all. These insidious English knew not how deadly she was with a knife— even if they had taken hers for the moment.

But Serge stepped into the clearing of his own volition, spotted her and headed straight over, plopping himself down onto her blanket.

"Dani, what did you go and get yourself into?"

"A nest of English spies."

Halston dropped his cup of tea to the ground. "What did you say?"

She swallowed, her tongue freezing against the roof of her mouth. What *had* she done?

Or rather, what had Serge done?

Repercussions of her simple mistake echoed through her body. Serge had spoken to her in English—had probably been speaking to the servant in English since the man first found him by the river.

And she'd answered him back.

In English.

"You speak our tongue." Halston narrowed his eyes at her. "You've understood every word we've said."

"I knew she was hiding something." Kessler spit into the ground by the fire.

She was going to kill her brother. Slowly. Torturously. She turned so her back faced Halston, though that didn't stop the growing vibrations from his footsteps as he approached.

"What were you thinking?" she whispered to her brother furiously. "How dare you let them know we speak their language? We're their prisoners, and you just gave away one of our advantages."

"Calm down, Dani." Serge reached over to pat her

back. "They're nice. Besides, it's not like they've got us tied up or anything."

If he only knew.

"Why didn't you tell us you spoke English?" Halston's irate voice boomed from above her, all traces of mercy and consideration vanished in the storm of his anger. "Well?"

She didn't need to turn around to know where he stood. She could *feel* his nearness, the heat of his legs boring into her back, the fury of his rage rolling off him. The hair on the back of her neck prickled in instinctive dread, and she bit the side of her lip. But really, there was only one thing to say. In English, unfortunately. "I demand you let us go."

"You're not going anywhere."

She jumped at the underlying bite to his words, then glanced at Serge, who stared up at the Englishman with wide eyes.

"What exactly did you overhear earlier, before Farnsworth found you in the shrubs?"

Before Farnsworth had found her? Something about traveling at night and being lost and a sarcastic comment that involved asking the gendarmes for directions—which was about the time she'd decided to go find a gendarmerie post herself and turn the men in.

And also happened to be about the time she'd made too much noise backing through the shrubs.

She licked her lips. "Nothing terribly significant."

"Turn around."

She startled again, the edge in his voice warning her not to disobey.

He crouched before her, his large, looming body so close all moisture leached from her mouth. "I don't believe you."

"I didn't…that is…I don't…I mean…um…"

"Tell me—Dani, is it?" His gray-blue eyes flashed at her.

"Danielle," Serge piped up. "Just the family calls her Dani."

"Danielle." The name sounded long and cool on his tongue, an oddity considering the way the rest of his words smoldered. "What is it you think we're going to do to you?"

She squeezed her eye shut. Take her and Serge to England, throw them in a dungeon and leave them to starve. Or maybe he wouldn't take them to England but kill them here in the woods and bury…

"Danielle, look at me."

She forced her eyes open. "I know not."

"I'm not going to harm you, merely offer you a few napoleons—a business proposition, if you will. Are you familiar with business?"

She nodded, afraid to speak an answer lest he somehow trap her with her own words. She was already quite trapped enough with the way his intense eyes refused to let hers go and the way his strong body hovered so near her own.

"Our *papa* lets land and farms." Serge, evidently, didn't feel quite so trapped. The dunce. "And he owns a share in a clothing manufactory. We know all about business."

The man's eyes left her gaze, only to run slowly down the rest of her hunched form. "And you're good with a blade…know English rather well."

"Our *maman* taught us the English," Serge spoke up again, and Danielle clamped her jaw so tightly her teeth ground together. Would the boy never learn to hold his tongue? "She used to be a governess, she did, and insisted we learn it. Then there's our aunt and uncle across the channel, so we've got to know English for when we go over there to visit."

Halston's eyebrows rose. "You have relatives on the other side of the channel?"

"Hush, Serge," she gritted.

"And you visit them despite the war?"

Serge finally closed his mouth, but it was too late. Gregory's calculating eyes gleamed in triumph.

The kind of triumph that could only mean her own defeat.

"You're perfect, then. I'm in need of a guide to the channel, and you have the ability to take us there."

Every muscle in her body turned hard as stone as she stared at the abhorrent man. Help men from the country that had killed her brother? The man had to be mad. "Do you think me a traitor? I care not how much coin you can offer. I will not aid English spies. Not now and not ever."

Chapter Three

"Spies?" Gregory sputtered. "You think we're spies?"

The accusation was laughable, really, if it didn't carry such deadly implications should they be caught and imprisoned as such. "Last I checked, English spies don't get themselves lost or need maps. English spies speak flawless French, and if you met an English spy on the street, you'd never know."

The color that had suffused the woman's cheeks just moments before drained away, and her jaw fell open for the slightest of instants before she hardened it again. "You're still Englishmen. In my country. In the middle of a war. You can have no honest reason for being here, or you would not dread being spotted by the gendarmes. Do you expect me to take your guineas or napoleons or whatever other coins you offer and let you continue on your way to the channel with no objection?"

He sent a gaze toward the heavens. "No. I want you to *help* us get to the channel."

She turned her back to him.

"I'll pay you well. I've only a few guineas now, but I can promise two thousand pounds sterling if you see us safely to the coast."

The woman still didn't deign to face him. "I told you once. I don't want your filthy English money."

Heat surged up the back of his neck. "My money is far from filthy."

"Dani, don't be a fool." The youth nudged his sister. At least one of them had a fraction of sense. "Just think of it. Two thousand pounds is enough to buy up more of the clothing manufactory. Why, you could start your own factory for that sum."

She swiped a strand of hair from her face. "I don't want to start my own factory. I just want to go home."

A large, uncomfortable lump settled inside Gregory's stomach. Yet another thing he'd never learned at Eton or Cambridge: How to hold people hostage and drag them across half a country against their will. But the woman knew too much for him to allow a different course of action. "You and your brother are coming with us to the coast. You can either aid us with our journey and be paid in turn, or you can fight us—in which case you'll be restrained and towed along. But either way, if you're caught with our party, your fate will be the same as ours."

Danielle looked out over the tangle of shrubs that circled them, then to the larger trees in the forest beyond. Planning her escape, most likely. She could handle a blade well, but she would make a poor spy. Every thought and plan flitted across her expressive blue eyes a half instant before she acted.

She sighed. "If you're in northern France headed toward the coast, I suppose you escaped from Verdun."

He watched her with the same hard gaze he would use on anyone he distrusted. And in the selfsame manner, he held his tongue. Let her think they'd come from Verdun, where Napoleon had interred all the English he'd rounded up after the peace treaty failed. Yes, that was the most reasonable assumption, and if Westerfield and Kessler *had* been interred there instead of imprisoned in a forgotten fortress, they'd likely be following this very path back to the channel.

But then, had Westerfield and Kessler been in Verdun, he'd have known their whereabouts long ago and been able to send Westerfield money to procure apartments and buy wares, set Westerfield up with a household and purchase new clothes. From the reports Gregory had heard, Verdun functioned as any normal British city would, with people attending the theater as well as gaming halls, making calls and going about everyday business. The only difference was the English weren't allowed outside the city's impenetrable walls.

But Westerfield and Kessler hadn't been imprisoned in a place where they could get sunshine and a decent meal, much less the other trappings of ordinary life, not with the crimes they'd been accused of committing. Oh, no. They'd been held in one of Napoleon's secret prisons, instead, deprived of the most basic comforts, and Westerfield had fallen deathly ill because of it.

Danielle already suspected them of being spies. If she knew the whole of it, she'd never agree to help. "Think about whether you'll aid or hinder us. But know this, I won't let you escape again as easily as last time."

Gregory stood and moved to the other side of the fire, keeping one eye on her. She'd promised she wouldn't run.

If only he believed her.

Kessler wrinkled his nose as he ate a bite of salt pork, watching Danielle and her brother the way a hawk did a field mouse while Farnsworth tried coaxing tea down Westerfield's throat. His brother only coughed in response, and a thin stream of liquid trailed down his chin to dampen the blankets beneath his head. Gregory turned away, his jaw working back and forth. Could nothing go as planned?

He was a man of business. He made his living off predictions and plans. He predicted the Exchange, rates on interest, returns on investments and likelihood of growth for various industries. He also predicted people. His father would never invest in a shipyard—too risky given that ships would be lost during the war. Yet shipping could offer a great return on investments, and a man like Kessler would have no trouble putting money toward such a venture.

When he'd come to France, it hadn't been on a whim. He'd had a plan, which was why he'd hired a guide, purchased coarse French clothing and carried both guineas and napoleons on his person. Yet he'd still ended up here, dependent on two French strangers for the safety of himself, his servant, his brother and Kessler.

Father God, am I doing something wrong? Please save my brother and get us safely to England.

"Can I have some?" Serge came around the side of the small fire, his eyes locked on the salt pork sitting beside Kessler. "I didn't get supper."

At least the young man wouldn't choose to starve— unlike his stubborn sister.

Kessler thrust a piece at him. "What's your name, boy?"

"Serge." The youth settled beside Kessler, scarfed down his pork in three bites and reached for another piece.

Gregory sat on the soft earth between his brother and Kessler and took some meat for himself. Danielle merely glowered at them from across the fire, arms crossed and back rigid. Good. For some unfathomable reason, he preferred that rigid silhouette to the sight of her hunched over, arms wrapped around herself and eyes blinking as she pleaded for him not to tie her.

"Serge what?" Kessler took another piece of salt pork. "Have you a surname?"

"Serge Belanger."

"Belanger?" Gregory set his salt pork aside. "And you say you have relatives in England?"

The boy's brow furrowed. "*Oui*, an aunt and an uncle that moved there during the Terror."

"Are you by chance related to Michel and Isabelle Belanger? They live near Hastings and have a furniture factory."

The boy stopped chewing. "How do you know *Oncle* Michel and *Tante* Isabelle?"

Gregory ran his eyes over the lad. He didn't look at all similar to Michel Belanger, but why would he lie about such a thing? "I'm Belanger's man of business."

Much to his mother's dismay. She'd wanted him to join the church, but his brother and the other noblemen whose accounts he handled certainly didn't complain about the money he made them. And if he happened to take on a client or two from the merchant class in exchange for a certain percentage of the money made on their investments, then so be it.

The boy's nose scrunched. "What's that?"

"I manage his investments." He glanced at Danielle across the fire. Was she surprised he knew her aunt and uncle?

The stubborn woman's jaw was still set and her body angled away from him.

"Man of business." Serge rolled the words over his tongue. "Sounds like some fancy English farce of a position that no one needs."

Kessler smirked. "Halston probably makes more money in one day than your father does in a year."

Gregory rolled his shoulders. He was a bit adept at making money, yes. So much of it, at least, that whatever he spent on clothes or conveyances or housing, he easily made up and then some within the month. Which was why he allotted a large chunk to the Hastings Orphanage and a series of foundling hospitals and poorhouses in other areas of England.

"You don't look all that rich." Serge eyed Gregory.

Kessler laughed, the first time the man had likely smiled in two years. "Yes, Halston, why don't you look rich?"

Gregory rubbed the back of his neck. "I usually don't traipse about the French countryside disguised as a peasant and trying to evade the law."

"You're disguised as a peasant?" The boy's nose wrinkled again. "With boots as fine as that but unmended holes in your trousers? Being rich sure don't give you much sense, does it?"

"What, precisely, is wrong with my garments?"

"No peasant would let those holes in their trousers without sewing them up right quick—they need their clothes to last, not fall apart. No peasant would spend the money for boots like that, and no peasant would stand as straight as you do."

Gregory stared down at his boots. Did they truly give him away? He'd wanted sturdy leather ones that wouldn't pain his feet while walking. Who could fault him for that? His first guide certainly hadn't objected when he'd chosen his disguise.

Then again, his first guide had probably intended to betray him all along.

"From where do you hail?" Kessler asked Serge.

Gregory blinked and looked back at the boy. He probably should have asked that before demanding that Danielle and Serge take them to the coast. If this was their first time traveling inland, would they make competent enough guides? Knowing English and having family across the channel didn't exactly mean the woman and her brother could effectively lead them.

Though the woman's skill with a knife would certainly be useful.

"Abbeville," the boy stated.

Kessler merely stared.

"It's near the coast. Just inland a bit from Saint-Valery-sur-Somme. Do you know Saint-Valery?"

"I do," Gregory answered. "It's somewhat across the channel from Hastings." Which made the boy and his sister perfect guides for his purposes. They were likely familiar with the roads and terrain between here and the channel and could guide them with far less risk of getting caught than Gregory and the others could ever manage on their own. And he needed that, since the prison guards would have already notified cities, towns and gendarmerie posts of their escape.

Serge reached for more salt pork—what had to be his fifth or sixth piece of the leathery meat—but Kessler clamped down on his hand. "If you're from the coast, what are you doing so far inland?"

"We were in Reims visiting our *tante* and *oncle* and trying to find a husband for Dani." The boy scowled at his sister. "No one wants her, though."

Gregory had been taking a sip of water and choked at the boy's words. No Frenchman wanted her? He glanced at Serge's silent sister through the smoke of the small flames. What was wrong with the men of this country? Could they not see the crystalline color of her eyes or the smooth, pale skin of her face? The riotous black waves that fell about her shoulders?

No, her hair would have been up. The men wouldn't have known how magnificent it looked free. But even so, the rest of her was enough to bend any man's mind toward marriage, wasn't it?

Well, maybe not if she decided to hold a knife to her suitors' necks.

"Stow it, Serge." Warning dripped from Danielle's voice.

The boy shrugged. "What? They asked. I'm just being honest."

"Then stop talking all together. Why are you volunteering information to these strangers? Your mouth is what got us into trouble in the first place, Mr. I'm-going-to-forget-I-have-a-brain-and-speak-English-when-I-should-be-speaking-French."

"On the contrary," Westerfield's weak voice filled the air behind them. "I believe his excellent English quite proves his possession of said brain."

The youth laughed at that, his face alight with pride. "See that, Dani? He thinks my brain is just fine."

"Though I question the intelligence of any Frenchman who doesn't want your sister." Kessler watched Danielle with a predatory glint to his eyes.

"Don't even think about it," Gregory muttered.

"I wouldn't dare," Kessler answered airily.

But Kessler had already had thought of it—and done it—in England, and his gaze said he'd thought of such with Danielle just now.

She glanced between the two of them, as though sensing the tension. Then again, a deaf, blind mute could likely sense the tension between him and Kessler.

Serge, however, stuffed another piece of salt pork in

his mouth and spoke around it. "Well, some of the men might want Dani if she tried being nice. She stomped on one landowner's toe and then slapped him, and he was the richest of the lot of them."

Danielle threw up her hands. "He tried to…" But she suddenly clamped her mouth shut, color flooding her cheeks. "Never mind. Just keep quiet, Serge."

"On the contrary, I'm rather curious now that you've brought it up." Kessler's harsh voice floated over the campsite. "What precisely did this Frenchman attempt, Danielle?"

She hardened her jaw.

"Enough." Gregory stood. So Danielle was beautiful, any man could see that. But she didn't deserve to be taken advantage of—especially by someone like Kessler. "Kessler, go to the stream and get more water. Westerfield might need some in the night."

Kessler's eyebrows shot up. "You expect me to haul water? Have Farnsworth do it."

Gregory glanced at Farnsworth, sitting near the fire and stuffing salt pork into his mouth as greedily as Serge. "Farnsworth is about to unroll the bedding."

His valet shot up and rushed to the pile of blankets, still chewing awkwardly.

"But if you're too cowardly to walk to the stream by yourself," Gregory continued, "I'm sure Serge will accompany you."

"That's hardly necessary." Kessler pushed stiffly to his feet, grabbed the one small bucket they had and stalked off into the darkness.

Gregory watched the other man go, and not a moment too soon. Did he think he could take advantage of—

"Don't." Westerfield's voice drew Gregory's attention away. "Those thoughts won't do you any good now."

He approached his brother and kneeled, speaking low enough the others couldn't hear. "How can I not think of what happened at times like this? When he looks at Danielle as though he would devour her?"

"Put it behind you."

How could he, when dreams of Suzanna's tearstained face still came to him in the darkest hours of the night? He could picture the scene in his mind as clearly as though it was happening this very moment. Coming in from a late night in the village, he'd found Suzanna in the stable, her dress undone and her crumpled form sobbing into the hay.

So he'd called Kessler out, and Kessler had injured him in the duel. When infection claimed his leg, his father had been so furious, he'd sworn retribution on Kessler, and Kessler had fled to France. The sordid tale might have ended there were it not for Westerfield. Why his brother would up and leave England to find Kessler, Gregory would never understand. But leave England Westerfield had, only to end up disappearing after the peace treaty failed.

"Careful, Halston, you don't know the full of it," Westerfield rasped.

No, he clearly didn't, because Westerfield's decision to come to France and bring Kessler home still made no sense. But one thing was clear: were it not for the duel, Westerfield wouldn't be gravely ill, and the rest of them wouldn't be stuck in a country they were at war with.

Then again, other parts of the story were as clear as water on a cold winter morning. "When you're a guest in someone's home, you shouldn't make free use of the serving girls. That isn't difficult to understand."

Never mind that it was a common enough practice among the ton. Never mind that Kessler's own father never would have taught him otherwise—had probably been the leading example, in fact.

Wrong was still wrong, and it shouldn't take a vicar pointing his bony finger at Kessler to sear the man's conscience.

And listen to him, waxing moral. Perhaps he should have joined the church, as Mother had wanted, rather than become a man of business.

But then he wouldn't have those two thousand pounds to pay the Belanger siblings for taking his party to the coast. Nor would he have the funds he contributed to the Hastings Orphanage or the foundling hospitals.

And he probably wouldn't have known about Suzanna because he would have been seeing to his parish in some far-off village instead of staying at his family's country home for a visit.

He didn't regret what he'd done.

Which only proved to nearly everyone he knew that he'd gone mad at some point since he'd graduated from Cambridge, because titled members of the ton didn't call out future earls over a serving girl. A duel could be fought over a lady, certainly, but never a servant.

Westerfield coughed again, his hacking more violent this time.

Gregory touched his forehead. "You're getting worse."

"I'm f-f-fine," Westerfield stammered through a sickening wheeze.

But he wasn't fine. His skin was hot and clammy, and his once-strong body lay pale and emaciated. "I'll go for a physician if you but give the word."

And he would. It mattered not how many napoleons

or guineas he'd have to use to buy the physician's silence. His brother needed to live.

"The cough isn't so bad, really." But Westerfield couldn't even speak the words without letting loose a smaller cough.

Something rustled by the fire, and Gregory turned to find Serge sitting back beside his sister. Farnsworth had busied himself making up pallets to sleep upon, and Kessler had returned. He set down his pail of water and approached the Belanger siblings, a length of rope in his hand.

Not again. Gregory pushed wearily to his feet.

"Be kind," Westerfield warned.

Why should he? Hadn't he told the man to leave Danielle be? Not that Kessler would ever deign to listen to a mere third son when he was a future earl.

Kessler crossed his arms and waited for him. "We can't have her escaping in the night."

"She's not some slave to be bound at your whim."

Danielle scooted closer to the trees while Serge's wide-eyed gaze moved from him to Kessler and back.

Kessler held up the rope. "She'll escape by morning if you don't tie her, and we'll likely awaken to gendarmes and bayonet tips."

"She promised not to run."

"And you're risking our capture on the word of a woman who held a knife to your valet's throat and pretended not to speak English?"

"The knife to my throat was rather uncalled-for, if I can say so," Farnsworth spoke from where he unrolled the final blanket for his own bed.

"Don't tie my sister, please," Serge's pleading eyes sought Gregory rather than Kessler. A smart boy, that Serge Belanger.

Gregory heaved a sigh. Kessler was right—much as he hated to admit it. Perhaps she would keep her word, but she was also the sort to use her wits and cunning to seek any loophole she could find. Danielle had promised she wouldn't run, but she'd never said for how long. She was likely just waiting for night to fall and everyone else to sleep. If he didn't tie the woman, they'd be rotting in prison cells come tomorrow evening.

"Fine, but let me do it." He jerked the rope away from Kessler.

"*Non*! You can't." Tears flooded the boy's eyes. "She'll promise to be good and not escape, won't you, Dani? She doesn't deserve it, I swear."

Gregory wouldn't say she didn't deserve it—his cheek still throbbed where she'd scratched him—but he'd no desire to humiliate the woman, either. This wasn't about what she deserved—it was about protecting himself and his brother.

"Do you need me to hold her?" Farnsworth approached while Kessler stalked around the fire to his pallet.

"Please don't." Danielle looked up, her blue eyes entreating him in the firelight.

This would be easier if she screamed or attempted to run. Instead she sat too still, like one of his sister's dolls propped on a shelf.

He paused, and Westerfield coughed again from where he lay. As beautiful and earnest as she might seem, he couldn't risk his brother, risk them all, based on the word of a woman who'd already proved herself untrustworthy.

He knelt behind her. "Put your hands behind your back."

She kept her fists anchored firmly by her sides and looked away but couldn't hide the slight tremble in her jaw.

He tugged her hands behind her back, her skin far too soft for one who seemed so fierce.

Blast! He was letting her charms play tricks on his mind. So she was beautiful. He'd seen many a beautiful woman before, all dressed in finer clothes than Danielle Belanger, with jewels dangling from their necks and fingers and coiffures. Simpering, delicate creatures who wouldn't have lasted five minutes in the woods, let alone know how to use a knife or attempt to escape a band of strange men.

But Danielle didn't fight him now. She didn't speak, didn't even look at him as he began to tie.

Why wasn't she begging, pleading, attempting to struggle?

A faint bead of moisture slipped down her cheek to glisten in the firelight, and she sucked in a long, quivering breath. Perfect. Instead of fighting him like the woman two hours ago would have done, she now struggled against tears.

Yet another thing Eton and Cambridge hadn't taught him. How to tie up a captive woman so she couldn't escape. Or what to do with one when she cried.

Useless schools, the both of them.

He tightened the knot as much as he dared against her tender wrists, then stood, tossing another length of rope to Serge. "Tie your sister's ankles."

"Non." Hatred radiated from the boy's eyes.

"Either you tie her legs, or I will. But in the end, her ankles will still be bound."

Serge reached for the remainder of rope, and Gregory dug the heel of his boot into the dirt as he watched. He was making a muck of everything. Serge hadn't despised him until now. Sure, Danielle had wanted naught to do with them from the first, but the boy had been much more amicable, helpful even.

Gregory couldn't let them escape and call in gendarmes, yet neither could they travel to the coast with two guides who hated them. He had to find some way to make amends and change their minds about helping, or this was going to be the longest, most miserable journey in the history of Europe.

But how exactly could he convince a humiliated woman and her angry brother to help him? Somehow, he didn't think a nice little apology was going to repair things.

Danielle lay back on her makeshift pallet, her hands bound behind her back and her ankles tied tightly together while hot tears of mortification welled behind her eyes. She had no one to blame but herself for this situation, she supposed. She was too rash, always too rash. *Papa* and *Maman* had told her so numerous times over the years, but what did she do over and over again? Run headlong into a situation, waiting until she had herself well and truly tangled before she stopped to think that maybe, just maybe, she should have slowed down enough to mull things over before she'd acted.

'Twas probably the reason no decent man wished to wed her. Who wanted to be bound for life to a woman who always created trouble?

Like tonight, she should have agreed to guide Halston and his friends. Why had she not thought it through first? She could have guided them straight to a gendarmerie post and no one would have been the wiser until it was too late. Instead, she'd proudly defied them.

Why, oh, why hadn't she just pretended to be a simple girl from the provinces, eager to do anything for a bit of coin?

Maybe because she was neither simple nor willing to do anything for coin. Her parents had instilled principles into her far too well. Plus, she was a terrible liar and likely would have given herself away.

Even so, no one had ever warned her having principles and staying fixed on doing what was right could lead her here. To being tied up while a bunch of Englishmen milled around. To being forced into acting as a guide when she should be running through the woods toward a gendarmerie post.

"Don't cry, Dani." Serge plopped down beside her, chewing yet another piece of salt pork as he faced her on the blankets. "Everything will be all right."

"Easy for you to say…" She pressed her eyes shut. How could she even look at her brother while she lay trussed up like some animal? "You're not the one being made into a spectacle."

He sighed, long and heavy. "Dani, if you don't want to be a spectacle, then don't act like one."

"I wasn't trying…oh, forget it." She moistened her parched lips and glanced at Kessler and Halston sitting beside the sickbed arguing over something or other. "At least they didn't tie you, too. That should make our escape easy enough."

Serge cast a quick glance toward the darkened woods. "Figured we'd wait until everyone was asleep, and then I'd untie you."

Untie her. Like she was some captive animal rather than a person. A fresh wave of humiliation welled inside her chest. "Lie down here and get some sleep. The sooner we go to bed, the sooner everyone else will."

Serge scrambled down onto the blankets beside her.

"Are you going to pretend sleep? If we both truly sleep, we might miss our chance."

She winced as rope bit into her wrists. Of course, if she stopped trying to loosen her bindings, they probably wouldn't bite so much. Serge would be freeing her in a few hours, so she could stop struggling and simply wait. But truly, how was she to sit docilely and not attempt to loosen the ropes even a little?

"Danielle?" Serge blinked up at her. "Are you going to stay awake, then?"

"Don't worry, even if I doze off, I won't be able to sleep long with these ropes cutting into my skin."

His eyes turned soft as he watched her. "I'm sorry, Dani. Really, I am. The Englishmen seemed nice enough, and they've got that sick man on the other side of the fire. I didn't think they'd hurt us."

"Of course they'll hurt us. Have you forgotten we're at war with them?"

"But they're people just the same. And if one of us was sick and needed help, I'd like to think…" His words trailed off as another grotesque cough filled the air.

"That doesn't mean we need to be nice to them," she snapped. "Or that they need to be nice to us. Now lie down and sleep. You'll need all your strength if you're going to keep up with me tonight."

"All right." He rolled over, presenting his back to her as he snuggled in for slumber.

On the other side of the fire, Halston pushed his tall form up from where he sat and approached. In his hands he held a blanket torn into strips and then knotted together formed a makeshift rope. Were they planning to gag her as well?

"Non." Danielle scooted herself back on the pallet as best she could with both her hands and feet tied.

"It's not for you but your brother."

"For me?" Serge pushed himself up to a sitting position.

"You can't tie him. He hasn't—" She clamped her mouth shut. She was going to give their escape plan away if she panicked again.

Halston quirked an arrogant, dark eyebrow at her. "You were saying?"

"Nothing."

"Put your hands behind your back, Serge," he commanded.

Her brother's gaze shot fiery little arrows toward the Englishman. "I didn't do anything."

"It's whether you plan to do anything once the rest of us are asleep that I question."

"So you're going to tie me with a blanket?" he scoffed.

"We're out of rope. It will have to do."

And with those words, the man knelt down to tie her brother, cutting off their best chance at escape.

Chapter Four

"Serge, you have to be quieter," Danielle hissed into the darkness.

The admonishment did little good. Her brother still clomped behind her, his boots rustling old leaves and snapping twigs.

'Twas hardly astonishing the boy had trouble killing a squirrel. The entire forest would hear him coming a full kilometer away. "You're going to awaken the English and lead them straight to us."

The noise of mud sucking at his feet drowned out her words.

She rolled her eyes and moved soundlessly behind an ancient maple tree. They'd best just focus on getting away fast—since "quiet" wasn't working for them. She surveyed the darkened trees. The clouds now blanketed the moon and stars, making the forest so black it obscured trees a meter in front of her. But the darkness would also make following them nigh impossible.

If not for Serge and his incessant noise.

He came up beside her, panting. "How do you move so fast in the dark? I can hardly follow you."

"There's a thick stand of firs several meters ahead."

She reached back to take hold of his wrist, keeping her eyes pinned on the goal ahead. "If we can get there, the English will have no hope of—"

"Finding you?" A hand reached out to clasp her upper arm.

She squealed at the sound of the familiar English voice.

"Serge, *t'enfuis*! Run!" She shoved her brother away before Halston could grab him, as well. At least one of them would be free to find a gendarmerie post.

Serge's heavy footfalls crashed into the darkness while a narrow beam of lantern light found her face.

"Where, exactly, did you intend to go this late?" Halston asked.

The oaf. He deserved to have his other cheek scratched as badly as the first. She curled her fingers into fists at her side.

He chuckled, clearly guessing the direction of her thoughts. "I wouldn't attempt it again if I were you."

She jerked her chin up. "Where I go is none of your concern."

"Is that so?"

"Of course."

"You'll have to forgive me for not believing you, seeing how when you feigned sleep two hours ago, I left both you and your brother *bound*."

The word cracked through the woods with such force she couldn't help but cringe. "Mayhap we didn't like being bound."

His hand dug harder into her arm. "Wretched woman."

She couldn't make out more than his shadow with the way he held the light to shine on her alone, but she could well imagine him gritting his teeth as he called her wretched, just like *Papa* always did when he said she was insufferable.

Not that she was either wretched or insufferable.

"My brother has spent the past year and a half trapped in your horrid country for the heinous crime of traveling here when our two countries were at peace and not managing to leave before we were once again at war." Frustration ground across the edges of his words. "When I came to rescue him, the French guide I paid quite handsomely betrayed us. Now Westerfield might well be dying, and he needs help. I've offered you two thousand pounds to take us to the channel, a sum that should be of great use to you and your family, and you look down as me as though I'm no more than dung on the heel of your boot. What must I do to convince you to help us? Offer you another thousand pounds?"

"That man is your brother? The sick one with the wretched cough?"

He probably raised that arrogant eyebrow at her, except she couldn't see it in the black. "Does it make a difference?"

It didn't. Or rather, it shouldn't. But his brother? Could she blame him for wanting to protect his family? And what if his claim about not being spies was true? "When you learned he fell ill, you came over from England solely to get him out of Verdun?"

"Again, why does it matter?" His voice was hard, as though he hadn't a drop of mercy anywhere inside his tall, lanky form.

"Because…because…" *Because I had an older brother once, and if he'd been trapped in your country, I would have done anything to save him.*

But Laurent wasn't trapped in England. He was dead.

And she, Serge and Julien—Laurent's twin—were all absent a brother because of England's navy.

She licked her lips and looked away from Halston's shadow. "You're right. It doesn't matter."

"That's not what you were thinking."

She attempted to yank her arm away. Serge had had ample time to escape, and if she could free herself, he'd never be able to catch her in the woods. But Halston only tightened his hold on her arm.

"So are you going to take me back to camp and tie me up again?"

"What were you about to say concerning my brother?"

She glared at him and tapped her foot impatiently against the soft earth. "Sometimes it's better to keep your mouth shut. Or do they not teach such manners in your country?"

He laughed then, so bold and loud the sound echoed off trees. "The woman who held a knife to my valet's throat and scratched my cheek is now lecturing me about manners? Forgive me if I hesitate to heed your advice."

Her stomach coiled into a knot. "Fine. Perhaps I wished your brother dead a few moments back."

"You were right. You should have left that thought to yourself." His voice, relaxed and curious only seconds ago, now resonated hard and cold. He turned her back toward camp and thrust her forward, his hand never leaving her arm.

She swallowed tightly. She hadn't meant to offend, not really. The words had just slipped out. What else did he expect when she'd been thinking of Laurent? If he was bound and determined to drag her to the coast with him, he'd best learn to accept her harshly honest ways.

She peeked back over her shoulder. Halston's jaw was set at a hard angle, while the rest of him remained shrouded in darkness. "I didn't mean it like that. I had a brother once, 'tis all."

He shoved her forward with greater force. "You still have one, by the look of it."

"An older one named Laurent. He served in the navy."

The grip around her shoulder loosened a fraction.

"Your country captured his frigate and killed him. Mayhap I don't actually wish your brother dead, but in some ways it seems fair, does it not? A brother for a brother?"

Halston pulled her to a stop, though he didn't turn her to face him. It was just as well. She hardly wanted to look into an Englishman's eyes when she spoke of Laurent. So they stood in the darkness, with only the faint sound of the flowing stream permeating the eerie silence.

"I'm sorry for your loss." His words, once he finally spoke them, rang with sympathy.

Did she want sympathy from an Englishman?

She blinked and looked down, only to find her arms had somehow slid around her ribs and wrapped about her body in a lonely hug. "I should think you'd be glad to hear of a fallen French sailor. We're your enemies."

"I'm not happy to hear of any life lost, even a Frenchman's."

Moisture burned in her eyes.

"And yes, I did enter France for the sole purpose of finding my brother and bringing him home. It only seemed right, seeing how it's my fault he left England in the first place and our middle brother is making a muck of the marquessate in Westerfield's absence."

She craned her neck to glimpse Halston's face, partially visible with how he now held the lantern. His brother's being here was his fault? She'd not have guessed that. If anyone seemed the most blameworthy of his party, 'twas Kessler. "At least you had the courage to come to France and do right by him."

"Does that mean you'll help?"

She shifted from foot to foot. The wind whispered through the barren trees, and an owl let out a distant call. She should twist from his grip while it remained loose and run into the forest. He might catch her, but she was quick and quiet and had the cloak of darkness on her side. Somehow running seemed less dangerous than facing this tall man with sympathy in his voice.

"I don't trust you in the least. What if you're spies, only pretending to be internees from Verdun so that you can reach England and foil Napoleon's next military campaign?"

He chuckled. "You have quite the imagination, Danielle Belanger."

The breath in her lungs stilled at the sound of her full name on his tongue. Danielle Belanger. It hadn't sounded so...so...so tender when he used her Christian name earlier. Tender and full of compassion.

But he shouldn't have compassion for her, not when their countries were at war. "You expect an awful lot of me when you hail from the land that killed my brother."

"That's not an answer."

Even through the darkness, his gaze felt warm against her skin; she was aware of it in a way she didn't quite want to contemplate. The sensation might have been soft and comforting, if it wasn't quite so...unsettling.

She shouldn't help him. He had no reason to speak

truth to her and every reason to lie. About his "brother."
About why he was in France. About everything.

And yet, if he was going to lie, why admit his brother
had been interred because of him? Why plead for her
help rather than kill her?

Kill her...

Had she truly discovered spies speaking in English,
she and Serge would be dead by now. Suddenly cold,
she rubbed her hands up and down her arms. A faint
cough rang through the trees, as though the sick man
knew she stood in turmoil a few meters away, debating
whether or not to help.

What if the situation were reversed and that sick
man was Laurent, trapped in a hostile land? What if
her older brother hadn't been killed three years ago but
had somehow ended up in England and begged for some
Englishman's mercy? Would she not want that Englishman—or woman—to show kindness to her brother? To
help him return to France?

*For there is neither Jew nor Greek, there is neither
bond nor free, there is neither male nor female: for ye
are all one in Christ Jesus.*

She shoved the verse from her mind. She cared not
how many times *Papa* had read it from his old, large
Bible while the family sat around the table. Cared not
if Serge's words were right earlier when he'd said that
the English were people just as much as the French.
Those principles certainly didn't apply here and now.
Not with her enemies. Not with men from the country
that had killed Laurent and had warred with her own
nation for over a decade. Maybe there wasn't any difference between Jew and Greek, but there was certainly
a difference between English and French.

Wasn't there?

Another cough echoed through the woods, this one louder than the last. Westerfield wasn't going to live much longer if he didn't get help, and given the not-very-secret manner in which the Englishmen were traveling, they'd be discovered by the end of the week even without her and Serge seeking out some gendarmes. Another bout of imprisonment would finish the man off.

"So will you help?" Halston asked again.

Could she really leave these men to be caught, and one of them to likely die, just because they were from the wrong country?

Yes. Of course she could. That's what happened in war: people died if they were from the losing country. She raised her chin and swallowed thickly, meeting Halston's eyes.

And then the entirely wrong words came out of her mouth: "*Oui.* I'll help."

She would help? Had Gregory heard her right? Her eyes met his, no longer hard and determined but misty in the pale orange glow from the lantern. His knees nearly folded beneath him in relief. Perhaps all wasn't lost. Perhaps he could get help for Westerfield and make it to the coast undetected. Perhaps—

"But I won't let you tie me or my brother again. If we're going to work together, you'll have to trust us."

The hope that had filled his chest deflated. "Trust you? What reason have I to trust you?"

"What reason have I to trust you're who you claim and the sick man is really your brother? That you harbor no secrets of the state, or..."

He held up a hand. "All right. I agree. No more ropes."

"Or torn blankets that act as ropes."

He shoved a hand into his hair. "Or torn blankets."

"Do you really mean it, Dani?" a voice piped up from the woods. "We're going to help them after they tied us up like trussed pigs?"

Danielle whirled toward the voice. "I thought I told you to run. You should be halfway to a gendarmerie post by now."

A loud, awkward rustling sounded to their left, and Serge clomped from the darkness into the dim circle of lantern light. "I couldn't just leave you. What if he tried to hurt you?"

She rolled her eyes—a rather common habit, that. "And what would you have done if he'd hurt me?"

"I still have my knife, remember?"

Gregory frowned. "Is that how the two of you escaped? Farnsworth missed one of your knives?"

Serge turned to him and crossed his arms. "No. *You* missed the knife."

Evidently he hadn't searched the boy thoroughly enough before tying him. Then again, he hadn't exactly searched the boy at all, had he? He'd simply assumed Farnsworth had seen to it. Yet another thing he'd failed at this day. Though truly, he might well suggest that the faculty add a class on how to properly manage an abduction when he next visited Cambridge. With the wars facing Britain these days, one never knew if alumni would end up abducting an enemy of the crown.

But how many knives Danielle and Serge Belanger had or where they were strapped mattered little so long as they planned to use those knives to help rather than thwart them.

Gregory raised his eyes to the heavens, darker than tar with a layer of clouds covering the stars and moon. *Thank You, God, for bringing them to help us.*

Because maybe now he could begin to undo the mess he'd started with that duel two years ago. Maybe now they'd be able to reach the coast safely. And maybe, just maybe, he could save his brother's life.

Chapter Five

"Where are your ropes?"

Danielle propped an eye open and stared up into the gray light of dawn, partially covered by the silhouette of a rather irritated blond man towering over her.

"We left you tied," Kessler added when she failed to reply.

She yawned. "Halston untied us."

"Halston?"

She nodded and snuggled back into the blankets. Usually she'd little trouble getting up of a morn, but then, usually she didn't stay awake into the wee hours of the night, either. And she had a long day ahead of her if she was going to lead this party of useless aristocrats through the countryside without any of them getting caught.

Kessler crouched down and hauled her up by her shoulders until she sat, then he leaned in, his mouth mere inches from her nose. "That's *Lord Gregory* to you."

She rolled her eyes. Of course he'd expect her to use their ridiculous English titles. Lord Kessler and Lord Westerfield and Lord Gregory could leave off the "lord" part of their own names and call her and Serge by their Christian names, but was she good enough to call Halston "Halston" or Kessler "Kessler"?

Not to their way of thinking. Arrogant, stubborn, insensitive oafs. This was precisely why France had gotten rid of its aristocracy.

"You forget yourself, *Kessler.*" She spit his name from her mouth while she twisted out of his hold. "You're in France now, not England. We don't have lords and ladies, just citizens."

"Of all the ridiculous notions. Of course you have lords and ladies. Who do you think runs this wretched country of yours?"

"Citizens, as I said." She stood, shaking out her wrinkled skirts and shoving her matted hair over her shoulder. "That's why we voted for Napoleon—because citizens are in charge. Which is more than a country with a tyrannical king like yours will ever understand."

"King George is not tyrannical." Kessler shoved to his feet, his bony, emaciated arms doing little to add to the authority of his stance as he crossed them over his chest.

"No? Did your people vote to elect him king?"

"Don't be ridiculous."

"Then it's tyranny."

"It's sound monarchial leadership. A much better way to run a country than putting a bunch of half-wits that know nothing about governing a nation in charge simply because people voted for them. One half-wit voting for another doesn't mean either should be in charge of the masses."

Her skin turned hot despite the cool winter air and her lack of cloak. There weren't lords and ladies, aristocrats and peasants before God. There were just people. All equal, all of value.

Just like there's not a difference between Jew and Greek, English and French.

She shoved the uncomfortable thought aside and glared at Kessler.

People were people, all the same and all equally important. And those people should have a say in who governed them.

"What about your servant Farnsworth there?" She gestured toward the stiff man rolling up the blankets where Halston and Kessler had slept. "Have you ever asked him whether he likes your King George?"

"Me?" Farnsworth squeaked. "I like King George well enough. Um, long live the king?"

Kessler cleared his throat, a smirk playing on his lips.

So perhaps attacking England's monarch wasn't the best way to make her point. "Fine then, Farnsworth. You like your king. Do you also like spending every moment of the day serving Kessler here?"

"He serves Halston," Kessler gritted.

She kept her eyes on Farnsworth, who'd stopped rolling blankets and was now looking at her. "Perhaps you'd like to be a duke from here on out and let Kessler and Halston serve you."

"I…uh…"

"After all, what makes Kessler and Halston worthy of being served? Because they were born into the right families and you weren't? Wouldn't you much rather be part of a country that values all people equally? That will allow you to stand on your own merits rather than condemn you to a life of servitude because of who your parents are?"

"That's enough," Halston's brother rasped from the sickbed.

She looked around, her cheeks turning suddenly hot. Had she woken Westerfield? That had not been her intent. Mayhap she'd spoken a little too much—or perhaps a shade too loudly—if she interrupted a dying man's sleep. But at least her words had achieved something. Farnsworth still stared at her, as though no one had ever bothered to tell him he was valuable.

Kessler stalked away, his back rigid and shoulders tight, not stopping to help Farnsworth with the blankets. No. His precious blue-blooded heritage had put him too far above such menial tasks.

She'd visited *Tante* Isabelle and *Oncle* Michel in England enough to understand the divisions of social classes.

At least her country's own *Révolution* had stripped the nobility of their titles. Was it bloody and violent? Yes. Had innocent people lost their lives? Far too many. But now France had freedom from the tyranny of aristocracy. Now its citizens were equals. Now her country acknowledged the value of all people rather than placing some above the rest.

She pressed her lips together. According to the stories she'd heard, *Tante* Isabelle had once viewed life in much the same way as Kessler. She had been born the daughter of a duke and raised with every luxury, yet her aunt had lost everything—and everyone—that mattered to her when the *Révolution* started. But she'd come to understand what truly mattered most in life. Love for God and family, respect for others. *Tante* Isabelle was a good lady, aristocratic birth or not.

Which was certainly more than she could say of *Lord* Kessler.

She turned her nose up at the man, now taking a sip of water while Farnsworth scrambled to clean up camp, then looked around the rest of the clearing. "Where are Serge and Halston?"

Kessler's jaw worked back and forth. "That's *Lord Gregory* to you."

She rolled her eyes.

"They went hunting." Farnsworth shoved some folded blankets into a sack lying by the fire. "First thing this morn. They wanted to bring back breakfast, I believe."

Hunting? Serge? She rolled her eyes again.

Almost predictably, a rustling sounded from the bushes and a moment later Halston stepped into the clearing, his hands empty of any game. "Actually, we returned in time to hear the argument. Or at least the end of it."

"What are you trying to do, Dani?" Serge followed Halston into the campsite, his hands also empty. What a surprise. "Alert all of France to where we are? You shouldn't shout so."

She cringed even as her cheeks grew warm. Mayhap she could have expressed her opinion more quietly.

And docilely.

And why was she thinking about being quiet or docile? A man like Kessler deserved to be yelled at.

"It was a rather interesting opinion." A bone-rattling cough emanated from Westerfield's chest.

"Indeed." Halston quirked an eyebrow at her, his eyes alight as though he was almost tempted to smile at her.

Smile!

"It was a rather amusing argument, to be sure." His bright eyes dared her to challenge him. "I assume you plan to call me Halston rather than Lord Gregory as we travel?"

"You're in France now, not England. I'll call you the same as your brother does and nothing else." She turned her back to him and bent to roll up her blankets. Maybe she should leave the lot of them in the woods after all. They'd probably learn more about humanity and people in a French prison than they ever would back in their precious England.

Gregory tried not to smile. Truly, he did. Something told him the warrior woman wouldn't take too kindly to the grin that tugged at the corners of his mouth. But goodness, was she magnificent. All that glorious black hair cascading freely down her head and over her shoulders, those crisp blue eyes practically burning holes in anyone who dared look at her, and the proud, regal way she held herself despite being nothing more than a peasant.

What he wouldn't give to meet a woman like her back in London. Instead, the ton was filled with simpering little dolls who hadn't the courage to voice whatever thoughts passed through their brains—if any thoughts were there in the first place. He was rather doubtful of that with some of the debutantes.

"You're staring," Serge growled from beside him. "At my sister. With an asinine grin on your face."

Right. Gregory cleared his throat and tore his gaze away from Danielle only to find a none-too-happy Serge glaring at him. "Um…sorry about that."

"Since when did she agree to travel with us?" Westerfield somehow managed to speak a full sentence without coughing.

"Last night, evidently, while the rest of us were abed," Kessler snapped. "Which makes me wonder…"

Kessler turned accusatory eyes on him, and Gregory stiffened. The man had no place making such crass insinuations after what Kessler had done to Suzanna.

"I offered her an extra thousand pounds," he proclaimed.

Danielle's gaze flew to his. Would she declare the money wasn't anything close to the reason she'd agreed to help?

Danielle pressed her lips together and then swung her gaze away. "Actually, I believe Halston is mistaken. He offered to pay me an extra *two* thousand pounds, totaling four thousand altogether."

His jaw fell open. "I did—"

"Just pay it." Westerfield propped himself up on his side and coughed. "You can afford it."

Danielle quirked the side of her mouth up in an uneven grin, but kept quiet—likely for only the second or third time in her life. "All right, then, let's eat some salt pork and pack up camp. The day's already wasting."

Gregory looked back to Serge, still standing beside him. "She's going to push us mercilessly, isn't she?"

The boy scratched behind his ear. "That was the reason you wanted her to guide you, right?"

Chapter Six

"Dani, slow down," Serge called.

Danielle rolled her eyes but paused at the top of the little knoll she'd just climbed, scanning the road that led down the incline before starting up another, larger hill.

"Oof!"

"Westerfield, can you walk?" Halston's voice echoed up the hill.

"I don't think he's awake, my lord."

"Kessler, come back here and help us."

More scuffles sounded behind her, as they had for most of the day. She dared not turn around and look. She carried her own sack plus a bundle of blankets and had no trouble keeping a good pace. Why couldn't the Englishmen manage the same?

Not that she begrudged an ill man for traveling slowly, but they had a channel to reach, did they not? With four others to aid him, certainly Westerfield could move faster.

She surveyed the valley and next hill lying before them—one that they should have crested hours ago—and tapped her foot on the ground. Every extra moment the Englishmen lingered in the country increased their chances of getting caught. But she hadn't considered how badly an ailing man would slow them down. They'd be fortunate to make it to the top of the next hill by nightfall, when she'd wanted to be halfway to Saint-Quentin.

Footsteps sounded behind her, their gait slow and weary. She turned to find Halston, his breathing hard and his dark hair disheveled and damp despite the cool air.

A faint odor of sweat mixed with the chilled breeze. "How long until we make camp?"

"Tired, *my lord*?"

"I can continue if you can."

It was an empty boast. He might stand there before her with arms crossed and back straight, but his shoulders sagged and dark shadows haunted the skin beneath his eyes.

"We'll stop at the top of the next hill."

His eyes traced the road down the little incline and up the larger one. "We have to rest before then. Westerfield won't be able to—"

"Then you should have brought a cart to carry him." She snapped the words quicker than intended, given that Westerfield struggled for breath when merely lying on his back. But she could hardly lead a band of four Englishmen to safety if the group traveled slower than an arthritic turtle.

Halston rubbed the back of his neck. "I didn't anticipate him being ill when I made plans for this escape."

"Just like you didn't anticipate the possibility of your guide deserting you? It seems you didn't make plans for much of anything, *my lord*."

"Don't mock my choices." He stepped closer, the shoulders that had been lifeless now rigid as granite.

His tall, lanky body loomed over hers until she could see naught but the coarse brown fabric of his peasant's coat, feel little but the heat radiating from him despite the dank, cold air. "You have no idea what I've sacrificed to find Westerfield."

"I have some idea." Because she would have sacrificed the same for Laurent—as would Serge and Julien—had she news her brother was alive somewhere in England.

But his guide's desertion made little sense. Halston was hardly the first person to rescue people from Verdun, and the consulate couldn't afford to put a price of two thousand pounds sterling on every escapee's head. So why would the guide turn down such a sum from Halston and attempt to foil an escape?

"Whether you understand matters little." He shoved a finger at her chest. "My brother needs rest now, or at least at the top of this hill."

She glanced back at the others, only halfway up the small incline, all hoisting their own sacks and helping Westerfield as he staggered drunkenly up the road that had taken her only a minute to walk.

Halston was being impossible. "You hired me to get you to England, yet you travel so slowly someone is bound to discover us. What do you expect from me? Shall I stand atop this hill and command the land between here and the coast to fall into the sea so we can sail safely to England? Or better yet, I'll blink my eyes and we'll instantly be transported to the coast."

"I refuse to let my brother get sicker. I refuse to let him die." Halston voice rumbled low and deep in his chest. "If anyone's life is risked, it should be mine." He was crowding her again, his eyes hot and intense.

"Pneumonia won't just hop from your brother's body

to yours because you wish it. And it hardly matters which of you—"

"He has pneumonia?" Halston reached out and wrapped a hand in the fabric of her cloak. Smoky, hope-filled eyes stared down at her, while the stubble on his chin cast a faint shadow over a jaw clenched hard with determination. "You know what's wrong with him?"

She bit the inside of her cheek. "Mayhap I spoke too hastily. I am hardly a physician. It might not be pneumonia. He could have pleurisy or some other foul lung disease."

Halston's hand fisted tighter in her coat, dragging her so close his lean body eclipsed any view of the others. "Surely, if you know what's wrong with him, you're familiar with some type of treatment."

"You're not listening." She wrapped her hands around his wrist and jerked his hands away from her coat, then took a step back. "I said I don't know what's wrong with him, and I don't. The only thing I know is that he shouldn't be walking in his condition. But then, we hardly have any choice since you haven't a cart to carry him. If you want answers beyond that, you'll have to find a physician."

"If finding a physician is my only chance to save Westerfield, you should have stated so this morning. We could have spent the day looking for one instead of traveling."

"And what do you suppose would have happened when this physician came to camp and learned his patient was English?"

"I can afford to buy his silence."

"Like you bought your last guide's silence?"

Halston's eyes flashed.

She stared right back at him, her chest heaving as she glowered into his ominous, aristocratic face.

"Dani! There's horses!"

She swiveled her head, first toward Serge, who was nearly at the top of the knoll with Westerfield, and then toward the larger hill in the distance. A quickly moving party of shadowed horses thundered down the opposite incline, the faint vibrations of their hoofbeats rattling the ground now that she was quiet enough to sense the motion.

"To the woods. Posthaste!" She turned and raced into the woods, running ahead of the group to find a patch of brambles thick enough to conceal them. Why hadn't she been paying better attention? She'd been standing atop a little hill, visible to all the world, as she argued with the infuriating man.

He deserved a comeuppance for distracting her—except she hadn't time for such things if she wanted everyone to be safe. Finding a hollow behind a tangle of spindly shrubs, she dropped her sack and blanket and rushed back out of the woods. The others had already helped Westerfield onto the dead winter grass lining the road.

"Follow the deer trail into the forest and then crouch down behind the brambles." She pointed toward the narrow path of trampled grass, then reached up to take Halston's sack from him. "Here. I can carry this while you help."

"Make haste." Serge glanced back toward the road, where the horses had disappeared in the valley between the hills. "A few more moments, and they'll be upon us."

"This is taking too long," Halston muttered, aiding his brother from behind while Kessler and Farnsworth dragged Westerfield from each side. "Stand back. I'll carry him."

"But my lord, you cannot—" Farnsworth's words dropped away as Halston did exactly as he'd proclaimed. He bent to swoop his brother up, supporting the limp man's back and legs with his arms. He didn't even look back as he barreled into the woods, Kessler and Farnsworth following close behind.

Danielle stared after him. So mayhap he wasn't that insufferable, caring for his ill brother with such unwavering purpose.

"Dani, are you coming?" Serge called from the opening in the brambles.

"Oui." She forced her feet forward, pausing at the start of the woods to move some tangled branches in front of the now-trampled path. Hopefully the soldiers wouldn't notice the newly beaten down grass.

Then again, if the soldiers had seen her and Halston standing atop the hill but passed no one on the road, they might stop and search. Should she and Serge go back to the road as though they'd been the only ones traveling?

There wasn't time. The beasts' hooves pounded loud and close, and Serge had already disappeared into the thicket. She'd little choice but to heft Halston's sack and creep carefully back to the others.

"Who are they?" Kessler whispered.

Serge shifted to peer through the brush, the road barely visible between the shrubs' snarled limbs. "Military."

"Military?" Kessler looked through the brambles, as well. "Between Saint-Quentin and Reims? Did you see their uniforms?"

Serge scowled. "This is France, not England. Only the military have horses here."

"Only the military?"

"You forget we've been at war with most of Europe for over a decade." Danielle, too, peered over her brother's shoulder, then turned back to face the men. "The military confiscated any horses of value long ago. Now hush. No more speaking until they've passed."

She watched the horses as they raced past, not slowing enough for any of the riders to notice the trampled grass leading off into the woods. The gendarmes' unmistakable uniforms stood out against the muted grays and browns of winter. Dark blue coats trimmed with white, tan breeches, black boots and bicorne hats. Her heartbeat rivaled the thump-thump, thump-thump, thump-thump of the horses' hooves. The sight of those familiar uniforms had never struck fear in her before, but how close had they been to discovering her and the Englishmen? Another half minute, or Serge failing to call out a warning, and...

Westerfield loosed a chest-rattling cough, and his eyes flickered opened for the barest of moments. "What's happening?"

She glared in his direction while reaching down and gripping the knife strapped to her ankle. Beside her, Serge reached for the blade settled into the waist of his trousers.

Halston bent and whispered something to his brother, but noise from the trampling beasts obliterated his words. The same noise must have prevented the gendarmes from hearing Westerfield's cough as well, because not a single gendarme glanced at the woods that concealed them.

Thank You, Father.

Wherever the men were headed, they certainly made haste, passing quickly until the clomp of hooves gradually faded. She stared warily through the brush, knife clenched in her hand and eyes alert until the last of them disappeared down the hill.

"I'm sorry," Westerfield rasped, his voice haggard and gravelly. "I—I didn't…" Another bout of coughing overtook him, the sound ringing through the forest while his body convulsed and his lungs wheezed for breath.

Danielle ran her eyes over the ill man and rubbed the tender space where a headache was building at the sides of her forehead. Was this how Laurent had died? In a foreign land at the mercy of some stranger?

Non. She couldn't think of such things now, not with a group of Englishmen to protect. Besides, Laurent's death at the hands of the British navy would have been swift and ruthless. A jab of a bayonet or firing of a musket. No mercy from the English. No one scrambling to save his life. "We need to get to Saint-Quentin, posthaste. We're traveling much too slowly."

"No. We need to travel slowly for Westerfield," Kessler retorted, his eyes still on the road as though he expected one of the gendarmes to return.

"That's not much of an option." At least not if he wanted his friend to live.

Halston's brows drew down. "Why is Saint-Quentin so important? You didn't mention it this morn. And don't tell me it's because of a gendarmerie post you're planning to visit."

She squeezed her knife extra hard as she shoved it back in its sheath. She'd promised the man she would help, had she not? "I didn't realize how sick your brother was. We need medicine and a cart to carry him."

"You can get medicine?" Halston's eyes rested on hers, that expectant expression back on his face.

Best not to give the man too much hope, not when his brother looked so sickly he might not live through the night. "I can try, but I promise you nothing beyond that."

She drew in a deep breath and looked away.

"How far is Saint-Quentin?" Kessler demanded.

"From where we left this morn, it should have taken us two full days, but at the rate we're traveling, we've got nearly two days left." If Westerfield even lived two days.

Perhaps she should have paid closer attention when they stopped for midday meal. Perhaps she should have walked slower from the beginning, offered to help with the ill man herself and not have pushed the group so hard.

The man's skin was no longer merely pale but held the gray hue of death, and a faint trace of blue tinged his lips. Saint-Quentin, medicine and a cart might only be a day and a half away, but it would do them little good if Westerfield couldn't live long enough to get supplies.

She looked away from the man, whose labored breathing filled the little thicket. He was the reason she'd agreed to help, but she hadn't realized the journey to the channel would kill him faster than any gendarme who discovered their whereabouts.

Danielle rose from her crouched position, as gracefully and naturally as a deer moving through a field—save for the tight set of her back. "Since we've stopped, we may as well settle farther back in the woods and make camp."

Gregory rolled his weary shoulders, careful not to

disturb where Westerfield leaned against his chest. The woman might wish to be nearer Saint-Quentin, but she and Serge were the only ones not exhausted from their travels. Plus, the group had barely made the woods in time to escape the gendarmes. If someone had tripped or Westerfield fallen, they'd all be staring down musket barrels about now.

"Serge, you scout ahead for a stream." Danielle pointed toward the thick trees growing behind the brambles. "We'll camp at least a kilometer back, and in thick patch of woods so our fire won't be spotted."

"Oui." Serge took off obediently, crashing through the barren branches.

Danielle bent to collect the sack of supplies and bundle of blankets, then paused, her worried gaze landing on Westerfield. "Westerfield, can you travel a bit farther tonight?"

Westerfield opened his eyes only long enough to give a faint nod before his eyelids drifted closed again.

Gregory reached out and laid a hand against his brother's burning forehead. "Perhaps we won't make it as deep into the woods as you're hoping, Danielle."

Her rigid shoulders fell just a bit. "That means a greater chance of being discovered."

Possibly, but his brother needed rest, not to be dragged half-conscious through brush. "You three go on ahead. I'll carry Westerfield after you find a spot to camp."

Danielle sighed and rubbed at the pale, creamy skin beside her eyes. "Fine, but don't wear yourself out to the point where you're as ill as your brother."

Kessler rose slowly, muttering something unintelligible as he took up his sack and a bundle of blankets before following Danielle into the woods.

Only Farnsworth remained behind. "Lord Gregory, you haven't the strength to carry Lord Westerfield."

Gregory looked down at his brother, his gray pallor and closed eyes, the sweat beaded on his forehead despite the cold January air. His chest rattled subtly with each shallow breath he took. "Perhaps, but 'tis worth it to aid my brother."

"Very well, sir." Farnsworth rose, taking up his own sack and the last of the blankets before moving off in the same direction as the others.

Gregory slumped back against a tree trunk, shifting his brother carefully so as not to disturb Westerfield's rest. He used his sleeve to dab at the sweat beaded along Westerfield's hairline.

Pneumonia, she had said.

Pneumonia killed people in England who were able to rest abed all day with servants to wait on their every need. If pneumonia could steal the life of a person such as that, what hope did Westerfield have of surviving?

Gregory bent his head over his brother's chest, his eyes suspiciously hot and moist. "Oh, Westerfield, what have I done? You were never supposed to die because of me."

But die Westerfield would, and all because Gregory and Kessler had fought a foolish duel over a serving girl.

Chapter Seven

Where was she?

Gregory shifted his gaze around the small clearing, searching for the familiar form of a tall, willowy woman shrouded in a brown cloak. To his right, Serge rummaged around in the packs, while Kessler sat on his own pallet eating salt fish and drinking the water that Farnsworth and Serge had dragged up from the stream. But Danielle was nowhere to be seen.

"Serge…"

Westerfield's wretched coughing sound interrupted his words.

Gregory turned back toward his brother, whose wheezy lungs gasped for air between each cough.

"Here, will this help?" He positioned himself behind Westerfield's back and raised his brother's painfully thin torso, but the new position did little to dissuade the coughs.

Had he truly hoped to ease the pneumonia simply by changing his brother's position? Westerfield had spent all day upright and that had done little good. Gregory set his brother down on the bed of blankets and withdrew his hands.

Footsteps thudded on the damp earth behind him, then Kessler squatted down and pressed a hand against Westerfield's brow.

"He sounds as though he's getting worse."

He is.

"Westerfield?" Kessler leaned over him. "Can you hear me? Is there anything we can do to make you more comfortable?"

Westerfield's eyelids flickered, and Gregory met Kessler's gaze over the sickly body. Did Kessler feel any guilt? Any bit of responsibility for Westerfield being so sick?

But Kessler's eyes were hard and flat as always, without silent apology or any hint of remorse.

Shuffling sounded from the woods, and Gregory raised his head to find Danielle approaching the little clearing, a makeshift rope filled with rabbits and squirrels dangling from her hand.

She'd been hunting? He hadn't even noticed her absence until a few minutes ago. Then again, she hadn't bothered to tell him she was leaving. She could have run off and escaped or gone in search of some gendarmes, and none of them would have realized until too late.

He needed to have a conversation with her about traipsing off into the woods. He might trust her enough not to bind her at night, but in return, she could take someone else with her on her hunting forays—or at least inform them when she was going.

Serge stood from where he sat by the fire eating salt pork and headed toward his sister. "I'll help you skin."

"Well, well, looks like the hoyden is good for something more than yelling at us to move faster." Kessler pushed away from Westerfield and approached the fire.

Danielle didn't even glance up from skinning the rabbit. "Repeat after me, *Lord* Kessler, 'Thank you.'"

"I think not. You're being paid well to take us to the coast, and such an exorbitant fee should include your hunting skills. Though I do appreciate your admitting I'm a lord."

Danielle dropped the animal she'd been skinning and rose to face Kessler, mobcap askew as hair tumbled from its perch atop her head. "Oh, how could I resist calling you by anything but your proper title, *my lord*? I wouldn't want you to go more than two minutes without someone reminding you of how superior you are to us commoners."

Farnsworth choked and dropped the flask of water he'd been holding. At least Serge had sense enough to not make a sound and reached for another squirrel.

"I don't need to be reminded every two minutes, but twice an hour should be sufficient, wouldn't you say, Lord Gregory?" Kessler cast a glance in his direction.

Gregory let out a quiet groan and stood. Another minute of this, and Danielle would have a knife at Kessler's throat.

"Well, I'd actually prefer to be called *lord* three times an hour now that I think about it." Kessler looked down his nose at Danielle.

She curled her bottom lip. "I should leave you to starve."

"Enough, please," Westerfield rasped.

Danielle's chest heaved as she drew in a breath, but then she took a step back from Kessler and ducked her head, almost as though suddenly embarrassed. "I'm sorry, Westerfield. I meant not to disturb you."

She approached Westerfield, passing Gregory, who stood halfway between his brother and the fire. "Now perhaps you should rest. I've given some thought to the morrow, and I don't think you should travel but sleep and attempt to gather your strength."

They weren't traveling tomorrow? Gregory moved back to his brother. Hadn't she proclaimed they needed to travel faster to reach Saint-Quentin?

"Don't stop—" Westerfield's eyelids fluttered open and he wheezed, attempting to prop himself up on his arm only to fall back down on his blankets "—on account of me."

A horrid coughing filled the air, and Danielle crouched down, helping Westerfield to sit up as the convulsions racked his body. Her actions seemed to ease his brother in a way Gregory's hadn't a few minutes earlier, as though a woman's touch was all that Westerfield needed to heal. Most unfair, that.

"Easy now. There's no need to alarm yourself." Danielle spoke in tones so soft and gentle Gregory almost didn't recognize her voice.

Would she speak that kindly to a child, perhaps one of her own? The orange flicker of firelight cast dancing shadows across Danielle's body. She'd make a good mother one day. A good wife, too, even with her penchant for knives.

And why was he thinking about Danielle Belanger as either a wife or a mother?

"Must...reach England," Westerfield choked out through a fading cough. "Can't...keep stopping."

"Lie back now." Danielle helped Westerfield onto the pallet and smoothed a hand across his brow. "You'll never see England if we keep today's pace. You need sleep and medicine, a cart to lie on while the rest of us walk. I'm a fool for not seeing it sooner. I nearly killed you today."

Gregory narrowed his eyes at Danielle. Sleep, medicine and a cart for Westerfield sounded wonderful, but how would they ever acquire them if they camped here rather than went to Saint-Quentin?

As though sensing his question, she looked up. "I know I intended for us all to travel together, but I didn't realize how ill your brother was. Serge and I will leave for supplies at dawn then return the following evening."

"No."

"There's no other choice." Westerfield looked up, his eyes pale and weak. "Not if I'm going to live."

"I agree with Halston." Kessler spoke from the other side of the fire, his eyes watching Danielle closely in the flickering light. "You and your brother aren't leaving this camp without us."

"It's not that you can't rest while Danielle travels to Saint-Quentin," Gregory clamped a firm hand on her shoulder. "But Danielle and Serge aren't going alone. I won't have it."

Danielle's eyes snapped to his. He could almost hear the sharp words that would likely spill from her mouth were she not kneeling beside Westerfield. *How dare you tell me what you will or won't allow? I'm neither your slave nor your servant and need no permission to do as I please.*

She jerked away from him and rose. "Rest, Westerfield. I'll make some bone broth for you after a bit." She stalked to the fire, where she set about impaling a rabbit on a makeshift spit.

Gregory followed. "You and Serge aren't going off alone for two days."

"Absolutely not," Kessler proclaimed. At least the man agreed with him for once rather than argued.

She crouched beside Serge, who'd already started

roasting one of the squirrels. "No? Would you rather your brother died from lack of medicine and harsh travel?"

Gregory's throat muscles constricted. "Of course not, but neither am I fool enough to let the two of you head off toward the coast without us. What's to keep you from announcing our campsite to some gendarmes and then continuing on your merry way home? If you want to go, I'll accompany you."

"Oh, that would be lovely. One word out of your mouth in Saint-Quentin, and the gendarmes will have us surrounded. Not to mention the way you walk and sit and act like a gentleman yet dress like an addle-headed peasant. We'd not last five minutes before someone reported you. If you want your brother to live, Serge and I will go alone."

"I don't trust you."

She held his eyes with her own. "And I don't trust you. But if I wanted to tell gendarmes about you, I could have flagged down the ones that rode past earlier. And I certainly wouldn't make you a camp and hunt some food before turning traitor."

"She's trying to trick you." Kessler sat on his pallet and flicked a stray twig off his coat. "Either you or I should go and leave the boy here."

Gregory rubbed the back of his neck. Kessler could bluster and object all night long, but she was right. Both he and Kessler would likely give themselves away. If he wanted his brother to live, trusting her and Serge wasn't just his best choice...

It was his only choice.

Danielle cast her gaze to the side and swallowed tightly. A gendarme stood not a meter away, surveying the crowd headed into Saint-Quentin's fortified walls. His blue coat and black bicorne hat made him stand out like a red fox against a field of snow, and his broad shoulders and thick torso turned her throat dry. He looked strong enough to wrestle any man present to the ground.

"Don't look so nervous," Serge whispered from beside her. "Are you trying to draw attention to us?"

"*Non.* Of course not." She licked her lips and cut another glance toward the gendarme.

Serge sighed. "That's precisely what I mean. Stop."

"Stop what?" She took a step to the side, only to bump an elderly woman holding a little boy's hand. What were all these people doing here? And why the delay at the gate ahead? "I'm not doing anything."

"Besides licking your lips and swallowing and staring at the gendarme every two seconds? Your face is paler than milk, and your hands are shaking. If I were *Papa* looking for spies, I'd have noticed you long ago."

"So I'm not good at keeping secrets!" She could fight her way out of almost any battle, but asking her to lie convincingly was quite a different matter.

"Hush, Dani. You're going to make him…"

But it was too late. The gendarme had already left his post at the side of the road and started shoving through people toward them.

Entering Saint-Quentin was supposed to be a simple task—slip in without anyone noticing them and leave a couple of hours later with their supplies. No throngs of people, no line at the gate, no waiting for two hours to inch a few feet closer to the city's fortified walls.

Within a matter of seconds, polished black boots met her own muddy ones.

"Papers, now!" the gendarme boomed in a voice so loud half the throng quieted.

Danielle sucked in a deep breath. Calm. She needed to be calm. He had no reason to suspect her of any illegal activity. All she need do was reach into her pocket and produce her citizenship papers.

Except her hands shook so badly she could barely find her pocket. She crinkled the papers before passing them off.

"You're from Abbeville? What brings you to Saint-Quentin?"

"We've been visiting our *tante* in Reims for the past three months and needed to stop by Saint-Quentin for supplies on the way home."

How did Serge's voice manage to sound calm and unmoved when they could be imprisoned if this gendarme discovered they were helping enemies?

"Visiting your aunt?" Disbelief dripped from the gendarme's voice. "I see no valise or supplies."

"We camped outside the city last night and hoped to slip in and out quickly this morning." Serge spoke the words easily, as though omitting the four Englishmen that camped with him was as natural as swallowing a mouthful of water. "We never expected such a throng."

"Is that so?" He jabbed a blunt, stubby finger into her shoulder.

She jerked her eyes up to meet the gendarme's, and she found herself staring into a chiseled face with hard brown eyes, an overlarge nose and eyebrows spaced too far apart.

He shoved a handbill in front of her face—a handbill with a rather accurate sketch of Kessler and Westerfield plastered on the front. "Have you seen these men?"

Her stomach cramped. Was that the reason for this

crowd? Were gendarmes searching the city gates for Kessler and Westerfield?

She raised her right foot ever so subtly. She could have her knife in hand in under a second to defend herself.

But just as she inched her palm down, Serge's hand gripped her wrist. Hard.

"Please, sir. My sister and I just want to get into the city for a few supplies. That's all. Mayhap you can explain why there's such a crowd?"

The gendarme jerked the handbill away from her face. "Perhaps you wouldn't have heard if you've been traveling, but two British spies escaped from prison five nights ago. We've got strict orders to search the papers of every person entering the city."

Spies? Danielle's eyes dropped to the handbill in the gendarme's hand and the bold word printed just below Westerfield and Kessler's faces. *Espions.* Spies. Threats to her country's liberty. They were supposed to be just Englishmen interred at Verdun with all the other captive English, not spies. At least according to Gregory.

Sweat beaded on the back of her neck. But spies imprisoned in a dungeon made more sense. That was the type of place where men would be nigh starved, or get sick and die of pneumonia. The type of place much more fitting for what she saw of Kessler and Westerfield's too-thin bodies than the city where Napoleon held his British visitors.

"I ask again, have you seen anything suspicious?" The gendarme's hard gaze refused to let hers go.

"N-n-n…" *Nothing terribly suspicious, no.* But the words wouldn't come. Halston had lied to her. He'd made his brother and Kessler out to be like any other

British captives, living a life of normalcy and ease inside the walled city of Verdun.

"Non." Serge's answer rang clearly over the crowd. "We've been fine, haven't we, Dani? Nothing suspicious."

"Nothing suspicious," she finally muttered. But her stomach churned sickeningly.

She and Halston had much to discuss when they returned to camp.

If she decided to go back at all.

Chapter Eight

"Come, Westerfield. Another swallow." Gregory lifted his brother's shoulders while Farnsworth held a flask of broth to his lips, but Westerfield's eyelids didn't even flutter; nor did his throat move.

He laid his unconscious, wheezing brother gently back on the pallet.

"Would you like to try again, my lord?" Farnsworth twisted the lid securely onto the container. "Perhaps just water this time, rather than bone broth?"

Gregory pressed his eyes shut. What was the use? Westerfield wasn't even conscious, let alone eating or drinking. "No."

"Very well, sir." Farnsworth stood, flask in hand. "Can I get you some food, then? Or perhaps some broth for yourself?"

He shook his head and stared out across the dreary little clearing, the clouds above casting a gray pall over the afternoon. What right did he have to eat or drink while his brother remained so ill?

Perhaps if Danielle returned with the medicine, Westerfield might take a turn for the better, but Danielle and Serge had promised to return by last night, and were now running a half day late.

A twig snapped in the woods, followed by the sound of boots on leaves. Gregory turned as Kessler stomped into camp. "Are they coming?"

Kessler's eyes were hard and angry. "They've deserted us. There's no sign of them."

Gregory stood on legs that felt leaden and aged beyond his eight and twenty years. "Then something must have detained them."

"Nothing detained them. That was the problem. You gave them a chance to run, and they took it."

He crossed his arms. "If that were true, we'd have been encircled by gendarmes two days ago."

"Perhaps they didn't turn us in, but they still left us." Kessler stalked to the fire, presenting his back as he helped himself to some water. "I told you not to let them go."

"You blame me for this?"

From where he sat on a fallen log, Farnsworth stopped sipping his bowl of broth, his eyes moving between the two of them.

"Why shouldn't I?" Kessler tipped his head back and drank deeply. "One of us should have gone with the wench instead of her brother, but you refused to listen."

"Danielle said we'd have been found out in under a minute," he growled at Kessler's back.

"'Danielle said,'" Kessler mocked. "Tell me, since when does London's richest man of business bow to the whim of some frog?"

He looked down at Westerfield, his face gray and faint breaths rattling inside his chest. "Since she's saving our lives."

"She's not saving our lives—she's deserting us. And

in the meantime we don't even have someone here who knows how to hunt."

"So you didn't find food, either? Not even a squirrel?" Gregory raked a hand through is hair. "Can you do anything besides stomp around camp and argue?"

"I'm skilled at a great many things, as you well know."

"I meant besides debauching maids." The words slipped out of his mouth before he thought to check them, crashing to the ground like large, insurmountable boulders.

"I beg your pardon," Kessler spoke slowly. Quietly.

"I'm sorry. I shouldn't have—"

"Oh, no. You should have. You definitely should have." Red rushed up Kessler's neck and cheeks all the way to the tips of his ears. "It's what you've been thinking all along, isn't it? Ever since you first pulled me from that wretched dungeon. In fact, if your brother hadn't been imprisoned beside me, you'd have left me to rot, would you not?"

"Do you deserve anything less than a dungeon after how you treated Suzanna?"

"You act as though I ravished your sister, not some serving girl."

Did Kessler hear his words? How arrogant they sounded? How cruel? How ruthless? Did Suzanna somehow not matter because she was in service? Perhaps Danielle had the right of it when she spoke of people's value not being based on who their parents were. "Serving girl or not, you were still wrong."

"And I tried apologizing!" A vein throbbed along Kessler's neck.

"Last I checked, you couldn't give a woman her virtue back with a mere apology."

"Can we calm down, my lords? I'm not sure all this shouting is good for Lord Westerfield." Farnsworth stuck a finger in his collar and tugged.

Kessler's jaw worked back and forth. "As I told you before the duel, you see only what you want to see, but what's the point of trying to explain when you're too self-righteous to listen? Perhaps I will go hunt more squirrel. That's certainly more appealing than being stuck in this camp with you." Kessler dropped the flask of water and stalked off toward the woods.

Gregory heaved in a giant breath of air. He should let Kessler walk away. Of course he should. Nothing good would come of fighting further.

But the sight of the other man retreating, his back straight and shoulders squared, his blond hair pulled back into its queue was so similar to when he'd walked away after Gregory confronted him about Suzanna. And again, when he'd walked away after the duel, leaving Gregory crumpled on the ground with a leg wound that had given way to an infection that nearly took his life.

Kessler wasn't going to walk away a third time.

"It's time we have this out." He charged forward and yanked Kessler around by the shoulder.

"My lords…" Farnsworth shouted.

Gregory swung his fist into Kessler's stomach, and Kessler stumbled back, bumping into one of the tripod legs near the fire.

"Look out for the broth and fire," Farnsworth finished, but too late.

The little pot of broth tipped and extinguished the flames, emptying the last of their food—food that Westerfield needed.

Kessler jerked away from Gregory's hold. "This is ridiculous. I've apologized for Suzanna time and again.

The problem isn't with me. It's with you. You refuse to forgive me."

"You think *I'm* the problem? You're the one impossible to work with. Always too good to help find squirrel or pack up bedding or carry water. Staring at Danielle as though she's Suzanna."

"I don't look at Danielle that way."

Gregory lunged forward and gripped Kessler's coat by the collar, jerking him forward until their breaths tangled. "Don't lie to me. I've seen you look at her."

"I haven't set eyes on a woman in over a year," Kessler growled. "I can't help it if—"

"What are you fools doing?" A displeased feminine voice cut through the clearing.

Gregory dropped his hands from Kessler and took a step back. Danielle stood on the opposite side of the camp, her mass of hair tucked up beneath that tiny mobcap while stray wisps fell about her face.

She was back and safe. *Thank You, God.*

"You're late." Kessler tromped around the fire toward her. "What took you so long?"

Gregory gritted his teeth. Had the man learned nothing from their argument? "He means, ah…we hope you didn't meet with any trouble returning."

She propped a hand on her hip and surveyed the three of them, her eyes lingering on the spilled broth. "That's why you were fighting? Because I hadn't returned?"

"Ah…somewhat…"

"The business between Lord Gregory and myself is none of your concern." Kessler straightened the crumpled collar of his coat.

"Danielle." Farnsworth stood and headed toward her. "Did you get medicine for Lord Westerfield? Is there anything I can help with?"

"None of my concern." Danielle glared at Kessler, her voice going from curious to a low, deadly calm.

"Danielle?"

She didn't even look at Farnsworth, who had come to stop beside her. "Tell me, how much more of this journey is 'none of my concern'? And I'll not listen to any more of your lies."

Gregory furrowed his brow. "We've not lied to you, Danielle."

"No? Do you agree with your friend Kessler and claim everything is 'none of my concern,' as well?"

Gregory could hardly call the lout his friend. Westerfield's friend, perhaps. Though he'd never understood why.

"Like Kessler and Westerfield not being imprisoned in Verdun is 'none of my concern'?" Spite dripped from Danielle's voice.

Gregory winced. Had she discovered the truth about his brother and Kessler on her trip to Saint-Quentin? "Perhaps we should have explained more—"

"Like the fact that they're escaped spies?"

The blood drained from his face. He cast a glance at Kessler, but the other man looked as immovable and hardened as ever, while Danielle's voice grew louder with every word she uttered.

"I'll tell you what else is 'none of my concern.' All four of you." She spread her arm to encompass the camp.

"Dani." Serge broke through the trees. "I could hear you shouting from ten meters away. Calm down."

"It doesn't matter whether I'm calm or not." Danielle's creamy cheeks darkened to a dull pink. "We're leaving. Just give me a few minutes to show Farnsworth the medicines Westerfield needs. He doesn't deserve to die because of these two idiots."

Serge scratched his head. "Are they really spies?"

"Spies or not, I won't spend the next two weeks traveling with people I can't trust." She turned then and stalked to Westerfield, kneeling over him and unfolding a little pouch. "Farnsworth, I need your assistance."

The servant dropped to the ground beside her, leaving Serge to stand by himself. "But what about the cart and mule hidden by the road?"

"Leave them for Westerfield. They'd only slow us down."

"There's no need to leave them," Kessler boomed. "Because you're not breaking from our party."

Gregory turned to Kessler and gripped his arm before whispering, "Keep quiet, man. Do you want her to stop helping Westerfield?"

"We can't let her leave," Kessler whispered furiously. "She'll turn us in to the first gendarmerie post she comes across."

"If she was going to do that, she'd not have returned at all. Look at her." He gestured toward Danielle's hunched form studiously working beside his brother. "If nothing else, she wants Westerfield to live."

"And cares not whether the rest of us live or die."

Gregory blew out a breath. "I probably should have told her where you and Westerfield had been imprisoned."

"You mean you didn't?"

"She suspected we were spies as soon as she saw us. Do you think telling her everything would have convinced her to help? I thought it better to let her assume you were in Verdun."

Kessler crossed his arms over his chest. "So you lied?"

Gregory cleared his throat. "I...ah...didn't exactly correct her assumptions."

Kessler's upper lip curled into a vicious snarl. "And here you blame me for—"

"Do one of you want to go hunting with me?" Serge stepped around the fallen pot and smoking embers of the now-dead fire. "Dani will have to make poultices and then separate our things from yours, so we've got at least an hour."

Kessler looked down his nose at the boy.

"Go," Gregory urged. "I'll remain here and see if I can convince Danielle to stay."

"It's no use." Kessler jerked his chin toward where Danielle still knelt over Westerfield. "That woman is as stubborn as a mule."

"Perchance, but it's worth the try."

"Fine." Kessler huffed out a breath. "But don't think this conversation is finished. You're arrogant and self-righteous, Halston, and a hypocrite, as well. You always stand in judgment over us all as if you are free of wrongdoing. But you lied about where Westerfield and I were imprisoned. That's on your head, and if you can't make things right with Danielle I'll hold you accountable." He stalked off with Serge into the woods.

The muscle in Gregory's jaw clenched involuntarily. Kessler thought him arrogant and self-righteous? *Him?* What had he ever done besides give to the poor and aid the needy? He was the sole funder of the Hastings Orphanage and more generous than many a peer with his giving to London's various foundling hospitals and poorhouses.

And he'd never once debauched a woman, only helped the ones left destroyed in Kessler's wake. Suzanna had hardly been the first, just the most personal.

Yet Kessler had the gall to call him hypocritical for not correcting Danielle's assumptions about Verdun. It had seemed the wisest option at the time, nothing more and nothing less.

But evidently it hadn't been the best choice, not if Danielle wanted to leave them because of it.

He sighed and made his way across the small clearing toward Danielle. Though not yet evening, the gray winter light shone down on her through the spindly branches above, illuminating her round cheek and tapered jaw as she worked intently on his brother. A woman as beautiful and vibrant as she belonged somewhere like a London town house or ballroom, with maids to wait on her every need and a string of suitors following her.

But she wasn't in London. Nor was she aristocracy. She was a French peasant with an uncanny understanding of the woods and survival.

And she was his only hope of reaching England alive.

He stepped closer. "Danielle."

She held up a hand, not bothering to take her eyes from her work. "Farnsworth, I need some water."

Farnsworth jumped up and rushed for Kessler's discarded flask while Danielle took a little wooden mortar and pestle out of her pouch.

Gregory cleared his throat and tried again. "Danielle, I'm sorry. Truly."

Her shoulders stiffened.

"I want you to know—"

"Your words won't sway me, Halston. But if you want your brother's condition to improve, I suggest you stand back and let me work."

"Will this be enough?" Farnsworth returned with the half-empty container of water.

She took the container and looked inside. "*Merci*, Farnsworth. It will do for now."

Unstrapping the knife from her ankle, she cut into… an onion? She'd brought his dying brother an onion?

Farnsworth frowned at the flakey brown vegetable. "Do you think that will help?"

"Nothing can hurt at this stage." She placed the onion inside the mortar and first minced, then crushed it before adding it to the water. Then she took a head of garlic from her pouch and minced that as well.

Farnsworth pinched his nose. "That smells strong."

"Hopefully it's strong enough to cut through whatever has contaminated Westerfield's lungs." She put the garlic in the flask then took a scoop of an amber liquid—honey, perhaps?—and added it to the drink. "We need to let this sit for a while, but we'll make a plaster for his chest while we wait."

She set to work on that, cracking eggs and adding flour, getting a yellowish powder from a smaller pouch and combining it to the mixture.

Gregory clamped his lips together and watched her work. Perhaps she was French. Perhaps she was a peasant. But she was also the strongest, most dedicated woman he'd ever met. As soon as Westerfield had his medicine, the two of them were going to talk things through.

Or rather, he was going to fall down on his knees and beg her to stay.

Chapter Nine

Danielle stared down at Westerfield, bare to his waist with a yellow mustard plaster slathered atop his skin. Leaving his shirt open so the plaster could set, she covered him loosely with a blanket and rose to face Farnsworth.

"This is all I know to do. If it doesn't help, then…" She refused to speak the words, as if they'd prove true if she uttered them. Though 'twas a ridiculous notion. What good could come of garlic and onion and honey? But the apothecary's wife had given her the old remedy in lieu of other medicines or bloodletting, and at least she'd tried to save him.

"Give him as much of the onion and garlic water as he'll drink and keep the paste on his chest at all times. When you run out of either, make more. Do you have any questions?" She wiped a hand across her brow, damp with perspiration despite the chilly air.

"No, Citizen," Farnsworth answered. "Thank you for your help."

Citizen. She paused at the use of the word. Evidently her lectures weren't lost on all the Englishmen.

"I've things to prepare for our journey. If Serge returns, let him know I'm at the cart packing." The wagon and old mule would never have made it back to the camp without leaving a telltale trail through the woods, but she still had some of her supplies stored in the cart—which she should probably show Halston.

As though sensing she was thinking about him, Halston jumped up from his perch on a nearby log. "Danielle, wait. Let me explain."

"I'm done listening to your 'explanations.'"

His jaw fell open. Likely because she was the first woman to ignore his fancy words and pleading looks. Well, he could keep that jaw open for as long as he liked. She wasn't going to listen.

Farnsworth rested a hand on her forearm. "*Merci*, Citizen Belanger. You have been most helpful, and I'm sorry to see you go."

She laid a hand over his fingers. In some ways, she was sorry, too, but some things couldn't be helped. "I hope your Lord Westerfield lives."

"And the rest of us?"

She glanced around the campsite, still empty of Serge and Kessler. She didn't want these Englishmen dead, *non*, but neither could she continue to aid people who told her lies. "I hope you make it safely to England, but you must understand..."

He squeezed her arm. "I do. And Citizen, those words you spoke when you first agreed to journey with us—the ones about people being valuable and standing on their own merits?—I understand those, too. I think I even agree. Thank you."

She couldn't help the small smile that curved the edges of her mouth. Perhaps some of her ramblings and mutterings hadn't been futile after all. "You're valuable,

Farnsworth. Don't let anyone tell you differently because you weren't born to a duke or some other peer."

"I won't."

"Adieu." She cast a glance at Halston, still standing near the log, and blew out a little breath. Either she or Serge still needed to show someone where the cart was hidden, especially since one of the men would need to sleep with the mule and conveyance tonight. She could wait for Serge to return and have him bring Halston or Kessler where the cart was, but doing so would delay their departure.

Taking Halston with her now was the most obvious solution, even though the man would surely bludgeon her with all the reasons she shouldn't leave. She straightened her shoulders and took a step toward him. "I've hidden the cart and mule by the road. If you want to find the beast again, you'd best follow."

She headed away from the camp, the tromping of boots through the brush behind her indicating he followed.

"Danielle, wait. I wish to speak with you."

Could the man not understand? Another conversation would only lead to more arguments—arguments she had neither the strength nor inclination to endure. She moved lithely around branches and saplings, not quite quickly enough to lose Halston altogether, but not slowly enough that he could catch her.

"Danielle!" Her name echoed through the forest, louder this time than the last.

Was the clod trying to get them all captured? She paused for a moment, until the dreary gray of his greatcoat flashed through the trees, then started walking again.

"Danielle, please."

The cart and mule came into view, nestled in a patch of brambles near the road. She held out a handful of oats from her pocket as she approached. The old, tired animal had cost an exorbitant sum thanks to the military confiscating every reliable beast in France, but the extra money Halston had provided eventually convinced the cobbler who'd owned him to sell.

"There, boy," she whispered, stroking his head. "Rest easy tonight. You've got a big task ahead of you, taking Westerfield to the coast."

The gray animal nibbled the oats and then snorted.

Footsteps sounded in the trees to her left. "Danielle, did you not hear me calling for you?"

She pressed her fingers to her temple. "I've no desire to speak with you, I just brought you to show you the beast. Now that you've seen him, you can head back to camp."

"I wish to explain." Halston moved toward her, all wide shoulders and tall body and aristocratic bearing. His tousled brown hair hung over his forehead while a handful of twigs snagged the bottom of his coat.

"Save your words for someone who wants to hear them."

"Do you not wish to know why Westerfield and Kessler were imprisoned?"

"Non." It wasn't a lie. She didn't want to know, because she didn't care about a bunch of English spies who refused to treat her fairly despite how much she'd risked to help them.

So why did questions niggle in the back of her mind?

Halston settled himself against the side of the cart, arms crossed and hip leaning against the wood. "They were never interred at Verdun with the rest of the British."

"I understand that now, very much. *Merci*." She clamped her teeth down on her tongue. Hard.

"They were in Paris when the Peace of Amiens ended. I'm sure you remember how quickly the treaty fell apart, after which Napoleon rounded up all the British visiting France."

"Your king declared war and captured two of our frigates first."

He waved his hand in the air, as though it made little difference which country had been the first to break the treaty, which had been the first to declare war and then perform the act that began it. "The point is—"

"That your country started this war?"

He scowled. "You know it's not as simple as that."

She rubbed her hands together to ward off the encroaching cold. Perhaps it wasn't. Napoleon certainly hadn't abided by his terms of the treaty—not that she was about to admit France's guilt.

"Kessler and Westerfield attended a ball in Paris before the treaty broke. They were in the garden talking, but afterward someone accused them of overhearing…things."

"What kind of things?"

"Things that allowed them to be incarcerated as spies."

She stiffened. "I knew they were spies from the first."

And she'd been a fool for allowing herself to become tangled in their dastardly mission. But not anymore. She was washing her hands of them, bidding them good riddance and not looking—

"They're not spies." Halston straightened to his full height. "They were accused of spying. There's a difference."

She straightened her back, also, though any threatening effect her posture might have was likely lost on a man who towered over her. "And you expect me to believe this?"

His eyes turned from the color of fog over the ocean to the shade of deep, dark storm clouds. "When Napoleon rounded up his British visitors two days later, my brother and Kessler were thrown into a dungeon to molder, mostly with other Frenchmen accused of thwarting your beloved Napoleon. It took nearly a year and over ten thousand pounds for me to find them."

Ten thousand pounds just to find his brother? Something inside her chest tightened. But then, she'd known from the beginning that Halston was loyal and determined when it came to his brother's welfare. 'Twas the only reason she was still standing here, in his presence, instead of halfway home by now.

But his story was utterly ludicrous. Oh, he spoke his words smoothly, looked at her with those charming eyes and entreated her to believe him, but she was neither a schoolgirl nor a fool. "So Westerfield and Kessler were imprisoned after being tried and convicted as spies, but you claim they should be free? How surprising."

"They weren't tried," he growled. "They were simply imprisoned."

"After going before a magistrate."

"No magistrate, no tribunal, no trial. An officer close to Napoleon accused them of overhearing something about the navy at Boulogne. Then they were thrown into a dungeon and left to starve."

She furrowed her brow. Would Napoleon truly imprison someone on a flimsy accusation? Two British peers, no less? And if so, wouldn't England have tried to get the men back in some sort of prisoner exchange?

King George held four times the number of prisoners as Napoleon. It shouldn't be that difficult for the British government to arrange something with the French. "'Tis no secret about the navy stationed at Boulogne. Half of England knows of it, from what I understand. I can't think why that information is enough to imprison two men."

Halston paced the ground before her, his shoulders tight and gait stiff. "I know I've given you little reason to believe me, but I swear I speak the truth. My brother and Kessler were caught in the wrong place, but they were never spies."

Oui. He had given her little reason to believe him. Too little. And he had every reason to lie now, every reason to convince her Westerfield and Kessler sought not to harm her country. And yet, a part of her still believed him. Curse those beseeching, smoky-blue eyes and the honesty ringing from his voice. This man would be the death of her.

"What prison were they in? I've heard there's one in Bitche. Another in Sedan."

"No. Not Bitche. Not Sedan. Not anywhere near a city where people might know of them. They were held in a secret, forgotten dungeon northwest of Reims. One where the prisoners are starved of food and water. One where sickness runs rampant. 'Tis surprising Kessler's not deathly ill along with Westerfield, to hear Kessler tell it."

A secret prison where men were starved? 'Twas unthinkable. Or rather, it should be unthinkable. But in some ways, the information made entirely too much sense in light of *Papa*'s secret work. Did *Papa* know of these prisons?

Halston stopped his pacing and looked up at her. "Do you believe me?"

She eyed him. "You lied to me before. What's to prevent you from lying now?"

"I didn't lie. You assumed."

"I assumed?" She shoved herself away from the cart. "That's your excuse? I *assumed*?"

"I never said they were in Verdun. You supposed they were there, and I…ah, I…failed to correct you."

She glared up into the smooth planes of his handsome, blue-blooded face. "Exactly."

He laid a hand on her shoulder, gentle despite the way her body trembled with anger. "Not because I wanted to deceive you, but because I needed you, Danielle. I needed you."

He needed her? *Needed?* He had to be mistaken. People didn't need Danielle Belanger. Quite the opposite. She was always in the way. Always doing men's work. Always ruining the bread she attempted to bake and messing up her mending. Always underfoot. Always…

"Danielle?"

The sound of her name on his lips drew her gaze back to his face.

"Is something wrong?" His hand squeezed her shoulder. "Did I say something I ought not?"

She clamped her eyes shut lest the hotness building behind them turn into moisture and slip down her cheeks. "*Non*. You said nothing wrong."

"Then why do you cry?"

She blinked furiously, but the rebellious tears pooled in her eyes anyway. "I'm not crying." Because she wasn't. She refused.

He took her chin in his hand and raised it until their eyes met. "What did I do? Tell me. I know not."

She sniffled and swiped at a tear with the back of her hand. This was nonsensical. He could lie about where Westerfield and Kessler were imprisoned with little care and force her to lead them to the coast without concern, but the moment her eyes grew teary, he was suddenly undone.

"Nothing. You did nothing. I just wish…oh, never mind."

Gregory reached out and stroked a strand of hair behind her ear, her skin soft and warm. She stilled beneath his hand, her eyes on his in the dim light of the woods, her lips just a breath away from his own. He stared down at them, full and red from the bite of winter's chill. What would kissing them feel like? Fierceness and determination, like the woman he'd first met in the woods four days past? Or tenderness and sorrow like the hurting woman standing before him now? He inched forward the slightest bit, leaning his head down another inch.

"Stop." She gasped and jerked back, wrapping her arms about her middle. "You can't…we can't…" Her face flushed a dull pink, and she swallowed. "Don't do that again."

He blew out a breath and scrubbed a hand over his jaw. Had he nearly just kissed her? A peasant woman he could never pursue? And not just a peasant, but one whose country was preparing to invade his own? "I hardly think that will be possible, seeing how you're leaving in a few minutes."

She looked down at her feet and then peered back up at him. "You understand why I have to leave, do you not?"

She turned away and reached down with a trembling

hand for the sack that had slipped to the ground at some
point in their conversation.

"I was rather hoping you'd still help us."

"I can't."

"I'm sorry I wasn't more honest from the beginning." And he was. "I simply...I'd do anything to save
my brother, and I feared you'd leave if you knew he'd
been accused of spying."

She shoved another tress of falling hair behind her
ear and sniffled. "Like I'm leaving now?"

"A bit like that, yes."

"You rescued your brother and Kessler from a secret
prison." She opened another sack in the back of the cart
and collected a handful of supplies. "You only need to
reach the coast now. You'll be fine without me."

He'd be fine without her? The trip to Saint-Quentin
must have somehow addled her mind. "We won't last a
week, which I knew when I first came to France. That's
why I hired a guide. It's not my fault he deserted us."

"It is if you offered to pay him a measly two-thousand
guineas. The consulate has a bounty of double that on
Westerfield and Kessler's heads."

It did? Gregory's tongue turned dry as sawdust.
"How do you know such a thing?"

"Handbills are posted all over Saint-Quentin. When
you offered your guide that two thousand pounds, you
failed to consider how valuable British spies are to our
government. A couple of escapees from Verdun? Not
worth so much. But men who might impart war secrets to our enemies? And especially men of the peer-
age? They're valuable indeed. If Napoleon had a mind
to trade Kessler and Westerfield back to England for
money, King George would probably pay ten thousand
pounds apiece for their safe return. When your guide

betrayed you, he was likely thinking that your party was worth more money were he to catch you when you were free, especially if you already gave him part of the money promised."

He pressed his forefinger and thumb to the shallow indentations in his eyebrows. He had indeed paid his guide a handy sum once the man had located Westerfield and Kessler's prison. But then, why hadn't his guide laid a better trap? Had gendarmes meet them at the rendezvous spot once Kessler and Westerfield had been freed?

Because there wouldn't have been a large reward placed on their heads yet? "He probably still searches for us, then."

Danielle looked over her shoulder and surveyed the trees, as though scanning them for sudden danger. "*Oui.* And he would know the roads you planned to take, as well as where you've booked a boat along the channel."

"Berck. I have passage back to England arranged with some…er, fishermen in Berck. That's how I first found my guide, through the fishermen's recommendation."

Her eyes took on a knowing gleam. "You need not lie to me about the fishermen, Halston. I can discern the difference between a fisherman and smuggler."

Were his dealings that obvious? "The truth is, much of this business of getting Westerfield back to England has been unsavory. But he's not a spy, nor does he pose any threat to your country, and since I'm to blame for his capture, I need to see him freed and returned home. But I can't do any of that without you. None of us can hunt like you or scout out where to set camp. We don't know the back roads to the coast or the narrow paths to follow through the woods. And if anyone spots us, if we have to talk for any reason…"

She turned back to the wagon and picked up the bundle of clothing. "Here, take these back to the camp and make use of them. They should make your disguise more believable, provided you don't need to say anything in French."

He accepted the sack and dug through a few of the items. "These are finer than what we're wearing, and more colorful." Blue breeches instead of the drab gray or brown. A dark red waistcoat.

"That's because you don't pass for peasants, even in your rags. Your posture is too straight and your mannerisms too refined. Better to dress like members of the bourgeoisie."

She continued packing, taking things from various sacks in the back of the cart and transferring them all to the single one she held.

"Is there nothing I can do to change your mind about leaving us?"

"I should have never helped in the first place." She took a bundle of salt pork from his sack and placed it in her own.

"Then why did you?"

"Because I wanted Westerfield to live. Because if it were my brother stranded in England, I'd hope and pray someone, anyone…" She blew out a breath and gave her head a subtle shake. "*Non.* I was wrong to ever help. I knew not what I risked until I entered Saint-Quentin yesterday."

What *she* risked? "Your danger is little compared to ours."

She dropped her sack, her hand flying through the air so quickly he hadn't time to halt it before her palm struck his cheek. "How dare you. You think you're the only one who risks something on this journey? You know nothing. Nothing! Of who my family is, of how we could be hurt, of the dangers that await everyone I love were Serge and I to be caught."

His skin smarted from the slap, and he raised his hand to cover it. "No, I rather suppose I don't."

"My father's name might not be recognizable to you, but he's a member of Fouché's police force. He's been secretly reporting to the Minister of Police since the middle of the *Révolution*, long before Napoleon rose to power and gave Fouché his official role."

Gregory sank back against the cart. Her father was a member of some secret network? The same secret network that ran the prisons where Westerfield and Kessler had been? The same secret network that would have reported his brother and Kessler as spies in the first place?

"I failed to think about the consequences of helping you at first. Perhaps I believed in the back of my mind that if Serge and I were found and accused as traitors, *Papa* could use his connections to free us. But then when I went into Saint-Quentin and saw the gendarmes searching the crowds and handbills advertising your disappearance, I realized the truth. If Serge and I are found out, *Papa* won't be able to free us, and he'll likely be arrested and thrown into prison. And not just him, but the rest of my family. My *maman*, my four little sisters, one of whom has not yet reached her first year. How do you think a babe would fare inside the prison cell that held Kessler and your brother?"

A babe. Gregory's stomach churned. She was right. He hadn't considered what she was risking. Hadn't asked. Hadn't assumed she risked much at all. She seemed so sure and confident, so invincible. Able to conquer anyone or anything that stood in her way.

"I'm sorry." He'd spoken the words more times in this single conversation than he likely had in his past twenty-eight years. But they no longer seemed enough. "I should have been more honest from the start. I should have considered the threat to your family."

"I deserved to be told the truth. Just because I'm French and can't claim a marquess or earl as my father doesn't mean you can belittle me."

"I never thought it did."

Her throat worked back and forth. "You're lying again."

"I'm not lying. I'm only…I was so concerned about Westerfield that I…" He sighed, because truly, what more was there to say? He hadn't thought about the sacrifices this quest would require of her or her brother.

She stood beside the mule, her cheeks overly pink, her dark tresses slipping from their pins to fall in little waves about her shoulders and hurt rolling off her like waves from the sea. Both of them concerned for their families, both trying protect their kin. How could he fault her for wanting to shield those she loved?

Curse this senseless war that pitted them against each other. That took a good man like his brother and threw him in a dungeon to rot. That threatened a kind person like Danielle for helping others in need.

"Dani?" a voice called from the woods.

Danielle swallowed and swung her gaze toward the stand of firs behind him. "Over here."

"Oh, there you are." Serge appeared from behind a thick tree. "I must have gotten turned around a bit in the woods."

She raised an eyebrow at her brother. "Am I supposed to be surprised?"

Serge's eyes moved between them, honest and perceptive as always. "Is everything all right?"

She sighed wearily. "It's fine. I just…we were…discussing some things."

Serge glared his way. "Did he hurt you?"

"Not in the way you mean, *non*."

"Well, there's rabbit back at camp. I set it to roasting a bit ago. Thought we could eat before we head out."

She rubbed her temple, another tired gesture.

"Don't act as though eating rabbit is such a hardship. If we don't sup now, we'll be stuck having more salt pork for dinner." Serge grimaced. "That is, assuming you still want to head out tonight."

The breath clogged in Gregory's throat. Perchance she'd changed her mind. Maybe something in their conversation had made her understand—

"*Oui.*" She lifted her sack. "I still want to leave."

"But can we eat first?" Serge offered her a big, sloppy grin.

"If we hasten."

She started through the trees with Serge following closely behind, neither bothering to wait for Gregory nor even looking back.

Just like they wouldn't look back when they left for good in another half hour.

Chapter Ten

Danielle didn't wait for Halston as she threaded her way back to camp, nor did she look at Kessler once she and Serge entered the little clearing. Instead, she headed straight for Westerfield. She'd do a quick check of him, eat some food and then they would be on their way. The sooner she was gone, the better.

But leaving didn't feel better. It felt…

Uncomfortable. Awkward. Wrong.

Which was ridiculous. Of course it wasn't wrong for her to leave. Halston and Kessler didn't trust her; nor did they treat her as an equal.

Except for back in the woods. Halston apologized, nearly kissed you and understood why you wanted to leave. She shoved down the little voice whispering at the back of her mind and knelt beside Westerfield.

She laid a hand across his brow, still hot with fever and damp with sweat. "Westerfield? Can you hear me?"

His eyelids didn't even flicker.

All the more reason for her to go. She was starting to care too much for the ailing Englishman and his determined brother. For the servant with a soft heart and…

well, she couldn't think of anything to commend Kessler. But the rest of them were almost tolerable.

"Danielle?"

She turned abruptly. That she recognized the voice and the soft way her name rolled over Halston's lips was yet another thing that didn't bear thinking of. "Did you want something?"

"The food is ready." Halston held out a hand to help her up, his eyes flickering to his brother. "Is he any better?"

"I'm afraid not."

"Will he...?"

"I can't say for certain one way or the other." She headed toward the fire where everyone else had gathered and plopped onto the ground. The conversation was quiet—a word from Serge, a question from Farnsworth, but mostly silence without even Westerfield's cough to interrupt them. Perhaps the mustard plaster had been a mistake. At least the man had been making sounds that indicated he still lived before. Now he lay motionless as a corpse.

"Not hungry?" Halston asked from beside her.

She shook her head and stared down at her food, but that didn't stop the warmth of Halston's gaze from touching her face and washing through the rest of her body. Why was he sitting beside her, anyway? And why did he keep staring?

Because of the kiss? Her face heated. *Non.* It wasn't a kiss. It was an...an...an almost kiss.

Almost kiss? Did such a thing even exist?

It must. Otherwise the memory of his eyes gazing into hers, of his body shifting subtly forward, wouldn't keep running through her mind.

Why had she pulled away?

Why had she let him get so near in the first place?

And why did she now have the irresistible urge to jump up and seat herself on the other side of the fire? His presence had never bothered her before.

Well, mayhap once or twice, like the night he'd caught her trying to escape with Serge, or the argument she and Halston had gotten into while standing atop the—

"Dani!" Serge shouted from across the fire.

She jerked her gaze up to meet her brother's. "Is something wrong?"

He scrunched his forehead. "Are you all right?"

"Of course. Why wouldn't I be?"

"Um, mayhap because I had to call your name three times to get your attention."

Three times? Heat started somewhere in her chest and worked its way up over her throat and onto her face. Then Halston cleared his throat beside her, and her cheeks burned even hotter.

She scowled at her brother. "What did you want?"

"Are you ready to go?"

She glanced down at her still-full plate. *"Oui."*

After setting her dish on the ground, she pushed it nearer the fire and stood.

"Wait." Halston scrambled to his feet, his hand reaching out to grip her wrist. "I'm sorry for not telling you the truth about Verdun. I'm sorry for not considering all you risked by helping us. Please forgive me, and please stay."

She tried to tug her wrist away, but he only held tighter, the heat from his palm searing through the sleeve of her dress to her skin. "If anyone finds out how I've already aided you, my family will be imprisoned, possibly even killed."

"Then we'll pray for God's protection." The flickering firelight danced across his imploring eyes. "We've already seen God's hand on Westerfield, haven't we? Shouldn't my brother be dead by now?"

She slanted her gaze toward Westerfield's ominously silent figure. "Yes, he should have died. But either way—"

"I want to stay." Serge appeared at her side.

"How can you say that? With half of France searching for these men, you know what could happen if we're caught, what might happen to *Papa* and *Maman* and the children."

"And I know the verses *Papa* reads at the dinner table. *'For there is neither Jew nor Greek, there is neither bond nor free, there is neither male nor female: for ye are all one in Christ Jesus.'* If there's no difference between Jew or Greek to God, then why's there a difference between French and English? If we don't help them, they'll likely be imprisoned or killed. Isn't saving a life more important than taking sides?"

Suddenly cold, she rubbed her free hand over the arm Halston still held. Serge had turned those verses around. That wasn't how *Papa* meant them, surely it wasn't. It wasn't a question of taking sides. The Englishmen were her enemies, their countries had been at war for over a decade, and Laurent was dead as a result. Maybe there wasn't any difference between Jew and Greek, but there was certainly a difference between English and French.

Wasn't there?

"The verse also says there's no difference between servant and master," she croaked, eyeing Farnsworth from where he watched her across the fire.

"Then maybe Kessler and Halston will learn that themselves on our journey," Serge answered easily, as though the decision to stay was simple. As though they didn't risk both their own lives as well as the rest of the Belanger family's.

"But if we're caught—"

"Do you remember when *Papa* helped *Maman*? He could have been killed, but he helped her anyway."

The memories flooded her mind in a giant rush. She'd been a mere girl of three and ten when *Papa* had entered their lives. *Grandpère,* with all his power and devious intentions, had given *Maman* a cruel task, and *Maman* had fought rather than comply. "*Grandpère* would have killed her."

Serge rubbed his throat, the memory probably more terrifying for him than for her. After all, it hadn't been her neck beneath *Grandpère*'s blade. "He would have killed us all."

She drew in a breath and looked down, only to find that Halston no longer gripped her wrist. Instead he held her hand, slowly massaging the weary, calloused flesh while she spoke with Serge.

"*Papa* made the difference between *Maman*'s life and death." Serge flopped a patch of auburn hair out of his eyes. "The difference in our lives, too. Now we have a chance to do the same for someone else. I think we should stay."

Papa wasn't their *Papa* back then, of course, and he hadn't had to help them. After what *Maman* had been forced to do to him, he'd had every reason to leave the lot of them to *Grandpère*'s machinations. But he'd helped anyway. Because it was right. Because he could. Because God had given him the ability to correct a terrible wrong—and bring down the most prominent smuggling ring in northern France in the process.

"Will you stay?" Halston's words were soft, his touch

gentle and tender. Though probably not able to understand most of their French words, he seemed to grasp the meaning of their conversation.

It's treason, a voice rang inside her head. *You can't help these men without being a threat to your own country. The very kind of threat your father watches for and reports to the police.*

But God hadn't created countries; He'd created Adam and Eve. That was it. And so her family had oft sneaked across the channel to visit Uncle Michel and Aunt Isabelle in England, and Uncle Michel and Aunt Isabelle had visited them on more than one occasion, even while the wars between their countries raged on. Because English or French, it should make no difference.

What if Halston was right? What if God had caused the two of them to meet in the woods and helping them was indeed God's plan?

She inhaled deeply, drawing the cold winter air into her lungs. "All right. We can stay."

Danielle opened her eyes and stared up at the rough wooden planks linking the underside of the cart she'd purchased in Saint-Quentin. The mule snorted from where it lay tethered to a nearby tree, and two squirrels nattered close at hand. She stretched her arms, rolling out from beneath the small shelter where she'd slept last night. It seemed only right she stay with the beast. The Englishmen would have no idea how to care for the animal, and she wasn't about to send Serge to the cart and camp with four men by herself.

She yawned and looked up at the ever-gray sky above. Mayhap one day the sun would deign to shine on this forsaken road in northern France, but until then, nothing but bleak skies, bare trees and brown earth surrounded her.

She buttoned the top of her coat and shook out her tangled mass of hair. She should take time to put it to rights, but only after she checked on Westerfield.

He'd been so weak last night, his skin burning to the touch and body drenched with sweat, fluid rattling in his lungs with each shallow breath he took.

She bent to gather her blankets, bundling them in the back of the wagon before fishing out some oats for the mule. What would Halston do if Westerfield died? If ever love and determination had the power to save a person from death, then Westerfield deserved to live a thousand times over because of Halston's dedication.

The man wouldn't even entertain the possibility that his brother might die. He would make a perfect husband one day, considering how earnestly he cared for his family and how determined he was to do right by them.

Why couldn't there be some Frenchman like Halston in Abbeville? Marrying him wouldn't seem so terrible.

Or rather, someone *like* Halston. Certainly not the man himself. She'd never marry an Englishman who thought his country right for declaring war on hers, much less an aristocrat who believed himself above people like her and Serge and Farnsworth because of his parentage. Mayhap he cared about his family. Mayhap he would make some prim English girl a good husband. But his future had nothing to do with hers.

Which left her just as alone as before she'd journeyed to Reims three months ago. No decent man in Abbeville wanted her, nor did any in Reims. Probably because she couldn't manage to do a womanly thing to save her life. She could kill, skin and roast a rabbit, sure. But most men wanted bread to go with that rabbit and a wife who could mend their shirts rather than accidently put bigger holes in them.

She huffed, feeding the mule another handful of oats before tromping off toward camp. She was too wrapped up in this entire tortuous journey, trying to save an Englishman she shouldn't care about, nearly kissing another Englishman she shouldn't allow herself to look at.

But last night by the fire, with Halston massaging her hand—yet another thing she shouldn't have allowed—and Serge looking at her with those pleading eyes, the decision to stay had seemed so simple. So right.

This morning, that decision had turned into a giant mess.

One that put her family at risk.

One she'd not be able to easily get herself and her brother out of.

What had she agreed to? And why? Just because a rich, dashing man with imploring eyes had told her he needed her?

She was a fool to believe him, and not just once over but twice or thrice.

She growled and kicked at a tree root protruding from the forest floor. Not that the root bothered to move for her. Instead she jarred her toes against the front of her boot, causing them to protest in pain.

Then a cough echoed through the trees, and she stilled as more coughing filled the air. Westerfield had lived another night.

Mayhap all was not as hopeless as it seemed.

Chapter Eleven

The foul scents of animal and sweat mingled with the odor of ladies' perfumes. Gregory stepped away from a group of women behind him and closer to the wagon where Westerfield lay, only to find an elderly man standing on his right.

Where had all these people come from? Mere minutes ago, they'd been traveling along unhindered. The foot traffic had been heavy as they passed more and more houses interspersed with fields and the occasional woods, but Danielle had told them to expect people that morning when she mentioned they'd be journeying around the bustling city of Amiens.

As though traveling with such a crowd wasn't bad enough, now everyone had suddenly stopped, the press of bodies suffocating beneath the wan winter sun. Gregory shifted uncomfortably. They needed to move around this crowd before someone discovered that the only French thing about him was his clothing.

Westerfield blinked open his bleary eyes. "Why are we stopping?"

Gregory stepped closer to his brother. Fortunately no

one stood near the cart's right side to overhear Westerfield's use of English.

"There's some kind of holdup," he whispered in bumbled French.

Westerfield propped himself up on his elbows and looked around the throng of peasant travelers. A cough rumbled from deep in his chest, and the group of women standing behind the cart took several steps back. Good. Less chance of them overhearing his and Westerfield's accents.

"Anything to be concerned about?" Westerfield's soft voice was barely audible over the muted threads of conversation and animal noises.

"Besides all the people?" Gregory craned his neck, looking past Kessler, Serge, Farnsworth and Danielle in front of him to the throng traveling the worn dirt road. An endless sea of wide-brimmed peasant hats and assorted mobcaps stretched ahead. He stood on his toes, attempting to view what, if anything, clogged the road. Up at the very front of the mass, a series of black bicorne hats floated above the crowd.

Gregory's fingers clenched around the smooth little button at the top of his coat's pocket. They'd all likely be locked in a dungeon before sunset. "I believe there're gendarmes ahead."

Westerfield's face, which had regained color in the week Danielle had been treating him with herbs, grew suddenly pale. "No."

The man standing to Gregory's left grunted and frowned at them.

"L-lie down," he whispered in French. If only his accent weren't so horrid.

Westerfield sighed but returned to his prone position. "Ask Danielle what this is about."

What this was about? This could only be about one thing. Danielle had explained there would be more checkpoints as they neared the coast, but he'd assumed she'd evade the stations by taking hidden trails through the woods. Except woods didn't surround them now, only wide, open fields interspersed with more houses than he cared for. They'd not be able to strike off the road into one of the fields without being noticed.

Ahead, the crowd nearly enveloped Danielle's tall, slender body. Why wasn't she turning them around and leading them back the direction they'd come? She just stood beside Farnsworth as though unaware that gendarmes waited at the front of the crowd. Did she not know about them?

Impossible. Danielle wasn't the type to lead them into a crush like this without knowing what it was about. So why did she stand there?

Clearly, she'd misunderstood what he'd expected when he hired her to lead them *safely* out of France. Nothing safe lay in their current situation.

"Don't cause a commotion while I'm gone," Gregory growled at his brother. People pressed around him, their bodies close and cloying, almost suffocating as he shuffled his way toward Danielle. Some citizens stepped aside when they saw he headed deeper into the crowd while others seemed determined to stand in his way. He passed Serge, who guided the decrepit mule, and Kessler, who stood with his back too straight and shoulders too stiff to blend with the throng of common workers and travelers.

Not that his own posture likely blended well, either.

They all wore the clothes Danielle had purchased in Saint-Quentin, a little finer fabric and nicer cut than their former peasant garb. But Kessler still managed to carry himself like a member of the aristocracy rather than the bourgeoisie. Gregory glanced down at his thick woolen coat and mud-caked boots. Was he doing any better? He hunched his shoulders and attempted not to step so precisely.

He jostled his way around a broad-shouldered farmer, the last person standing between him and Danielle, then leaned down and placed his mouth beside her ear. "What are we doing standing here? You've got to get us out of this. Now."

She glared at him, an entire lecture conveyed in that single, direct look: *Your wretched lack of French is going to give us away.*

Had his whisper not been quiet enough? He looked around. The broad-shouldered man glared at him, certainly, but likely because he'd shoved his way past without offering an apology, not because the man had overheard his English. The mother and three small children standing ahead of them hadn't turned around, nor did the older woman in the thick coat standing to their right look disturbed.

Danielle placed a hand on his forehead. "Oh dear, André. You're right. You do seem to be coming down with a fever. Perhaps you should lay down in the cart with Pierre. Just make sure you have your papers in order first." Her French words rang loud but sweet over the crowd, and she softly patted his cheek.

He ground his teeth together. This was her answer? To start pretending they were sick? They'd spoken of such a plan before, yes, but only as a last resort. "I hired you to get us safely to the coast, not parade us under our enemies' noses. Find us another road."

The mother in front of them herded her children closer to her side and inched forward into the press of bodies, as did the older woman to their left. Even the large man at his back took a step away.

"Your stomach is bothering you, also?" Danielle arched away from him, once again speaking loudly. "Poor darling. I think it best you *lie down*. I hope you aren't adding to the foul miasmas in the air. We wouldn't want to get others sick, now would we? Let me help you back to the wagon."

Though the smile plastered on her face was serene, her eyes burned hot into his. She took his arm, a caring gesture to anyone who might be watching, but her fingers dug through the wool of his coat hard enough to bruise his skin.

She turned him back toward the wagon, and the burly farmer behind them moved quickly out of their path, as did the older woman standing behind him.

"Which do you think will cause more suspicion?" she whispered as she led him past Serge and Kessler. "Going through this checkpoint like the two hundred others in line, or turning a group of six people around while everyone watches us leave? We don't know if we can even get around on another road. They might all have checkpoints."

The crowd parted easily as they moved toward the back of the wagon. Evidently word of "illness" didn't take long to travel among a crowd.

Gregory ran a hand along his throat, loosening the coat's suddenly tight collar, and leaned closer to Danielle. "Have you forgotten four of us can't speak passable French?"

Her fingertips dug into his arm as she guided him around the back of the cart. "*Non*. But if the guards believe you to be ill, perhaps they will leave you alone. Lie in the cart and feign illness. Get your citizenship papers ready and prepare to answer to the French names you've assumed. And whatever you do, don't speak. Not even to each other."

But what if the gendarmes ask questions? What if they notice Kessler stands too straight? What if...?

Danielle stared pointedly at the back of the cart and then glared at him. His fingers clenched around the button atop his pocket once again. The plan was risky, but how could he argue here, surrounded by people who thought him ill—thanks to Danielle's lie? He scooted himself onto the aged wooden planks and forced out a cough that sounded about as convincing as his French.

Danielle sent him a brittle smile before she disappeared around the side of the wagon. She returned only a minute later with Kessler, his face set in firm lines that looked nothing like a sudden illness.

"This is ridiculous," he muttered.

Gregory attempted another false cough. "Just get your papers out and try to look sick."

"Don't tax your sore throats, cousins," Serge called over his shoulder with a glare that rivaled his sister's.

"Now get some rest. Serge and I will explain everything to the guards." Danielle looked out over the crowd. "I'm afraid my cousins have fallen rather ill. It might behoove you to stay away from the wagon."

A grandmother hefted a child in her arms and turned, working her way back through the crowd. The group of woman who had spent the past quarter hour tittering behind them stepped off the road and into the muddy field

As foolhardy as Danielle's plan seemed, it appeared to gull the crowd. But what about gendarmes?

The sun slanted toward the western sky by the time they reached the checkpoint, and Gregory's legs were cramped and aching from the nearly two hours he'd

spent scrunched in the little wagon bed with Westerfield and Kessler.

"Why are three men riding while the woman walks?"
a rough voice demanded.

Gregory stared at the wooden slats of the cart's side
and heaved in a breath. If he looked like he was struggling to breathe, would he appear more ill? Or would
he only look suspicious? Why had they not practiced
feigning illness earlier in the woods? He hadn't the
slightest clue how to convince a soldier he was ill. And
judging by the haughty tilt of Kessler's nose, neither did
his brother's friend.

"Papers." A gendarme appeared at the back of the
small wagon, his voice smoother than the one barking
orders from the front.

Kessler offered the man a weak cough as they handed
over their papers.

"I wouldn't get too close." Serge came around to
stand beside the gendarme. "They're quite ill."

"Ill?" the guard sneered. "Out of the cart, the lot
of you."

Gregory pressed his eyes shut and sucked in a shallow breath—neither of which calmed his racing heart.
This was it. They were about to be discovered and he
could do naught to stop it.

"Move faster," the gendarme commanded.

He climbed slowly down with no need to feign his
trembling legs and shaking hands.

Westerfield propped himself into a sitting position
and inched his way out of the wagon bed, his face growing pale with the effort. Gregory took hold of his shoulder and helped him stand, then the pair of them turned
to face the gendarme.

"That last one there has been sick for nigh on a fortnight." Serge jutted his chin at Westerfield. "But I think his ill humors are spreading. The others will be retching and emptying their bowels within the day if that's what they've caught."

Gregory doubled over and groaned. Did he sound like a man attempting to heave his stomach contents?

He could only hope.

He kicked Kessler in the back of his ankle, and the other man bent and attempted to cough.

Serge gave a sudden, loud cough, as well—one that actually sounded real. "Could be some miasmas in the air, too."

No sympathy flickered in the gendarme's eyes as he ran his gaze over them and then scanned their papers.

Farnsworth came up beside Kessler as if afraid the man were too weak to stand and propped him up by the shoulder, while Serge sidled closer to the gendarme, his eyes wide and innocent looking, and coughed again.

Despite winter's chill, sweat beaded on the back of Gregory's neck, and a drop trailed down between his shoulder blades. Would the man believe their story? *Please, God, let him believe.*

The gendarme scowled at Serge, who offered a tentative smile in return. Gregory groaned again, not because he feigned sickness but because the gendarme was going to see through them any second.

And where was Danielle? Hadn't she said she would do the talking?

He raised his head enough to scan the checkpoint. Several paces in front of the cart, Danielle talked to another gendarme—one standing far too close to her. She reached into her cloak and produced her papers. The man smiled brashly, his hand lingering on hers as he took her proof of citizenship.

Gregory tightened his jaw and rubbed his hand over his forehead, which had turned hot at the sight of Danielle with the leering stranger. If nothing else, he was faking a fever passably. He coughed again for good measure.

The gendarmes standing on the opposite side of the road took papers from the stream of travelers before allowing them to continue on their way. Most were detained for only a second before proceeding down the road. But then, most didn't have three men crammed into a cart, either.

A giggle sounded from the front of the cart. Danielle? Gregory looked over in time to see her bat her eyelashes and smile up at the gendarme, who stood close enough his coat brushed Danielle's skirt.

Since when did Danielle smile at anyone, let alone flutter her lashes?

Since when did she giggle?

Something hot crept through his veins, and he dug his fingers into the side of his leg to keep himself from stomping over and yanking her back beside him.

Or at least beside Serge.

Danielle's gendarme leaned closer and whispered something in her ear before pressing a hand to her cheek.

Her cheek! Right there, in the middle of the road, for all the world to see.

And Danielle did nothing to stop it.

"Stop staring," Westerfield rasped beside him in terrible French.

Gregory averted his gaze and launched into a coughing fit. Perhaps if he coughed loud enough, he might distract the gendarme with their papers from noticing Westerfield's terrible accent.

Instead the gendarme looked straight at him. "The four of you are from Dieppe?"

God, please let me get through the interrogation without uttering a word. Gregory swallowed and gave a silent nod.

"Why are you traveling with a boy from Abbeville?" The burly man's face was austere beneath the shadows of his hat.

"We're cousins, sir." Not a hint of untruth shone in Serge's wide brown eyes.

How did the boy manage to look so innocent?

"Cousins." Doubt rang from the gendarme's tone. "And what are you doing in Amiens?"

"We're traveling back from visiting our *grandmère* in Reims. She's ailing and not expected to live through the spring."

The gendarme's brows only furrowed more. "And why are none of you in service to our Consul?"

Serge pressed his lips together, and another bead of sweat trailed its way down Gregory's back.

Why had he not foreseen this question and thought up some believable excuse before now? He was a man of business. His entire livelihood hinged on making predictions so as to be prepared for various situations, and here he'd failed to anticipate a legitimate question.

Then again, most of his previous plans had focused on evading gendarmes, not speaking to them.

A deep, bone-jarring cough resonated from Westerfield's chest. His breath wheezed in and out of his lungs, and he doubled over, bracing himself on the wagon as spasms racked his body.

"Maurice! Claude!" one of the guards from the other side of the road shouted as he waved two old women past. "What's taking so long? Are they British, or aren't they?"

British? Was this checkpoint set up not just to check everyone's papers but to search specifically for British interlopers? Or worse, specifically for the "spies" who had escaped from north of Reims?

The moisture leeched from Gregory's mouth and the air grew hot and thick around him, the pressure of the gendarmes' gazes stifling and intolerable. Somewhere in the crowed behind him, a boy called out, followed by the sound of several deep chuckles and a mother's berating lecture. But Gregory couldn't distinguish the words. In truth, he could barely breathe, let alone move.

They'd be eating moldy bread and drinking stale water for dinner tonight, tortured into giving up any supposed knowledge they had of Napoleon's military plans on the morrow, and he could do nothing to prevent it.

"*Non*. Just a bunch of cowards." The gendarme shoved the handful of papers back at Gregory's chest so quickly it took him a moment to reach up and grasp them. "You can pass."

The breath rushed out of him. *Thank You, Father*.

The gendarme turned and stalked back to the group of women waiting next in line.

"Don't smile," Westerfield growled in his ear. "You'll give us away."

Gregory forced his mouth into a frown and turned to help Westerfield back into the wagon. But Danielle still stood with the gendarme in front of the cart, allowing the man to brush her chin with his thumb.

"Stop staring and get into the wagon." Kessler shoved him from behind.

Right. He climbed onto the uneven planks and lay

down, letting the wood block his view of Danielle being manhandled in front of everyone. If he watched her for another moment, he might well leap from the wagon and pull the lecherous fool off his guide—which would endanger everyone all over again.

Maybe the gendarme was right. Maybe he was no better than a coward.

"We'll camp here." Danielle surveyed the narrow patch of woods. It wasn't very big, but a nearby river afforded fresh water.

Halston shoved some hair back from his face and brushed past her. He'd barely looked at her since they passed the checkpoint two hours ago. Was he angry because she had made him lie back in the cart and feign sickness? Her plan had worked.

Westerfield groaned and blinked himself awake in the back of the cart. "That was close back there."

Much closer than she'd have preferred. "Do you need help getting down?"

"I'll assist him." Farnsworth moved to aid Westerfield.

She stood back as Westerfield climbed down from the wagon and walked slowly toward the woods. She'd continued her ministrations endlessly over the past seven days, and he was much improved. If they could avoid more checkpoints, Westerfield just might reach his homeland strong enough to make a full recovery. Then again, closer to the coast, they'd be seeing more and more gendarmes and enlisted men, especially with Napoleon's navy stationed at Boulogne. Hopefully they could continue on unnoticed, but each brush with a soldier brought greater risk of being discovered.

"Can you carry some blankets?" Serge reached into the cart and handed Kessler a bundle.

The man glowered but yanked the armful from her brother's hand and followed Halston into the woods.

She sighed and rolled her shoulders, still aching from how tightly she'd held them as they'd waited to pass the gendarmes earlier. Did these Englishmen not understand how exhausting keeping them safe was?

"Go on ahead with the others." She moved toward Serge, who was standing beside the mule. "I'll hide the cart and settle Clyde for the night."

Serge handed over Clyde's rope but rested a hand on her upper arm. "Are you well?"

"Fine."

"You've barely said two words since we left the checkpoint."

Because there'd been nothing to say.

"You let that gendarme touch you, Dani. I know how much you hate that."

A wave of revulsion swept through her. Yes, she'd let him touch her. And leer. And make suggestive comments. But she'd gotten Halston, Westerfield, Kessler and Farnsworth past danger by distracting one of the guards so badly the other guard had had to check five sets of papers by himself. That's what mattered most.

"Dani?" Serge stepped closer. "Are you certain you're all right?"

She gave a curt nod. She had to be all right. She didn't have any other choice.

Serge walked ahead, and she turned the mule and cart into the brush, finding a dense thicket where the beast could bed down undetected. She fished a handful of oats from her pocket and then got some barley from the back of the wagon before she left the old mule tethered to a tree. Her feet were tired, her back ached and her head throbbed. If only she could curl up under the cart for a nap, but she started into the woods along the path Serge had taken instead.

A rabbit scampered across the trail, and without thought, she bent to retrieve the knife from her ankle and threw it. At least they'd have fresh meat tonight.

She retrieved the hare and continued on, passing through dead grass and thickets and dark stands of trees before the voices of her companions finally floated through the forest, not overly loud but not quiet, either.

"If we face another checkpoint tomorrow, do you expect me to crawl into that cart and feign illness again?" Indignation rose from Kessler's voice.

Of course Kessler would argue. Hefting the rabbit she carried higher, Danielle hopped over a fallen log and skirted a mud puddle.

"It worked," Serge answered. "So unless you can think of a better plan—"

"There *has* to be a better plan," Halston interrupted. "We were nearly discovered."

"With no thanks to your sister, who was too busy flirting to bother helping us escape."

Danielle stepped into the camp, the rabbit bumping against her thigh. "It was a distraction, and it worked. The gendarme didn't even speak to you, let alone look your way."

"You mean to say you did that on purpose?" Halston stalked toward her.

She pressed her lips together, her stomach churning sickeningly at the memory.

"Kessler's right. We'll not do this again."

"When we hired you as our guide, we didn't know you'd turn out to be a doxy." Kessler's eyes shone hard and brittle in the waning winter light. "Otherwise I might have used your services long ago."

She took a step back, feeling her veins fill with ice. Did they think she liked having strange men touch her? Stare at her? Whisper invitations to meet them behind the gendarmerie post that night?

"She's not a doxy!" Serge shoved Kessler's chest. "Apologize."

Kessler tilted his nose haughtily down at Serge.

"I think we should all take a moment to calm ourselves." Farnsworth rose from where he'd helped Westerfield recline on a pallet.

"The moment for calm has long passed." Halston took her by the shoulder, his fingers digging through the thick fabric of her cloak into her skin. "I'll not have you behave in such a manner while with us."

Serge whirled toward Halston. "You act as though she's a courtesan, not a maid."

She tightened her grip on the rabbit. Did Halston not understand, either? Did he truly think her a…a…a…?

Doxy, prostitute, Cyprian, streetwalker. The horrid names ran through her head, one on top of the other.

"Is this why no one wants to marry your sister?" Kessler grabbed Serge's coat and swung Serge back to face him. "How many men has she behaved this way with?"

Danielle jerked away from Halston, her tongue so thick and clumsy in her mouth she could do little more than mumble. "No."

She dropped the rabbit to the ground at her feet. She had to leave this place. Now.

Chapter Twelve

It mattered not how dark the night became or how dangerous the forest floor grew beneath her feet, Danielle wasn't returning to camp.

Serge's call through the forest echoed with Halston's cry from somewhere behind her, but she kept moving, her mind spinning with horrendous memories.

Meet me behind the barracks after dark tonight. I know a quiet spot in the woods where we can go. That from the gendarme she'd met earlier today, the one who'd touched her and leered while all the crowd looked on.

Then there had been Citizen Fauchet in Reims. *You're an insufferable little ingrate who'll never marry but become a blight on her family's name.* He'd called her that after she'd used the heel of her boot to stomp on his toes. But then, the man had first put his hands on her waist and forced her against the wall while he attempted to kiss her.

Had Citizen Fauchet expected her to smile and be grateful for his hard grip and roaming hands? To welcome his breath that reeked of foul onions and half-rotted teeth?

Danielle hastened through the tangled trees and uneven ground until she reached the river, a narrow strip of water too deep to be considered a stream. The sandy banks unfurled like a twisting snake before her, and she followed the soft path until a large rock obstructed her way. No voice called behind her and no boots thumped against the fallen leaves blanketing the forest. The rock looked as good a place as any to rest, so she climbed atop the cool surface smoothed by years of wind and rain.

If only the words of Citizen Fauchet, Kessler and the gendarmes weren't so similar to her own brother's. *You're never going to find yourself a husband, Dani, if you don't settle your ways. Stop hunting with your papa and spending your days throwing knives. Take up spinning or embroidery or the like. And please try to keep quiet when you go to an assembly, don't start arguments like last night anymore.*

They were the last words Laurent had ever spoken to her. Four years, and she still recalled how the sunlight had filtered down over his mussed auburn hair as he'd stood in the yard beside her. Still remembered how his eyes had gone soft at the mention of her getting a husband.

The night before, one of the boys in town had pulled her outside the hall and tried taking liberties. She'd stomped his foot and screamed until both her parents and his, as well as anyone else who happened to be at the assembly, had arrived.

Laurent had somehow blamed her for the incident, saying if she'd only behaved in a more ladylike manner, the boy never would have approached her. Mayhap he'd meant his words as advice for her protection, but she hadn't taken them that way, *non*. Instead she'd told him to go back to his frigate, that she'd find a husband just fine without his help, and then she'd darted into the woods.

She'd brought back a fox and two rabbits later that night, but Laurent had already left a day early for the navy.

Two British men-of-war overtook Laurent's vessel before it even left the channel, taking away any chance of reconciling with her brother.

She sighed and stared out over the water covered in inky blackness, the sounds of the flowing river mixing with an owl's lonely call.

What about her made men want to be cruel? She well understood why no one wanted her to wife, but what allowed them to think base thoughts of her? She'd been traveling with the English for a week. Did none of them see her as a capable, decent woman?

Not even Halston?

But no, evidently he thought her as disreputable as Kessler did.

She shouldn't care. It wasn't as though Halston's opinion made any difference. She was nothing to him but a French peasant useful only as a guide. It mattered not if her mouth turned dry when she thought of how he'd almost kissed her a week past or how her heart had an inexplicable tendency to beat twice as hard when their eyes met over the campfire. She was French and insignificant, and he was a rich, titled member of the English ton.

When he'd almost kissed her, his thoughts had likely been the same as the gendarme's and Citizen Fauchet's. She was just as much of a doxy to him as she was to the others.

She buried her head in her hands.

Father, why? Why was she even helping the English? All she earned for her efforts was their disdain.

A rustling sounded to her right, followed by the muted padding of footsteps and the thin beam of a lantern. She peered into the shadows behind the light.

"I was beginning to think I'd lost you."

Halston. Why him? Of all people, couldn't Serge have followed her? Or better, no one.

"I'm sorry for how Kessler treated you back there."

How *Kessler* had treated her? What about how *he* had treated her? She turned her face away, but that didn't stop him from climbing onto the rock and sitting opposite her.

"I'm rather curious as to why you're not." His voice carried smooth and deep into the night.

She frowned but didn't bother to look at him. "Why I'm not what?"

"Married yet."

She wrapped her cloak tighter about her shoulders. "It's not because I'm some fallen woman."

"I didn't think it was."

The gentleness in his tone brought her gaze up to his for the barest of instants, then she picked up a broken stick lying near her feet and threw it into the creek. *I'm not married because I want a man who looks at me like* Papa *looks at* Maman.

But how could she explain that to Halston? How could she make him understand how it felt to be twenty-two and likely to die a haggard spinster who lived with one of her brothers and his family?

She shifted uncomfortably on the rock, but Halston sat beside her, waiting for some answer. Did he know how terrible she was at sitting still? At being quiet? At being patient? "I'm not married, because I'm a failure at every wifely responsibility imaginable."

He didn't agree, at least not immediately, but he certainly didn't argue either. Instead he just sat there, his smoky eyes surveying her for far too long. "You don't possess many typical feminine qualities, no."

She raised her chin and turned so her back faced him.

A gracious and feminine gesture, that.

"Don't, Danielle. I didn't intend it as an insult. Perhaps you wouldn't make a picturesque wife, but you have other estimable qualities. I was terrified back there at the checkpoint. Terrified and angry. When I first saw you flirting with the guard, I thought you'd gotten distracted by a handsome face."

"He wasn't handsome," she spit out before she could think better of it.

"Nor were you distracted. You saved us back there. But you ought not have played the coquette to do so. The manner in which the gendarme was looking at you…" He cleared his throat. "'Tis not wise to trifle with a man's affections in such a way."

"Affection is too kind a word for what he was thinking."

"Yes, quite. Which is why you mustn't do such a thing anymore, not even to protect us. If that gendarme had taken you into the woods or forced you to his barracks, what could I have done? Or Serge? Any of us? The part you played this afternoon was more dangerous than allowing both the gendarmes to turn their attentions on our papers."

When he stated things in such a manner, his anger over her behavior almost made sense. Almost made it seem that he cared about her as a person, not just as a means of getting him and his brother out of France.

Quiet lingered between them before Halston broke it once again. "Even so, I spoke poorly back at camp when I said I concurred with Kessler. I agreed that you shouldn't play coquette to keep our disguise, but I do not agree with any disparagement against your character. I know you are an honest and honorable woman. By the time I realized my mistake, you'd already fled. Please forgive me."

She fiddled with another twig lying by her knees. "Serge and I thought it best I not be involved with the gendarme checking papers. I'm a terrible liar. If you want me to hunt or fight, I can do so to the death. But if you want me to look you in the eye and tell you I wore blue yesterday rather than brown, well, I can't."

He chuckled low and deep in his throat. "I'm aware. How do you think I caught you after we first met and you decided to flee? I was prepared to give chase since your eyes gave your thoughts away. They always do, whether you're irritated with your brother or mad at Kessler or devising a way to keep us all safe."

She swallowed. Did he watch her eyes so much? And if so, what did he take away from those times when their eyes met over the campfire? When it seemed impossible to pull her gaze away despite whatever else might be happening around them? "'Tis a flaw I must work harder to overcome then."

"No, 'tis not a flaw but a trait I rather adore."

"Mayhap. But eyes that give my hidden thoughts away do not make me a desirable wife."

He turned her to face him fully "Is that what you want, then? A husband?"

"Oui." Her eyes turned suddenly hot and moist. A husband like *Papa* with how he sneaked up behind *Maman* to wrap her in his arms and rain kisses atop

her hair. "If you want to know the truth of it, I'm not married because…because…I want love."

"Love."

The word fell hard and flat between them.

Of course he wouldn't agree with her about the necessity of love in marriage. He was a member of the ton, and people like him didn't marry for love. "*Maman* wasn't always married to my current *Papa*. My first father…he wasn't kind. He didn't love *Maman*, and…and…made things hard for her. For all of us. I see the way *Maman* and *Papa* look at each other now, the way she can't stop having babies though half the town thinks she's mad for birthing the lot of us. And I…I…" She couldn't go on. Her throat was dry and swollen, her eyes burned, and her muddled mind was making a mess of her thoughts. Why had she confessed these things to Halston? He wasn't going to understand.

"You want the same." He wrapped his arms around the thick wool of her cloak and drew her near, her face resting against his chest. He held her close for a moment before anchoring a strand of hair behind her ear and tilting her chin up.

Her unshed tears turned his face blurry, which was just as well. She didn't need to stare into his eyes. Or have his strong arms wrapped around her. Or sit this close to him.

"People don't marry for love in my country, at least, not members of the ton. But I think the idea noble. If you want love, you're no fool for waiting."

She blinked. He didn't think her some heartsick child for wanting to marry a man who loved her and would treat her right? Who would cherish her the way *Papa* did *Maman*?

"I should have guessed you wouldn't be like other

women, that you'd want something different..." He lowered his head, his lips hovering only a handful of centimeters above hers. "Something more."

She drew in a breath, staring at the smooth, dull pink of his mouth in the lantern light. Then his lips touched hers, soft and warm...and unforgettable.

Gregory drew Danielle closer, memorizing everything from the coarseness of her wool coat to the slender form beneath it. The soft breath that burst from her lips an instant before he covered them and the moment her body finally relaxed in his embrace. He would keep her here, against his chest, in his arms all night if he could. And not just tonight, but tomorrow, and the day after that and maybe even the one after that.

She was so different from the debutantes that paraded themselves before him in London. So beautiful and vibrant and alive in his arms. Her heart might be sad, but her body hummed with life, her mouth with care.

Care for him specifically? Or was she merely responding to his kind words, the way he endeavored to look past her lack of propriety and womanly actions to the shining jewel beneath? Would she respond this way to a cobbler or fisherman or butcher if he took the time to appreciate Danielle as she was?

Perhaps so, and it was just as well. There could never be anything between a French peasant and a British lord. She knew it. He knew it. Everyone knew it. If things were different, if she'd been born higher, if he'd been born lower...

Even then, their countries would still be at war.

Gregory pulled away, breaking the kiss though part of him—a very loud, obnoxious part—clamored for more.

Danielle leaned back, her lips wet and her breath puffing white into the cold air. "That was…that was…" She pressed her hand to her mouth, as though trying to seal the feeling of his lips on hers indefinitely.

He ran a hand over her hair, so rich and black and wavy, always falling into her face despite how she tried forcing it up beneath her mobcap.

"Thank you," she whispered into the moonlight.

"Did you just thank me?" A small smile curved the edges of his lips. "For kissing you?"

"No. I mean, yes. I mean…" She sighed. "It's never felt like that before. Thank you for showing me…and for…for…"

The woman with a tongue sharp enough to cut a person in twain suddenly couldn't manage a coherent sentence, and he was responsible. His lips curved even more.

Tonight he could give her those things she craved—understanding, acceptance, care—on some forgotten rock on the banks of some nameless river. But tomorrow…

He suddenly didn't want tomorrow to come.

"We should go," she said, as though somehow privy to his thoughts. "We've been away so long the others might wonder." Despite her words, she made no effort to move away from him.

He pulled her back to his chest, wrapping his arms around her until she relaxed against him. Holding her in his arms, hearing the soft inhale and exhale of her breath against the night, feeling the wavy strands of her hair brush against his cheek, it all seemed so right.

Could it be? Had God more in mind than Danielle guiding them to the coast?

No, it wasn't possible. Otherwise Danielle would

have been born to gentry in England, not to peasants in France.

For there is neither Jew nor Greek, there is neither bond nor free, there is neither male nor female: for ye are all one in Christ Jesus. Why, of all the church services he'd attended throughout his life, had he never heard that verse before? And as strange as the concept might seem, 'no bond nor free, no Jew nor Greek'—*no French nor British, no peasant nor aristocrat*—God certainly hadn't created peasant and lord in the Garden of Eden.

Were Danielle's notions of equality and individual value right? Did "lady" and "lord" matter to God? What if the world of class structures and aristocracy in which he'd been brought up was wrong? Could he take a chance on love with Danielle despite her low birth?

But then, he'd tried fighting for a commoner before, and where had defending Suzanna gotten him?

Nearly killed, with a father so angry at Kessler that Kessler had run to the continent. And when Westerfield went to bring Kessler back, they ended up imprisoned for over a year.

If God truly saw no difference between lord and peasant, then surely his attempt to fight for Suzanna would have ended better.

"Halston?" Danielle settled her hands atop where his own rested on her arms and turned to face him in the dim lantern light. "Is something wrong? You're squeezing me rather hard."

"Sorry." He loosened his hold and brushed his hands lightly up and down her arms. "I got lost in my thoughts."

She reached up to smooth a patch of hair away from his face, then pulled his head down until it rested against hers. "Bad thoughts, by the look of how your brow is drawn together."

He blew out a breath. "Not bad, merely…necessary."

She smiled up at him, her lips so close her breath fanned his mouth. "Perhaps it's best you stop thinking them. They've turned you sullen."

If she only knew.

But then, she didn't know, and she didn't understand. She likely never would, because in her mind, there truly was no difference between lord and peasant, maybe not even a difference between British and French.

If only the rest of the world saw things as she did.

She trailed a thumb over his lips. "Did you hear me about leaving a few minutes ago? I don't want the others to come searching."

"Just a few minutes longer," he spoke against her thumb.

Because as soon as the sun rose in the eastern sky, this kiss, this conversation, this night and anything they'd shared within it would be over. So he pressed his lips softly to hers and then turned her around and pulled her against him one more time, savoring the feel of her.

He wasn't ready to go back quite yet.

He wasn't sure he'd ever be ready to go back.

Chapter Thirteen

Danielle gave the mule's rope a tug and glanced behind her at Halston. They'd been walking for the better part of the day despite the cold, incessant drizzle, and Halston hadn't so much as looked at her. Not even once.

How could he kiss her and hold her in his arms last night, then rise this morning and pretend nothing had happened? She'd felt his lips on hers, not imagined them. Heard the understanding in his voice. Savored the sensation of resting in his embrace.

And now he ignored her while he walked behind the wagon, chatting with Kessler as though the two of them were suddenly bosom friends. She glared over her shoulder once more, but he didn't raise his eyes to meet hers.

Didn't act as though she existed at all, let alone mattered.

"Dani, what's wrong? Are soldiers coming?" Serge peered through the softly falling drizzle at the flat road behind them.

"Non." She yanked Clyde's rope again, urging the beast faster, and squashed her wide-brimmed hat down farther on her head. The road unfurled endlessly before

them, though this stretch of it had never seemed so long before. Were it not for needing to take the English to the coast, she and Serge would be only four days from home. Instead, in four days' time, they'd pass by her hometown of Abbeville and head north for another half week until they reached the port town of Berck.

Would the smugglers Halston had made arrangements with decide the price on Westerfield and Kessler's heads was worth more than taking the Englishmen across the channel? She rubbed her forehead. That question led to another host of problems she'd yet to consider.

"Then what's wrong?" Serge's eyebrows furrowed as he studied her face. "Why have you been looking behind us all day?"

Her cheeks turned hot. "I've done nothing of the sort."

Serge glanced over his shoulder again, his gaze pausing on Halston before swinging back to her. Well, her brother could look between them all day if he so pleased, but he'd have to guess what had transpired between her and the esteemed Lord Gregory Halston. She wasn't about to volunteer the information.

"Did Halston upset you last night?"

Last night? Oh, no. He hadn't done anything to upset her then.

Today was a different matter entirely.

She growled deep in her throat and tugged Clyde's rope. Why had she let Halston bother her in the first place? She cared far too much for an English lord whom she couldn't have any future with and should probably hate. Their countries were at war, were they not? And she wasn't even supposed to be here. She should be living in Reims with a new French husband.

She gave the mule's rope another vigorous yank.

Clyde brayed loudly enough for all of Amiens and Abbeville to hear, then buckled his knees and dug his hooves into the ground.

"Dani, don't hold his rope so tight. Here, let me." Serge took the rope from her hand, but the mule kept his legs locked into place and only snorted at Serge.

"Is something wrong?" Westerfield propped himself up in the wagon bed.

"Can I be of assistance?" Farnsworth left his spot walking beside Westerfield and came toward them.

"Why isn't the beast moving?" That from Kessler.

Danielle rolled her eyes. Somehow she didn't think three British lords and a valet knew the first thing about getting a mule to move.

"Here, boy." Serge offered Clyde a small carrot.

The mule only snorted.

"What happened to make him stop?" Halston's eyes didn't even meet hers as he spoke.

The wretch.

"He tired of Dani constantly prodding him," Serge called back.

She huffed out a breath and stared at the ground beneath her feet. Unfortunately, refusing to meet everyone's eyes didn't prevent her from feeling the weight of all their gazes.

"How long until he'll move?"

"Make him move now. He's your animal. His purpose is to work for you, is it not?" Kessler's demanding voice rang through the chilling drizzle.

"Can we camp here for the night?" This from Farnsworth. "Perchance it's a bit early, but there's a little patch of woods."

"Right, I'm tired of being wet. Let's make camp." Of course Halston had to add his opinion as well.

"And leave the mule on the road for anyone to take?" At least Serge provided some reason.

"No one will take him if he refuses to move."

She didn't even bother to figure out who had added that gem of wisdom to the conversation.

"Make Danielle stay with him. She's the one who did this."

Danielle rolled her eyes. *Thank you, Kessler.* The man was abounding in gratitude.

Besides she wasn't the one who'd done this—well, mayhap she'd personally tugged Clyde's rope too hard and too often—but Halston should be blamed. He'd put her in a foul mood.

A faint tremor shook the earth beneath her feet. If she hadn't already been stopped and staring at the ground, she'd likely not have noticed. She jerked her head up, looking first in the direction they'd come and then the way they were headed. Against the endless expanse of gray sky and brown, muddy road, shadows moved too quickly for travelers on foot.

"Horsemen." Her single word quieted the others. "Into the woods, everyone but Serge and I. Posthaste."

The men scrambled to help Westerfield, though the marquess was now hale enough to need little aid.

"Do you want me to collect the blankets and supplies?" Farnsworth asked from the back of the wagon.

"*Non.* Better to let the cart look full, so it will seem as though Serge and I have need of it."

A moment later the men disappeared into the brush, with Halston pausing for a moment to place some twigs and shrubs over the path they'd taken. The man might not deign to look at her, but at least he'd learned something during their week of evading the law.

She headed to the back of the cart and rummaged

through the supplies, repositioning blankets and a sack of food to cover the spot where Westerfield had lain.

"What do you want us to do when they come?" Serge offered Clyde some oats, which he refused to take.

"What we're doing now. Try to get the beast moving. The horsemen might not even stop."

But the three horsemen slowed long before they reached the cart. Of course they did. Having them continue on their way without so much as a glance in her direction would be too much to ask on a day such as this.

The men rode with soldiers' straight posture and possessed horses, something only the military would have. Yet the edges of their uniform coats were frayed, their boots worn and muddy, and their jaws unshaven. They weren't military—at least not anymore.

"Well, well. Looks as though your beast is giving you trouble." The first rider, an average-sized man with dirty blond hair, grinned widely as he swung off his horse.

The back of her neck prickled. She'd rather meet a band of soldiers—in spite of the danger they represented to the Englishmen—than deserters who answered to no one but themselves. But she merely crossed her arms in the soggy drizzle and raised her chin. The slightest show of weakness, and men like this would take advantage. "He's merely being a stubborn mule."

"We've been traveling for over a week." Serge ruffled the tuft of hair atop Clyde's head. "He's weary."

"I'm sure he is." But the deserter didn't bother to inspect Clyde, just her, running lazy blue eyes down her body and then slowly back up again.

She could hardly say what he found so appealing, given the way her old brown cloak covered all but her face, and he didn't seem very interested in that. "Is there something we can help you with? You must be in a hurry to make it back to your regiment before nightfall."

"Actually, there is." A short, stocky man with a girth he certainly didn't gain by eating army rations lit from his horse. "Have you seen these men about?"

He shoved a handbill in front of her nose, but she didn't need to look at the sketches to know the man showed her likenesses of Westerfield and Kessler— the exact same handbill that had been plastered all over Saint-Quentin.

"We've a need to find them before we return to our regiment." The third man, tall, painfully thin and with hair and eyes the color of muddy water, spoke from atop his horse.

Her hands began to shake. One lie. That was all. Now if only she could tell it convincingly. "*Non.* I've not seen any such men."

"Sure you don't want to take a better look?" The stocky man held the handbill to her face once more. "You barely glanced at the paper."

Her cheeks grew cold. Had her hasty actions just given Westerfield and Kessler away? Oh, curse her wretched inability to lie! She slanted a glance toward the woods, but the trees and shrubs remained still as death, without any indication it harbored escapees.

"We've seen the papers before." Serge attempted to offer Clyde the carrot again. "They've been scattered everywhere from here to Saint-Quentin."

How did her brother look so calm with four Englishmen hiding not fifty meters away?

"He's right," Danielle managed over her thick, sluggish tongue. "We've been asked about them several times on our journey from Reims." At least that part wasn't a lie.

As though mad at her for telling a half-truth, the rain turned suddenly heavy, pounding the muddy earth and smearing the ink on handbill. The stocky man shoved the paper inside his coat, but his eyes trailed down her body much as the first man's eyes had. She waited for what would certainly come next—for him to lean over and whisper something about how beautiful she was or an invitation for her to meet him tonight.

Instead, the stocky man looked at the first deserter, now standing near the rear of the cart, and gave a faint nod of his head.

Her breathing turned shallow. Did these deserters have some sort of plan? How could she thwart it if she knew not their intentions?

"It's getting awfully wet out here. Maurice, what say you we head to that barn back yonder?" The first deserter jerked his head in the direction of a shadowed structure in the field ahead.

"Don't want to get wetter than we need to," the thin man atop the horse proclaimed.

"Looks like you've got some fresh rabbit back here, just waiting to be cooked." The blond pulled the rabbit she'd snared that morning up by his legs. "It's been a while since I had a fresh-cooked meal. You got the makings for stew back here?"

Danielle left the foul-breathed fat man and rushed to the side of the cart. If the first deserter kept rummaging, he'd discover not only some carrots and potatoes, but clothes enough for four other men. "Yes, of course. Did you want me to make some stew?"

The man pulled away, his lips curving slyly. "Well now, that sounds like a fine idea. You can cook while the rest of us dry out in the barn."

She glanced towards the woods. Once she and Serge

went into that barn, they'd be out of sight of the others, and anything could happen. She might be able to take on a single unsuspecting man, but not three with military training.

"Sorry, but our mule refuses to move. I'm afraid we won't be able to join you." Serge's voice cut through the driving rain. "We can offer you some salt pork, though."

"Salt pork." The blond spit at the ground. "I don't want no foul, salted meat, not when I can have fresh. Just see if I can't get your beast to move." He pulled a riding crop from the folds of his coat and brought it down on Clyde's back quarters.

Danielle flinched at the resonating slap of leather against beast, and Clyde let out a frightened bray.

"Get on with you." The soldier whipped the crop again, and the mule started forward, a thin line of blood appearing on his flank.

"See? One only needs to take a strong hand to a beast and obedience follows." The stocky deserter—Maurice, evidently—laughed in response and waddled toward his horse.

The man with the crop approached his horse as well, his gait strong and purposeful. But rather than mount, he grabbed the reins and turned back to her. "I find my legs in need of a stretch. Mayhap I'll walk beside you."

Danielle blew out a breath and glanced toward the woods one last time. Would Halston know something was wrong? The last place she and Serge should go was into some forsaken barn with a trio of army deserters.

But Halston and the others couldn't aid them without giving themselves away, and they'd come too far, were too close to the shore, to risk capture.

The stranger's shoulder bumped hers as they walked. "Your journey has been long, *oui*?"

Hadn't Serge said as much earlier? *"Oui."*

"It looks as though the rain might last through the night."

"Oui." She spoke more curtly that time—if it was possible to be curt with a one-word answer. She needed to get herself and Serge away from the deserters before they entered the barn. But how?

Their party left the road and began trekking across the mucky field. Serge still led the mule, but if she and Serge left the cart and sprinted toward the trees at the same time...

They had no chance of making shelter before the deserter beside her pulled out the pistol he most certainly carried. Then again, if they could manage—

Her foot hit a patch of uneven ground, and she lurched forward, causing a cold stream of water to sluice from her hat to beneath her cloak and then down her back.

"Easy there." The deserter reached out and gripped her elbow. Not the polite hold of a man attempting to help a woman, but the hard grip a criminal kept on a victim. "I'm sure you're weary. A nice, long night should revive you."

A nice, long night of rest, perhaps. But the gleam in his eye promised nothing nice in store for her. "I—I'm afraid my brother and I must hasten on our way to Abbeville as soon as I've prepared your stew."

The man laughed, low and quiet but lewd nonetheless. *"Non, ma chérie.* I think there'll be time for some entertainment before you depart."

Gregory pounded the side of his fist into the scratchy bark of an aged tree when the soldiers, Danielle and Serge left the road and started across a field.

"Easy there," Kessler whispered from behind him. "Stay quiet or you'll give us away."

"Why are they leaving with the soldiers?" He slammed his hand into the tree again. "This wasn't part of the plan. If we follow them through the trees, we might give ourselves away. But if we don't, we'll lose our guide." The guide he'd spent too long holding in his arms last night, too long dreaming about in his sleep.

"They're heading toward that barn," Westerfield spoke from where he leaned against a nearby oak.

"The barn?" His throat turned dry.

"Yes, my lord. That appears to be where they're going," Farnsworth concurred.

"But why?" Surely Danielle knew better than to go into a building with three strange men. Once inside, they might—

"To escape the rain, my lord. That's likely the reason."

Beside him, Kessler and Westerfield remained ominously silent. He'd found Suzanna in a barn on that fateful night two years ago. Had Kessler and Westerfield's thoughts wandered to the same place as his?

"No," he rasped into the chilling rain.

"After the way she behaved with that gendarme yesterday?" Kessler's eyes were hard and flat as stone. "Why else would she go to the barn?"

Gregory curled his hands into fists.

"It doesn't look as though she has much of a choice." Westerfield's calm voice floated through the rain.

Gregory swung his gaze back to Danielle. The soldier now gripped her arm, propelling her toward the barn without so much as an inch of space between them.

No choice, indeed. "We have to do something."

"She might be fine on her own, my lord." Farnsworth's words came out as a squeak, then he rubbed his thumb back and forth across his throat. "She's rather handy with a knife, if you recall."

Farnsworth was right. He shouldn't involve himself. Hadn't he decided as much last night? The last time he tried to protect a peasant woman, it had ended in disaster. And yet...

"There's three of them against a woman and a lad." He started toward the clearing, but a strong hand wrapped around his wrist and yanked him back.

"You're not going anywhere."

"Let go, Kessler."

"You'll give us away."

"And that justifies letting a woman be raped? Think of all she's done for you. For Westerfield. For all of us. She would have never met those soldiers were it not for helping us."

"You don't know that."

But he did. Day after day, she'd tirelessly urged their party onward, scouting the woods for danger and tending to Westerfield as he recovered. Now she was in trouble. The others might sit idly by and watch, but not him.

He jerked away from Kessler's grip and sprinted through the trees. Wrong was wrong, and sometimes a man needed to stand between wrong and its victim. Besides, the mere thought of another man touching Danielle, running his fingers through that thick, wavy hair, being close enough to breathe her scent...

Father God, please keep her safe. Rain pelted his face and blurred his vision as he darted across the field and flung wide the barn door.

Danielle spun around, her knife in one hand and a half-sliced potato in the other. Behind her, the soldiers all sat in the hay...

Eating some of the dried apples she'd traded a farmer for?

They'd gone into the barn for something as simple as food? He stepped inside. "I—I'm sorry. I thought…"

And with those handful of words—*English* words—he realized his mistake.

Danielle whirled toward the others and caught hold of one of the soldiers who'd been harmlessly eating. She pressed a knife to the blond man's throat, holding it steady, but that didn't stop the other two men from scrambling up. Serge jumped on the back of a tall, thin man and similarly held a blade to his throat. A soldier with a girth wide enough to rival that of King George drew a pistol and trained it on Gregory.

Gregory's hands were slick with sweat. He'd had one gun trained on him before. One, in all his twenty-eight years. And the last time it had resulted in a leg injury and infection so dire he'd nearly died.

"You're English." The man with the gun spit into the hay. "One of the men from the handbill. Put your hands out in front of you where I can see them"

Gregory's heart beat wildly against his ribs. He wasn't on the handbill—that was Westerfield. But the sketch looked similar enough to incriminate him—and speaking in English certainly didn't help. He glanced at Danielle, her eyes wide with terror as she gave him a subtle nod. He slowly extended his hands.

"First I'll tie you up, and then you're going to tell me where that friend of yours is." The man approached, the gun not wavering the slightest from where it pointed at Gregory's chest.

Was there something he could do? Some way to knock the pistol out of the man's hand or lunge for him?

He looked at Danielle again. She was keeping her

knife steady on one of the soldiers. Seeming to understand his thoughts, she mouthed the silent word *no*.

The stocky man stopped before Gregory, the gun only inches from his chest. He produced a rope from the folds of his coat. "Now you hold your wrists together, one on top of the other good and tight."

Knocking the gun away was the only way to secure Danielle and Serge's safety. And he certainly couldn't wait until his hands were tied to do so. He drew in a breath, long and slow, since it might well be the last time his lungs ever felt air, and then—

Crash! A large noise sounded behind him. Gregory lunged, slamming into the brute and landing them both in a mound of hay.

The click of the gun's trigger resonated through the barn, but no boom of gunpowder accompanied it.

Thank You, God.

"What's going on in here?" Kessler demanded from somewhere near the door—right about the time a fist landed on the side of Gregory's jaw.

Gregory attempted to pin down the man's arm before another fist flew toward his face.

"Do you want help, my lord?" Farnsworth's boots appeared near the man's head.

"Yes. Grab his—oof!"

An elbow landed square in the side of his cheek. The valet crouched and grabbed hold of the soldier's free arm, then pinned the flailing limb in the hay before doing likewise with the arm Gregory held. Still lying atop the beefy man, Gregory heaved in a breath and reached up to touch his throbbing cheek and jaw.

"Kessler, take up the pistol in the hay there and then fetch me that length of rope hanging on the wall opposite the door." Danielle's English command carried through the suddenly silent barn.

For likely the first time in his life, Kessler rushed to do someone's bidding.

Danielle released the knife from her soldier's throat for the barest of moments, only to bring the blunt end of the hilt down against his temple. He uttered not a single cry before he slumped forward into the hay.

The soldier beneath Gregory struggled anew, attempting to buck Farnsworth out of the way with his forehead and twisting his legs to wrench Gregory off. "There's three of you cursed Englishmen, not just two." He glanced at Danielle. "And she must be a traitor. I knew her behavior was suspect. Just you wait. I'm going to—"

Thunk!

Danielle had approached so quietly he'd not realized what she was about. She now stood over them, holding her knife as though ready to strike the man in the temple again if needed.

"We've got to leave, posthaste." Serge worked with Kessler to tie his soldier—already lying unconscious—to one of the posts supporting the barn's roof.

Danielle took another rope from the wall before returning to bind the fat soldier's arms and feet. Then she turned her furious eyes on Gregory. "What were you thinking, Halston? Five more minutes and we'd have been rid of them."

He rubbed his cheek, still tingling from the brute's thrashing. Disaster. Just as he should have predicted. Kessler had been correct. Why had he thought Danielle needed to be rescued? "I didn't know. I assumed—"

"We wouldn't have been rid of them, Dani." Serge tightened the knot that secured his soldier to the post.

"They had foul intentions and would not have been dissuaded."

Her face flushed as she deftly bound the stocky man's hands behind his back. Then she shifted to tie his feet. "We would have been fine. But now 'tis only a matter of time before someone finds these deserters or they escape on their own and tell their story."

Deserters? Gregory had thought—

"Not if we kill them."

The barn fell quiet in the wake of Kessler's words.

Danielle heaved in a breath, her eyes meeting Gregory's over the unconscious soldier's body. "Are you prepared to end three men's lives because you barged in here?"

What did he say to something like that? Had he truly saved her, as Serge seemed to think? Or had he made another terrible mistake?

Then again, it hardly mattered now that the deed was done. Kessler was right that killing these men meant an easier journey to the coast. If they were left alive, all of France would soon know not just about the "two" men from the handbill, but about at least one more Englishman and a French brother and sister aiding them.

Passing through another checkpoint would be impossible.

Merely meeting someone on the road could turn into a deadly situation if their descriptions were made public knowledge.

He looked down at his hands, turning them palm up against his thighs. He need only give the word, and they would be dead. But could he permanently stain his hands with another's blood?

He forced his gaze back up to Danielle's. "Let them live."

She jammed her knife back into the sheath at her ankle and stood in her usual brisk manner. "Serge, pack up the cart and ready Clyde. Farnsworth, I assume Westerfield is still hiding in the woods due to his condition?" The valet nodded. "Fetch him and then catch up with us. We're going to start across the field and keep close to the woods. If we make haste and travel through the night, we might evade spending the next ten years of our lives inside a dungeon."

Gregory could only pray she was right, and that he hadn't just signed everyone over to death by a guillotine's blade.

Chapter Fourteen

"Of all the insolent, ridiculous, foolhardy things for you to do."

Gregory took a step away from Kessler, but that didn't stop the other man's steady stream of complaining as they trudged through a darkened field. Despite the hat smashed low over his head, the rain somehow pelted his face and slowly soaked its way into the untreated wool of his greatcoat.

Ahead of them, Danielle held one of their two lanterns, and Serge gripped the mule's lead as the beast staggered on. Westerfield slept in the cart while Farnsworth held the second lantern and walked along beside it, leaving Gregory and Kessler to follow behind in the darkness.

They'd been walking for what felt like hours, though he knew not how late it was. If the ache in his feet and weariness in his muscles were any indication, dawn should already be lightening the eastern sky.

But no hint of light flickered on the horizon, nor did Danielle show any sign of stopping. All night she'd led them on, through muddy open fields and along back trails that the mule could follow. They'd not once stepped foot onto a road, a wise plan considering the deserters might have already been found and gendarmes could be combing the countryside for them. He only hoped the ceaseless rain would be enough to wash away the tracks from the mule and cart.

"You gave us away by barging into that barn." Kessler stopped and tilted his hat so the pooling water streamed to the ground in front of him.

"And I refuse to apologize for it."

"They would have fared perfectly well without our interference."

On this, Danielle and Kessler seemed to agree, but Serge was adamant that the deserters had more dastardly plans in store for Danielle—plans that she could not have evaded with only Serge to help. Gregory dropped his head, staring at the darkness that swallowed his feet. He'd merely wanted to protect the woman who'd done so much to help them, not get them all caught. "Right is right, Kessler. I can't change that because it happens to inconvenience you."

"Inconvenience?" Suppressed rage tightened Kessler's voice. "You think this is an inconvenience? You might single-handedly land us all in a dungeon."

Single-handedly?

Him?

The ingrate. "I got you *out* of the dungeon. I didn't put you in one."

"And come morning, a swarm of soldiers and gendarmes will be searching the woods for us."

"Perhaps if we all had listened to the lady in the first place, we wouldn't be in this situation." Farnsworth's ever-reasonable voice rang out from where he tromped beside the wagon.

"Lady?" Kessler sneered. "What lady? I see only servants and peasants before me. Certainly no ladies."

"That's enough," Gregory warned.

Unfortunately the warning wasn't enough—one never was for Kessler. "Since when do you speak out of turn, Farnsworth? I heard not your lord ask your opinion."

"Since you decided to attack Citizen Belanger." Hardness rang from Farnsworth's usually quiet voice.

Kessler rubbed his face. "We've been in this forsaken country too long, Halston. Even the servants are forgetting their place."

"Maybe I've realized my place isn't the one that Lord Halston gives me." Farnsworth stopped walking and faced Kessler in the dim light of the lantern. "Maybe I think that France has the right of it. No lords. No ladies. Everyone equal. Everyone a citizen."

Kessler stalked toward Farnsworth until his shadow blocked the light. A moment later, the unmistakable sound of flesh slapping flesh echoed across the field and Farnsworth's lantern crashed to the ground.

"Halt!" Danielle raced toward them, her own lantern swinging wildly. She set it on the back of the cart near where Westerfield blinked open his sleepy eyes. Gripping the knife that had been sheathed against her ankle, she wedged herself between Farnsworth and Kessler. "I care not whether you're a lord or some other esteemed member of society, Kessler. If you strike another person in my presence, you'll find a blade through your hand."

"Listen to her." Gregory grabbed the back of Kessler's collar and yanked him away from Danielle. She could handle herself with a blade, yes, but what manner of gentleman let his woman break up a fight while he looked on?

She is not your woman! a voice inside his head all but screamed. *She can never be your woman.*

But she could, if he held to her idea that all people were equal, that birth didn't place one person above another.

Kessler jerked away from him and straightened his ill-fitting greatcoat, a rather ludicrous action, since he stood soaked and weary in a forgotten field. "Don't tell me you hold to this foolishness, Halston. That you intend to start treating your valet as though he's your equal."

Of course he didn't intend such a thing. The notion was ridiculous.

But then, if Farnsworth was his equal, so was Danielle. And that prospect opened an entirely new realm of possibilities.

"Well?" Kessler straightened his glove.

Gregory's heartbeat thudded in his ears. He didn't need the light of dawn to know all eyes riveted to him, or that his answer was of great interest to one person in particular. Did he believe Danielle's words? Did he ascribe to France's theory that the common person had value? To God's theory that *all* people had value?

He couldn't.

Yet he could. Was not Danielle more valuable than any blue-blooded debutante he'd ever met?

He wet his lips. "I don't sanction you striking my servant, Kessler. Nor do I like you threatening the woman who has sacrificed her own safety and that of her family to help us."

He didn't need to look at Danielle to feel her disappointment in him. It rolled from her to him like waves from the sea to the beach. And why shouldn't it? Had he not taken her in his arms and kissed her as though he intended a future for them last night?

But he hadn't made her any promises, just that one mistake of kissing her.

Because certainly the kiss had been a mistake, had it not?

"You don't like me threatening a peasant," Kessler sneered. "I should hardly be surprised seeing how two years ago you challenged me to a duel over a serving girl."

"A serving girl?" Danielle looked at him as if she was about to pull her knife, though she didn't seem sure whose throat to hold it to, his or Kessler's. "Is that what all your incessant fighting has been about? A serving girl from two years past?"

So now she knew of his disastrous attempt to defend Suzanna's honor. Why was she upset about it? She of all people should be championing his efforts to protect a servant, not angry at him. Unless she thought he and Suzanna—

"I'll leave you lords to play your games without me." Danielle's voice rose over the waning drizzle. "Dawn is almost upon us, and someone needs to walk ahead and scout a campsite so we can stay hidden until nightfall. Farnsworth, you're welcome to hold the lantern and walk ahead with Serge."

Danielle's footsteps thudded against the muddy, sopping earth, though not even a lantern guided her now that Farnsworth had broken their spare.

He wasn't about to let her walk off alone while half the countryside searched for them. "Danielle, wait. I'll scout with you."

But of course she didn't wait. If anything, she quickened her pace.

* * *

Danielle hastened across the field, moving as rapidly as she could toward the dim line of trees in the dusky gray dawn. Halston called after her, but she didn't stop or even look over her shoulder, no. She was done with him.

With them.

With this whole wretched business.

She smeared a tear across her cheek as the implications of Halston's answer to Kessler sank in. He didn't think Farnsworth his equal. Had all her lectures on people's innate value had such little effect on him? Did his eyes get soft when she spoke of France and citizenship only as some cruel joke?

She'd thought he'd been listening, if not to her, then at least to Serge and his Bible verses about equality in God's eyes.

She'd altered her opinion of him, had she not? She'd first thought him an arrogant, spiteful British spy, the kind of man to smile in satisfaction when he learned of Laurent's death at the hands of the British navy. But he hadn't been happy to learn of Laurent's death, and she no longer saw him as spiteful or a spy—though the arrogant part still held.

But evidently Halston's view of Farnsworth was no different than when he'd first entered France.

And if he still thought of Farnsworth as his underling, he certainly didn't view her as his equal, either.

But how had he seen some unnamed serving girl differently? In England, men of Halston's station weren't supposed to fight duels over serving girls.

Knowing he had done so should make her happy. At least at some point in the past, he'd thought a serving girl's honor important.

So why did her heart feel as though it would burst into a thousand jagged pieces?

Because she wasn't the serving girl he'd fought for? He'd started a duel at some point in his past, yet he didn't see her as his equal and even admitted such to Kessler.

Halston was no different than any other aristocrat—than any other man. He'd taken what he wanted from their kiss last night and then left her once he was finished.

The difference this time was her. She'd been willing to give him what he desired. A kiss in the night, an hour spent burrowed in his arms.

And now he was finished with her.

It shouldn't matter. None of this should matter. She'd known better than to get involved with Halston from the first.

But then she'd spent the next week and a half traveling with him, watching as he tirelessly fought for his brother's life, as he did everything in his power to move a band of four men across a country filled with people who wished them dead.

As he watched her when she sat by the fire skinning a rabbit or roasting a squirrel.

As he kissed her as if she was valuable to him.

Lies, the lot of them. She broke into the trees and kept striding forward. Gray was already lightening the sky, providing a dim illumination by which she picked out the path with the fewest brambles and greatest gaps between trees. If gendarmes combed these woods, they'd be found in an instant, but what other choice had she unless she abandoned the mule? Though Westerfield had improved, he was hardly hale enough to walk the distances she required of the others every day, and he'd likely suffer a setback after being exposed to today's rain.

"Danielle."

A hand rested on her shoulder, and she jumped, then furiously swiped another tear off her face. It seemed as though the rain had finally stopped, so she hadn't even the respite of blaming the weather for the moisture on her cheek.

She turned to find Halston staring down at her. "What are you doing sneaking up on me in such a manner? You're going to get us all caught."

"I don't want you walking alone."

"I'm scouting. That's the point of a scout, one person goes ahead. Alone."

A lopsided smile tilted Halston's mouth. "You didn't look as though you were scouting, just crashing through the forest."

She glanced toward the field, but trees obscured the rest of their party from view. "Go back and leave me be."

"I won't leave you on your own."

"You will."

"Danielle, look at me."

"No. I'm not looking at you, I'm not talking to you, and I'm certainly not kissing you again." She clamped her mouth shut the instant the words left her mouth. What was she saying? Did her wretchedly honest tongue insist on giving away her every thought?

Gregory gripped her shoulders with one hand and raised her chin with the other so she had no choice but to look into his misty blue-gray eyes. "Kissing me? Is that what this is about?"

"Of course not." She attempted to jerk away, but she

was too weary to fight in earnest and his grip proved strong enough to hold her.

"Danielle."

"Don't say my name like that, all soft and compassionate. Like you...like you...care."

"I do care."

She fisted a hand in his coat. "People who care about each other don't steal kisses one night and then ignore the person they kissed the next day. They don't evade questions about each other, and they certainly don't—"

His mouth covered hers, the pressure of his lips cutting off her words while their breaths tangled hot and fast. She stilled beneath the onslaught. She had something important to tell him, had been right on the verge of explaining...

What?

And why had it mattered in the first place? Did anything matter except the feel of his arms around her and the pressure of his mouth on hers? Her hand that had been fisted in his coat loosened into a soft hold. He pulled her closer, the scents of damp wool and musky man surrounding her, the strength of Gregory Halston wrapping around her to form a protective barrier between this moment and the rest of forever.

But the rest of forever would come eventually. Most likely in the shape of a dungeon cell. The tasks of both caring for Westerfield and keeping these men out of prison now that they'd been discovered seemed impossible.

Almost as impossible as a future between her and Halston.

Which had been what she had been about to tell him before he'd kissed her. That he couldn't care about her. That there could never be anything more than friendship between them. No, not even friendship. They had a business arrangement. She got his party to the coast, and he paid her handsomely. Nothing but cold, hard business.

She wrenched herself away from his warmth, his lips still seeking hers for a fraction of a moment. "I just told you not to kiss me. Don't touch me. Don't kiss me. Don't do anything other than leave me alone."

His eyes blazed. "Why? Was my kiss not good enough for your passionate French blood? Because unless I misread something, you enjoyed that."

She backed up, but the two steps she took hardly seemed enough distance. Were the entire isle of Britain plunked down between them, it wouldn't seem enough distance to keep her emotions at bay. "You're a British lord. You can't go around kissing any woman you please."

Which wasn't true. In England, aristocrats probably did kiss any woman they pleased without any fear of repercussions. And most women were likely happy to reciprocate.

Just not her. She turned and stalked toward the trees.

Though the rain had stopped, the muddy earth sucked at her boots and made her steps sluggish rather than defiant. She fisted a hand in her hair then wrapped her arms around herself. She was a fool! A wretch! A weak, loathsome woman.

Why had she allowed herself to kiss him again? To enjoy it? Had a bigger clod ever walked the soil of France? She'd thought she was a failure already, when she'd killed her chances of procuring a husband first at home and then in Reims. But if she'd believed that that was the worst that could happen, then she'd been wrong. She'd never failed so hugely before as she had just moments ago—as she had this entire trip—by allowing herself to fall in love with a British lord.

In love.

Non. She couldn't be in love. Not with Gregory Halston, third son of the sixth Marquess of Westerfield.

She pressed a fist over her mouth to stem the sob building in her chest. She hadn't the time to stand there and cry. She was in these woods not to argue with Halston, or fall in love with him, but to find shelter for the rest of the party and then finish leading them to the coast.

She straightened and drew in a long, slow breath. Then she surveyed the woods, quiet but for the sound of…

No. There was no sound of chirping birds or scampering squirrels. The woods were dead silent.

She paused a moment more, waiting, surveying. A frisson of alarm swept through her, and she spun around.

"Get down." She raced toward Halston, who still stood beside the tree where they'd kissed.

"I beg your pardon?"

She slammed into his chest, knocking him to the ground the same instant the bang of a gunshot echoed through the woods. The thunderous noise barely registered before pain exploded in her back and head.

Then her world turned to blackness.

Chapter Fifteen

A gunshot rang through the quiet morning. The weight of Danielle's body crashed into Gregory and sent him sprawling. He landed on his back, Danielle half on top of him and half on the ground.

"Danielle!" He scrambled upright only to find sticky moisture seeping from her body. Tearing off his coat, he pressed it to her bloody side. Another shot cracked through the woods. He reached for his pistol and scanned the direction from which the shots came, but only the trees' vague shadows stood in the dim light.

A third shot split the air, and a musket ball whistled past his head to imbed itself in the tree behind him.

Hands shaking, he pointed his gun at one of the darker shadows—hopefully a man rather than a tree— and pulled the trigger. A dull click echoed through the woods. Dampness beaded on his forehead. His powder was too wet to ignite, though evidently his assailant hadn't been walking through the rain all night and had perfectly dry powder.

A shadow moved from the direction the gunshots had come, and Gregory scrambled for the knife sheathed to

Danielle's ankle. Not that he knew how to throw it, but having some sort of weapon was better than nothing.

"Halt, or we'll shoot you like we did the girl," a rusted voice called in French.

"Aren't they supposed to be worth more money alive than dead?" a younger voice asked.

Two figures emerged from the murky gray morning. Not gendarmes. Even in the fog, their thick woolen coats, worn boots and wide-brimmed hats revealed them to be farmers.

"Put your hands up now and drop that knife." The older man used the barrel of his musket to point at Gregory's head.

Gregory glanced into the man's hard, line-creased face and let the knife thud to the ground.

"Are you English? You got two seconds to prove it one way or another."

His chest tightened until he could barely take a breath. He looked down at Danielle, her face pale. Was she alive, or had that musket shot already stolen the life from her? She lay still as death, no rise and fall of her chest discernible beneath her cloak.

"Answer us."

"I'm English."

"Whooo-eee, *Père*!" The younger man's pistol dropped toward the ground while a ridiculous smile claimed his face. "We done caught them. That's some luck, there! Do you know how rich this is going to make us? We'll have coin for—"

"I'll double it." Gregory's heart thrummed against his ribs. "Whatever your government's price on our heads, I'll double it if you let us walk away without speaking a word of our presence."

The younger man tilted his head. "You got that kind of money with you?"

"Not all of it, but I can pay you half now and send the other after I reach England."

"No." The old farmer trained his rifle directly at Gregory's heart. "I'm not some filthy traitor about to let enemies of France go free. You'll—"

Thunk!

Gregory blinked. A knife protruded from the farmer's neck. It seemed to have appeared from nowhere, and yet he hadn't imagined the blade. The man's eyes glazed over and he fell to the ground, blood seeping into the earth around him.

Gregory looked behind him just as Serge burst through the trees, another knife poised to throw.

The younger farmer dropped his pistol to the ground and his hands flew up. "*Non*, wait. I didn't do anything. I wasn't going to—"

But Serge's knife was already flying through the air. It hit the younger man in the exact same place the first blade had struck his father, and he crumpled lifelessly.

"Dani!" Tears choked Serge's voice as he fell to his knees beside his sister. "Where is she hurt? Is she... is she...?" He ran his hands frantically over her body.

"I don't know." Gregory leaned down and placed his cheek near her mouth. The faint warmth of breath puffed onto his chilled skin. "She still breathes, but I don't know if the injury is fatal. They shot her in the side." Or so he thought, he could hardly be certain, given the little time between Danielle falling and the men firing again.

He pulled back the coat still balled against her body, only to find her blood had drenched far too much of the fabric.

"Put it back." Panic edged Serge's voice. "We've got to stop the bleeding."

Gregory's hands trembled as he stared down at the bloody coat. "One moment we were talking, and the next, we…we…" He pressed his eyes shut, a thick lump lodged in his throat. "She saved me. She knew. Somehow she sensed the danger before the first shot, and she…she…" She'd sacrificed herself for him, had thrown her body in front of his own and sent them both crashing to the ground.

But not soon enough.

Serge grabbed the coat from him and put it back against his sister's side. "Don't sit there like a dunce. Hold the coat to her. Is she hurt anywhere else?"

"I…I know not." He held the fabric against her bleeding wound while Serge searched for further injury. Perchance Serge knew something of medicine and healing traits. Gregory likely couldn't discern the difference between a broken bone and sprained ankle. Though he well understood that if Danielle had been shot in her gut, if there was damage inside her belly, her soft breaths wouldn't last much longer.

God, what have I done?

Had Danielle jumped in front of him because she thought he'd paid her to do such? *Get us safely to England* had been his words, but he'd never intended for her to sacrifice her own life for his.

"Is she dead?" Kessler's harsh voice resonated through the still morning.

Of course he would be the one to ask.

"Not if I can help it." Serge pointed at Kessler. "Cut some strips from the farmers' clothes. I'll need them for bandages, and I need ale to clean her wound. See if they have any on them."

"Is she...? Is the wound...?" Gregory clamped his teeth onto his confounded tongue, which was suddenly unable to utter a coherent sentence.

Serge met his gaze, his face drawn into worried lines. "I think the musket ball only grazed her side. If we clean and bandage it, mayhap she'll be all right." He slanted a glance back at his sister's face. "But I can't say for certain. She's better at healing than me."

"A side wound doesn't explain why she's unconscious." Westerfield spoke quietly from behind them.

"Non." Serge sank his teeth into his bottom lip.

Westerfield's hand landed on Gregory's shoulder, firm but gentle. "What happened, Halston?"

"I...we...she...she jumped in front of a musket ball to knock me to the ground. She realized the danger and..." Gregory let his voice trail off as his eyes clouded. He raised his hand to wipe a stray tear from his cheek only to have the coat fall away from her body, once more revealing her bloody side.

"Halston, you've got to keep the fabric pressed tight." Serge nearly shouted the words from where he sat examining Danielle's head.

"I'm sorry. I know. I simply..." His hands started trembling anew as he put the garment back into place and pressed it tighter against her motionless body. But his stomach churned with the memory of all the blood. *Her* blood.

"Move aside." His brother nudged his shoulder. "I'll hold the cloth."

"No." He couldn't abandon her now, even if his stomach lurched and his hands shook. He had to get her well. This was all his fault. He'd followed her when she didn't wish it, then argued with her. Kissed her. Distracted her from her task of scouting a safe haven for them. Surely their raised voices had alerted the farmers to their whereabouts.

"Will these be enough?" Farnsworth approached with strips of torn linen in his hands.

"They should suffice." Serge held out his hand for the linens.

"I found brandy." Kessler walked over, sniffing a rather large leather flask.

Using one hand to keep the coat in place, Gregory reached for the container. Certainly he could manage such a simple task as pouring brandy on her wound.

Kessler set the flask in his hands, but the leather barely touched his sweat-slickened fingers before it slipped and plopped onto the ground, soaking the damp earth with precious liquid.

"Halston!" Westerfield swooped up the flask. "Move aside. You're in no condition to help."

"But I need to." And he did. More than anything he'd ever done in his life, he needed to save Danielle.

Except Serge had pulled the coat away from Danielle's side again, leaving the mess of blood and cloth and skin open for all to see. Gregory's stomach cramped with nausea and he gagged.

Kessler hauled him up to his feet and shoved him to the side. "Move before you retch atop her, you fool."

On legs hardly stable enough to hold himself upright, Gregory stumbled toward a thick tree. Leaning against the scratchy bark, he slid down to sit so he could see Danielle. If she died…

Had it really been just last night he'd told Danielle to let those soldiers go free? Perhaps they all would have been better off killing the original men who'd discovered them.

Serge and Westerfield poured brandy over Danielle's

wound while Farnsworth and Kessler looked on. She didn't even move, let alone gasp in pain.

He'd prided himself on fighting for Suzanna, had thought standing for the honor of a common woman was somehow a noble and gracious sacrifice on his behalf.

How dull his own sacrifice shone when compared to Danielle's. He'd all but said she was beneath him when Kessler asked whether he held to Danielle's theory about people's value. Yet here she had nearly forfeited her life to save his.

And why should he be surprised? She'd put herself in harm's way since she first agreed to help. That was what real sacrifice looked like, not challenging Kessler to a field at dawn out of anger or coming to France to save the brother he'd inadvertently put there. She'd had no reason to save him and every cause to destroy him, and yet she'd taken a musket ball in his stead. Her actions made all he had done for Suzanna and Westerfield in the past two years, all his giving to the orphans and hospitals, everything about his very life, seem paltry.

"You must be cold, my lord." Farnsworth approached, one of the thick woolen blankets from the cart in his hand. "Wrap this around yourself."

Gregory looked down at his rough linen sleeves. Though he'd spent the past half hour without his coat, he felt no cold or damp or anything at all…

Besides the large, aching hole in his chest that Danielle Belanger had once filled.

Chapter Sixteen

Pain tore through Danielle's head. It felt as though someone had taken her sharpest knife and sliced open her skull, then left the metal blade embedded in her head. She shifted and groaned, only to have a fresh slash of agony sear her.

"Dani?"

She turned her head toward the tender voice—a mistake considering the wave of nausea that followed.

"Dani, are you awake?"

She blinked and found herself staring up at unfamiliar trees, their branches bare against the dim sky. Halston hovered beside her, his face so close she could almost press her lips to his cheek—not that she intended to do such a thing again.

"You're calling me Dani now?" More pain, bright as lightning across a dark sky and hot as a fire on the coldest winter night.

"You took a musket ball and smashed your head against a rock because of me…"

A musket ball. That explained the burning in her side, which seemed to grow worse the longer she forced her eyes open.

"That should give me license to call you Dani and you liberty to call me Gregory."

She rested her head back against the makeshift pallet and closed her eyes. Whatever he chose to call her wasn't worth the anguish of arguing at the moment.

A hand pressed against her cheek, the touch cool yet comforting, so perfect she nearly rolled closer to Halston...Gregory...whoever he was supposed to be.

Clearly her injuries had addled her mind if something as simple as a touch had her turning soft.

"Don't do that again, do you hear me? Taking a bullet for me is not your job."

She forced her eyes open to find herself staring into the handsome—if aristocratic—lines of his face. Saving him hadn't been something she'd planned, just instinct. She'd sensed danger one second and moved to protect him in the next, that was all.

But if she'd had time to think? If she'd had enough seconds to warn him and take cover for herself...?

She'd have still stood between him and the gunmen.

Because she loved him, as pointless as it was. And so she'd throw herself in front of a musket ball time and again if it meant she could keep him safe.

But he wouldn't want to hear such things. He was some high-and-mighty British lord who saw value in her skills alone, not in her person.

She looked away from his somber blue gaze. "Where are we?" It certainly wasn't the same patch of woods where she'd been shot.

"I know not. We've walked through the forest for the past two days with Serge guiding us. You've been hot with fever and in and out of consciousness. Farnsworth and Serge took to giving you that garlic and onion po-tion you used on Westerfield to good effect—your fever seemed to abate."

He moved a hand to her forehead, but she raised her own to pull his away. She didn't need him touching her, not now. Not tomorrow. Not ever again.

"We had to leave the cart and mule behind. They couldn't travel through the brush."

Non. She wouldn't have guessed they could. But then, how had the men moved her? She looked at Gregory again, at his strong shoulders and lean torso hidden behind a gray coat far different from the one she'd purchased him in Saint-Quentin. Had he carried her for two days while she remained unconscious? She would have been helpless. Completely at his mercy. Totally under his protection.

Her heart quickened against her ribs. She'd rather rest in Kessler's arms than his.

But Kessler was weak from his time in prison, and Gregory hovered beside her.

"Did you...?" The rest of the words clogged in her throat, so she shifted her gaze away instead. Some questions one was better off not having answers for. "My side is sore and I'm feeling tired. Mayhap you should let me rest."

Danielle leaned against a tree and heaved in a breath, pressing her eyes shut for the briefest of moments. Her head pounded. Her side burned. Her throat felt as though it had been deprived of water for a fortnight. She only needed a moment or two of rest. And some water. She wouldn't complain about opiates to dull the pain in her side and head either. Or a nap.

Ahead of her, Serge continued to lead the men through the densest patches of trees and brambles, taking them through fallen, decaying leaves where they'd leave no footprints and getting them closer to Berck with every step. He was handling the task quite well, just like he'd done well cleaning her side and head and bandaging her wounds. Apparently he'd even done well throwing his knives—at least according to Gregory's account of the attack.

"Dani?" Gregory paused on the deer path ahead and surveyed the woods behind him until his gaze landed on her.

"Coming." She pushed off the tree and took a shaky step forward. The throbbing in her head turned from dull to sharp, and her side wept in protest. What had possessed her to attempt so much walking three days after she'd been shot? She should have known her body was too weak. But then, what other choice had she?

Gregory stalked toward her, his gait strong and purposeful. "You're ill. Let me carry you."

Definitely not something she would allow.

He laid a hand on her shoulder, but she shrugged it off, refusing to look up into those foggy eyes sure to be filled with sympathy and concern. "I'm fine. I kept pace all morning. I can walk all afternoon, as well."

"No. You cannot." With a deft movement, he swept her up, bracing her back with one arm while slipping his other beneath her knees.

"Let me down!" She pounded her fists against his chest, never mind that pain ripped through her side at the movement.

"Dani, hush!" Serge appeared beside her, while Kessler, Farnsworth and Westerfield looked on from farther up the trail. "Gendarmes will still be searching for us."

She clamped her lips shut. Her brother was right. What had she been thinking?

But then, she probably hadn't been thinking: her head hurt too much for that and her body felt too weary. Hot tears of mortification welled behind her eyes. She just needed sleep and something to dull the pain in her side and clear the ache in her head.

Both were luxuries that would cost them too much time. She looked at her brother. "Tell Gregory to put me down. I don't want to be carried."

"You don't have a choice." Gregory's voice rumbled from deep in his chest—a rumble she felt as much as heard given the way he cradled her against him.

"Forsooth, Dani. You can't walk all day, not after getting yourself shot."

"I can."

Gregory shifted her in his arms as though she weighed no more than a newborn chick. "Even if you can—which I doubt—I refuse to allow it. This is the third time you've fallen behind since our last meal."

Serge reached out to grasp her hand, his eyes pleading. "If you push too hard, you'll hurt yourself again. Do you remember how sick Westerfield got after that day you made him walk too far?"

She shook her head, though that only sent more pain skittering through her. How ill she felt mattered not. She couldn't lie here cocooned in Gregory's arms. Couldn't spend her afternoon with her head pressed against his chest so that she heard every beat of his heart and draw of his breath, smelled his familiar scent mixed with the aroma of clean air and winter's dampness. Her heart would shatter.

"Then l-let someone else carry me."

Gregory's arms stiffened around her.

Serge's eyebrows drew down into a frown. "Kessler and Westerfield are too weak from their prison stay, and Halston is stronger than Farnsworth. He's the best choice."

But I can't manage it. She turned her face into Gregory's thick coat. 'Twas useless to argue any longer, not with both Gregory and Serge set against her. Some part of her brain knew they were right, that she shouldn't be walking, that her head and side hurt much worse now than when they'd started that morn and that Gregory was the best person to carry her. But none of it made her current position in Gregory's arms any less humiliating.

Just like none of it would make forgetting his scent any easier, or the steadiness of his heartbeat, the feel of his arms, or her love for him.

"Spread the blanket for Danielle first." Gregory's arms ached as he held Danielle against his chest while she slept, her breath puffing little clouds into the cool winter air. But he wouldn't complain, not now and not ever, if it meant he could hold her for a minute longer.

Beside him, Farnsworth scrambled to do his bidding. Dusk had yet to fall over the forest, though that was probably Serge's intent. They'd stop early and sleep as the sun when down, then wake after dark and continue their journey when blackness covered the earth.

"Did you want some salt fish, Halston? Kessler?" Westerfield dug into one of their sacks for food.

Gregory gave him a slight nod and turned back to find Danielle's blankets spread to form a makeshift bed amid some fallen pine needles. He laid her down, her rich black hair fanning against the pallet beneath her. She'd slept poorly in his arms, twisting and writhing, crying out and waking far too often. Hopefully now that she had a stationary bed, her sleep would be more peaceful.

Gregory pulled two thick, woolen blankets up to her chin, then swept a lock of tangled hair away from her forehead. *God, heal her. Keep her well and give her strength.* He leaned down and placed a tender kiss on her forehead, then pushed to his feet and started toward Westerfield with the salt fish. 'Twould be no fire tonight, just as there had been no fire in the four days since they'd passed the checkpoint near Reims.

Four days? Had it really been only half a week ago? Four weeks seemed more appropriate given their near captures, Danielle's injury and the way they'd pushed tirelessly to the coast.

He approached Westerfield and Kessler and reached for the salt fish, but Westerfield didn't release it.

"Be careful with her, Halston."

He glanced over his shoulder toward where Danielle slept. "I only stumbled that once." The rough terrain and the way his arms grew fatigued after hours of holding her was sure to tire any man.

"That's not what he means." Kessler's voice was quiet yet hard, a sharp blade sheathed in satin. "You're getting too close to her."

Gregory's weary arms tensed. "I beg your pardon?"

"You heard me," Kessler spit.

Westerfield rubbed his brow. "Calm down, the both of you. Halston, I understand Danielle has done much for us. She's special, certainly. But don't get attached. In a few more days, we'll depart for England, and she won't be coming with us."

As though he needed Westerfield's reminder.

"She's French, Halston." Kessler's voice held no understanding. "And not just French, but a peasant. Unless you plan on making her your mistress when you reach London, you ought not—"

"How dare you!" Before Gregory could stop himself, his fist swung toward Kessler's jaw. It connected with a crack, and Kessler's head jerked back.

"Stop it." Westerfield attempted to step between them, but Kessler merely sidestepped and swung his own fist toward Gregory's nose.

Gregory barely managed to block the punch.

"I've been in your place." Kessler pulled his fist back and readied it again despite the large red mark on his jaw. "Do you think you're the only one to fall for a woman beneath your station? Heed my warning and stay away from her."

"I can't envision you caring for any person, let alone a woman beneath you."

Kessler lunged, sending them both sprawling against the damp, muddy earth. The breath whooshed from Gregory's body, and he struggled to fill his lungs while Kessler's hand tightened around his collar.

"What do you think Suzanna was?" Kessler landed a punch square in the side of Gregory's cheekbone, sending a vicious spike of pain radiating through his skull. "Do you know how things started between her and me? The same way they're starting between you and Danielle. I know what you thought two years ago, but I'm not some ape who forced myself onto her. That night you found her in the stable after I left? That wasn't the first time—it was the last. That's why she was crying. Because I'd told her no more."

"What?" Gregory's fingers turned cold, numb even, and a hollowness opened inside his chest.

Kessler still loomed above him, his fist poised to strike again and his other hand holding Gregory's collar.

But Gregory hadn't the strength to fight in light of what he'd just heard. He sought Westerfield's eyes from where he towered above the both of them. "Did you know this?"

Westerfield shoved a hand into his hair. "I suspected."

"Why...why didn't you say anything?

Westerfield blew out a breath. "I pleaded with you to call off the duel, remember?"

"And I apologized," Kessler reminded him none too kindly.

"But I thought..." That his brother was being an oaf. That Kessler and Westerfield cared not for the woman's honor because she was a mere serving girl. He'd never imagined the woman herself had voluntarily surrendered her honor to Kessler.

"Let me up," Gregory muttered.

Kessler tilted his arrogant nose down at him. "Why, so you can send another fist into my face?"

Gregory reached up and grasped Kessler's bony wrist, squeezing until Kessler released him. He stood with the grace of an arthritic farmer who'd spent nearly a century working fields, then hobbled into the woods.

His cheek throbbed, and his head still ached with the impact of Kessler's fist. Traipsing alone through the woods with no lantern probably wasn't the most intelligent activity, but he needed space, a chance to breathe without people staring at him. A moment to think.

He kicked a stone with the tip of his boot. The heavy rock rolled only a few inches before coming to rest in the wet soil. Had he really been so blinded to Kessler and Suzanna's relationship? Had the truth been staring at him, and he'd failed to see it because...because... because...

Why *hadn't* he seen what was going on between Kessler and Suzanna? Why hadn't someone from his family stopped the duel if his mistake had been so obvious? Though he supposed Westerfield had tried to stop things, and he'd been too stubborn to listen.

Gregory trudged deeper into the woods, his stride quickening as the throbbing in his cheek settled. When he'd looked at the situation with Kessler and Suzanna, he'd seen only what he wanted to see. That Kessler had forced himself on a girl Gregory had once jumped off haymows with, taken fishing and sneaked sweet biscuits with from the kitchen. When he'd found Suzanna lying in the hay, her hair in disarray and her dress disheveled, he'd assumed the obvious.

But he'd been wrong. And because he'd been wrong and too stubborn to consider otherwise, he'd taken a musket ball to the leg and Kessler had run off to France. The next two years of his, Kessler's and Westerfield's lives had been altered because he wouldn't listen.

Gregory paused beside a tree and heaved a ragged breath. And here he was, little better than Kessler with his own improper behavior making trouble for them all.

But no, he was better than Kessler. He had to be. He gave donations to the Hastings Orphanage, the foundling hospitals and poorhouses littered across London. He saw that his clerks were well provided for and earned a better-than-average income. He made certain workers in the shipyards and factories he invested in were treated fairly. He wasn't some arrogant, self-obsessed man, no. He saw the needs of others every day and did what he could to provide for them. That made him better than Kessler, did it not?

But do you behave any better with Danielle than Kessler did with Suzanna?

He'd kissed her and held her close.

And he was still planning to leave her.

"Because I don't have a choice!" he shouted into the trees.

Perchance she was the most fascinating woman he'd ever met. Perchance she made him smile and entertain thoughts of children with her flashing eyes and dark locks, flying kites through Hyde Park, of evenings sitting by the parlor fire with his wife curled up beside him.

Perchance.

Yet he was going to leave it all behind because she was beneath him.

Because he was like Kessler.

"No," he rasped, his throat raw.

He wasn't being like Kessler. He was being plain, sensible, honest. If he married a peasant—a *French* peasant who was at war with his country—his entire family would suffer. He would forever be a blight on the House of Westerfield. He would have to leave London and might well lose his clients despite how much money he made them on the Exchange.

His younger sister Lilliana was set to debut next year. Would she be able to find a husband if her older brother tarnished the family's reputation by marrying a French peasant? Perhaps. An aged and fat fourth son of a baronet or something of the like. No young, dashing member of the ton would touch her.

And what about Westerfield? Once in England, he would have to search for another wife since his late wife had produced no heirs. But what society damsel would accept a French peasant as sister-in-law? And Mother, his dear mother. She'd already lost Father, had nearly lost her eldest son. Now was she to have her youngest live in exile from the life in which he'd been raised?

Edmund, his middle brother who was comfortably

married and settled—even if he hadn't a mind for business or running a marquessate—would also suffer a certain loss of reputation, which his wife would find hard to forgive. Surely family harmony and the well-being of those he loved was more important than his own selfish desires.

It was too much to ask of his family. He couldn't wed Danielle, no matter how much Danielle meant to him. No matter how much he cared for…or loved the woman.

But no, he couldn't love her. Certainly his feelings hadn't gone that far. Not yet. And he would have to keep them that way: firmly under control. Firmly removed. Anything else would lead to naught but heartache for both of them.

She sacrificed herself for you, might well have ended up dead so that you could go on living.

He worked the side of his jaw back and forth, a faint moisture creeping into his eyes. Perhaps Danielle had been willing to sacrifice her life for him, but her actions couldn't change the world in which they lived. Taking a musket ball in her side wouldn't make either France or England accept them were they to marry.

His brother and Kessler had been right to pull him aside and remind him. Four more days until the coast. Certainly he could keep himself detached for so short a time.

"Move, and I'll kill you."

Gregory's blood froze at the sound of the deep, unfamiliar voice, speaking in French-accented English.

"Open your hands and put them where I can see them."

Heart thudding in his ears, he did as commanded, staring up at the tall, wide-shouldered man who towered naught but a yard away. Hair the color of midnight curled beneath the edges of his wide-brimmed hat, but from his stance it was clear that this man was no farmer. A gendarme, perchance? But he didn't wear the blue coat of France's military police, either.

And he held not a pistol but a blade poised over his shoulder, ready to throw.

"What's your name?"

Gregory kept his eyes riveted to the knife. Had he been too lost in thought to hear the other man approach? Or did the stranger move through the woods with the same quiet grace as Danielle? "Gregory Halston."

"Gregory Halston," the man repeated, his dark eyes hard in the hazy light of the forest. "Take me to your camp."

He knew not who this man was, but one thing was certain, he would die in this forsaken part of the forest before he'd lead him back to an injured Danielle, recovering Westerfield, and a lad of six and ten.

Gregory met the man's gaze, his pulse thudding hard against his throat. "This way." He nodded toward the patch of forest in the opposite direction of the camp.

With one lithe movement the man was beside him, the cold blade of the knife pressed against his throat. There hadn't even been time to struggle.

"Don't waste my time with your English lies." The man spoke in a deathly quiet voice. "I'm going to your camp, not the opposite direction. You can go there with me, or I can kill you now."

Chapter Seventeen

Why hadn't he been more careful when tromping away from the camp?

The man with a knife to Gregory's throat looked through the woods in the exact direction Gregory had come, at the very path of fallen leaves his boots had trampled. Clearly he would find the camp with or without help.

"I—I'll take you," he managed despite the blade biting into his skin. And he'd spend every second they walked praying God would protect the others.

Gregory's body trembled as he started back. Somehow the man kept the blade near enough his throat that he didn't dare attempt to trip him or look for a tree branch or rock to slam into the man's head. Yet the blade was loose enough he didn't fear it slicing his skin as they moved through the woods.

Dear God, protect the others. Somehow warn them of this man coming. Perhaps Serge could have his knife in hand when we enter the clearing. And perchance Danielle could be awake—something told him she'd still be able to throw a knife from her sickbed. Even if this man kills me, Father, let the others live and escape. Get Westerfield and—

"Faster." The man shoved him over the uneven forest floor.

When leaving the camp, it seemed as though he walked quite a ways, but within mere moments he glimpsed the dull blue of Serge's coat through the trees. The lad was crouched by the fire, his back to them, eating salt pork by the look of it. So much for Serge having his knife ready. The grays and browns of the other's coats were also huddled near the fire. Gregory slanted a glance through the trees toward where Danielle lay, but the fir boughs were too dense to make out her form.

Father, let her be awake...and holding her knife.

"Not so quick," the man whispered. Then the stranger hauled him back against his chest and pressed the blade snug against Gregory's throat. "We'll do this part together."

He moved forward, using Gregory as a shield between him and the others.

God, get us out of this alive! But it didn't seem possible, not with the way this stranger had everyone at an advantage.

"Anyone moves, and he dies," the man boomed in a voice that would commandeer the obedience of King George himself.

Serge sprang to his feet and whirled around.

Gregory closed his eyes. Did it hurt when one had his throat slit? Or was the death instant?

"Papa!"

"Serge," the man blundered.

Papa? Gregory's eyes flew open. The burly man behind him was Danielle and Serge's father?

No, certainly not. Because if anything, the man pressed the blade harder against his neck rather than releasing him.

Nevertheless, Serge scampered toward them with a giant grin plastered to his face.

"Papa?" On her pallet, Danielle blinked sleep from her eyes.

"The rest of you sit in a straight line in front of that blanket, hands placed open on the dirt in front of you." The man must have made some gesture to indicate which pallet he talked about, because Farnsworth, Kessler and Westerfield instantly obeyed while Serge stopped just a few feet away.

"Papa, non!" Danielle scrambled off her blankets far too hastily for a woman who had been shot just days before and raced toward them. "What are you doing? Take that knife away. Gregory's done nothing."

"Dani?" The man's voice turned quiet and the knife trembled slightly. "What have they done to you?"

Gregory took in Danielle's appearance. Dirty linen was wrapped over the gash in her head while her hair tumbled wild and matted to the middle of her back. Shadows smudged the fragile skin beneath her eyes, and her cheeks were drawn with worry. The bandage wrapped about her side peeked out from the large musket ball hole in her cloak, while dried blood no one had bothered to wash stained the left side of the wool.

She bore little resemblance to the beautiful, vital woman he'd first met in the woods. Why had he not realized it before now?

"They've done nothing, *Papa*." She pressed her hand to her head wound. "Some farmers shot at me, and I hit my head against a rock. Serge put a blade in each of their necks, though. I'm told it was quite impressive throwing."

Serge's narrow shoulders straightened and he nodded. *"Oui.* I heard the gunshots and found Dani in time to attack the farmers. You'd have been right proud, *Papa*, had you seen me throw."

"The man you're holding there, Gregor—er, Halston..." Danielle gestured to him. "He's done nothing to hurt us, and I've agreed to help him and his companions reach England."

"Help them?" the towering man shouted. He thrust Gregory forward and used his knife to point to the others. "Sit down at the end of the row. The slightest movement from any of you, and you'll each find a knife in your throat."

The man likely had enough knives concealed on his person to make good on his threat. Gregory hastened to the group and plopped onto the dirt beside Westerfield. His neck burned where the blade had pressed against it, but he dared not cover the tender flesh with his hand. Instead, he splayed his hands on the dirt before him, then glanced up at the stranger with dark hair and an even darker look upon his face. Strange how he'd thought little of taking on the three army deserters in the barn, but in the presence of this powerful man, he dared not move. He was the lord, not this common Frenchman.

But the common Frenchman wore his power and influence more comfortably than a seventh-generation duke.

Her father was livid. He didn't need to speak for Danielle to sense the fury coursing through his body. Serge took a subtle step away, placing himself between *Papa* and the others, but rather than follow Serge's example, she straightened her shoulders, met her father's gaze and took a step forward. "Two of them were wrongfully imprisoned, and—"

"They're British, are they not? Our enemies? The only thing wrongful about their imprisonment is that the other two weren't included."

She cringed, partly because of the truth behind her father's words, partly because of the force and loathing with which he spoke them, and partly because of the fresh pain tearing through her side. "*Oui*, but—"

"But nothing!" *Papa* reached into the folds of his coat and tossed Serge several pieces of rope. "Bind their hands and feet. I'll see them to the gendarmerie post in Abbeville while you two start for home. I only pray I won't be interrogated about the 'beautiful dark-haired woman and gangly youth' seen traveling with them when I turn them over to Captain Montfort."

"*Non!* You can't take them. I don't…that is…why…" She sucked in a breath and forced her thoughts into a semblance of order. "How did you even come to search for us? How did you know we were with them?"

Papa reached to the waist of his pants and sheathed his knife—not that he couldn't have it in hand again in an instant. "When your aunt's letter from Reims arrived and explained how sorry she was about the way thing had ended between you and Citizen Fauchet, I started to wonder why you hadn't beaten the letter home. You aren't known for traveling slowly, Danielle. In the meantime, I got word to be on the lookout for two escaped English spies from north of Reims. Three days ago I received news that some deserters had been found. These deserters talked about three Englishmen with a dark-haired Frenchwoman and a youth aiding them."

She bit the side of her lip. "Did you hear about the gunshots? About the farmers Serge killed?"

His gaze grew hard. "We'll say the Englishmen killed them."

She wrapped her arms around her waist, pushing down the pain that seared through her body with the action. "*Non*. I refuse to lie. I'll march straight into

Captain Montfort's office and tell him every last thing that transpired."

"So your brother will end up beneath the guillotine's blade while you're taken to some forgotten dungeon?"

Her throat turned dry. "I'll claim I killed the farmers."

"I see. You'll lie to protect your brother but not yourself." Frustration tinged her father's gruff voice. "Time with the English has clearly addled your brain."

"Don't stand there and judge me. You know not how much I've risked, what we've endured these past two weeks."

"Oh, no. I understand very well." He shifted angrily from one foot to the other. "You've risked my work as an informant. Our home. The lives of your mother and sisters, of myself. *I'll* not risk any of that over English buffoons for another instant. Whatever possessed you to help them? Have you not spent the past decade living beneath my roof, eating at my table? Did you learn nothing when I taught you of the First Republic, the Consulate? The hope our country has of ridding itself of tyranny? And you want to *help* people who would see France under the reign of another Bourbon king?"

She swallowed hard. He spoke truth, far too much truth. England's king wanted nothing more than to see a Bourbon reinstated on the French throne and all the advances her country had made over the past fifteen years undone. If England won this war, France would go back to how it had been before the *Révolution*. No more liberty or equality for the masses. Peasants heavily taxed while aristocrats lived in excess. Commoners starved for bread and clamoring after only a handful of jobs while the queen ate cakes at Versailles.

Papa's first wife had taken ill and died, half from

starving and half from illness, during those days. Many others would die of disease or starvation once more if King George had his way. 'Twas why England's tyranny had to be stopped.

'Twas why she never should have agreed to aid Gregory.

"We learned about the *Révolution, Papa*," Serge's soft voice wafted across the camp from where he stood with the ropes still dangling from his hands. "And we also learned when you taught us from the Bible. *'For there is neither Jew nor Greek, slave nor free, male nor female in Christ.'* If there's neither Jew nor Greek, why should God see a difference between French and English? He sent His Son to die for the English along with the French, did He not?"

Papa crossed his arms, his face dark and stony, but at least he didn't reach for his knife.

"Westerfield was near death when we found them," she added into the silence. "And both he and Kessler were so thin it looked as though they'd been starved. I fought them at first, was going to leave and turn them into the gendarmerie post, but then I remembered Laurent."

"*Oui*, Laurent," her father croaked. "How do you think he would feel knowing you're risking all you cherish to help men from the country that killed him?"

She gripped her hands together in front of her stomach. "What if he didn't die? What if he was injured but somehow made it to England? Would you want the first Englishman who happened upon him to drag him to the gaol? Or would you want someone to aid him so he could return home?"

Papa rubbed the back of his neck, his forehead drawing down into a frown. "'Tis not as simple as the two of you make this to be. They are our enemies and would likely kill us if they found one of us on their soil."

"They didn't kill Dani and me when we went over during the peace," Serge piped up.

"Yes, well, things change rather quickly when one nation declares war on the other," *Papa* muttered.

"These men know *Tante* Isabelle and *Oncle* Michel. Gregor—er, Halston is their man of business."

"And that's a reason to let them live? Some mutual acquaintance in England?"

"He's not a mutual acquaintance, he's your brother!" Danielle threw up her hands and whirled away from her father. A fresh stab of pain seared through her side. Her head was pounding now, so badly she could hardly form coherent words, and tears blurred her eyes. She needed to lie down, but she couldn't let herself rest when her father was about to cart the man she loved off to prison. "Do you think *Oncle* Michel would take up relations with a dishonorable man? The Englishmen are people just like us. Two of them were wrongly imprisoned when the peace ended and then kept in a forsaken dungeon and nigh starved. We should…"

She pressed a hand to her side, trying to stop the pain bursting through her, and sucked in a shallow breath.

"Dani?" Her father and Gregory spoke her name in unison.

But rather than look at them, she stared down at her hand, her fingers covered in a sticky red. "I—I think I need to…"

They were the last words she formed as gray clouded her vision and blackness overtook her.

Chapter Eighteen

"Why isn't she waking up?" Gregory repositioned the wet cloth he held against Danielle's forehead and stared down at her pale cheeks. "Because she walked too far earlier? I told her not to walk."

"Mayhap. Or it could be the pain from her side, loss of blood." Her father kept his gaze locked on Danielle's side as he poured water on her wound. "How much did she bleed when she was shot?"

The vision of his coat soaked with Danielle's blood flashed across his mind, and he pressed his lips together.

"Too much." Serge came up behind Belanger with a shallow bowl in hand. "Here's the water you asked for."

Belanger set the bowl he was using aside and reached for the steaming liquid, dipping a rag in it before cleansing his daughter's side once more. "Today was the first time you let her walk by herself?"

"She insisted." But the excuse felt paltry on Gregory's tongue. He should have carried her from the moment they left camp that morn, even if he had to bind her hands and feet and toss her over his shoulder.

Serge plopped down beside his father, the boy's attention on the ugly wound in his sister's side. "You know how she can be, *Papa*. She had it in her mind that she was well enough to walk, so she nigh fainted before she let Halston carry her."

Belanger's eyes met his over Danielle's body. "The *lord* carried my daughter, did he?"

Gregory nearly cringed at the use of his title. How was it this French family could make what all of England honored into something that sounded reprehensible? "It seemed only fair. She was protecting me when she got shot. I'm the reason she...she's..." He dropped his gaze back to Danielle's colorless face.

"She was protecting you? That's a story I should probably hear," Belanger growled.

"Shouldn't we try to rouse her first?" Serge reached for her hand lying motionless on her stomach and squeezed. "She's been out an awfully long time."

"We need to stitch her." Belanger's jaw remained hard. "Which should have been done after the gunshot and is likely why the wound reopened."

"Oh." Serge bit the side of his lip. "I probably should have known that."

Belanger raised an eyebrow at his son.

"If you stitch it now, will she heal?" Gregory asked, perhaps a bit too quickly since Belanger stared at him in that odd manner again.

"She should, though she'll likely bear a scar." Her father trailed a gentle finger around the wound. "Serge, go fetch my bag."

The boy scampered off and was back in an instant, rummaging through the sack to produce a needle and thread.

Belanger took the supplies in hand. "While I sew,

Lord Halston is going to tell me exactly how he got my daughter shot."

Gregory worked a finger beneath his collar and loosened the suddenly tight fabric. "I...ah—"

"There wasn't much to it." Serge raised his shoulder and let it drop. "We'd gotten into a scuffle with some deserters and were being looked for. Two farmers happened upon Dani and Halston, then fired at Dani. Halston should tell you about the first time they met instead. It's much more interesting."

Serge's voice was entirely too cheerful, and Gregory scowled. "Just a mom—"

"Dani here tackled Halston's valet and held a knife to his throat," Serge volunteered. "Which somehow made Halston decide she would do a good job of getting them to the coast. So then he kidnapped us, even tied Dani up for a bit until she agreed to help on her own."

"You tied my daughter up?" Belanger's shout likely alerted half the countryside to their presence

Gregory shoved a second finger beneath his collar and tugged harder. Danielle was right about her brother. The boy never knew when to close his mouth. "I, ah... couldn't exactly have her running to the nearest gendarmerie post and accusing us of being spies."

The worn lines around Belanger's eyes crinkled while he worked on Dani's side. "I see you've been introduced to her full charm."

Her full charm? Yes, he'd been introduced to all of it. The fierce way she'd fought against them at first, then for them once she'd decided to help. The tireless manner in which she'd cared for Westerfield, the quick rebukes she'd spit at Kessler.

The passionate way she'd kissed him.

His mouth turned dry at the sudden memory—

memories, as there had been two kisses. His gaze drifted to her lips, a dull, chapped pink on a face devoid of color. What would they feel like if he touched his mouth to hers now? Cold like the rest of her face? Soft despite their chapped state? Or perchance a kiss would wake her as it had the princess in the story of Sleeping Beauty.

Belanger's throat cleared, and Gregory glanced up, heat flooding the back of his neck.

"Care to state your thoughts?"

"Ah…your daughter is…well…"

Belanger shifted back and crossed his arms, revealing that Danielle's side was tightly sewn together. When had Belanger finished?

Likely sometime while he'd been staring at her lips.

Exactly how long had he stared?

And how long had her father watched him?

"You were saying?"

"I…" He looked back toward camp and pushed to his feet. "Perhaps I should check on the others."

"I think not. Sit down, Halston, and let Serge see to the others. I've a story to tell you."

Gregory turned back to the older man. A story? He could well imagine what the story might be—a tale of a man who fell in love with the wrong woman and then ended up in prison for the rest of his life. Nevertheless, Gregory sank into the dirt beside Danielle's freshly wrapped side while her father moved to probe the knot on her head.

"Before I ever met Danielle, when she was a mere child of three and ten, she'd sneaked into my house and stolen the knife from above my mantel. She'd also taken a chicken from the coop, but she knew not how to grip a knife or kill a chicken. So she dragged the thing, half dead, to the woods lining one of my fields, and when I came upon her, she had that knife raised like a warrior above her prey, ready for the kill strike."

Danielle gave a little gasp, and her hand opened before fisting tightly on her belly.

"Dani?" Gregory took her hand and glanced at Belanger, his fingers still probing her injury. "Dani, are you awake? Can you hear me? You swooned, darling. We think it's because your wound started bleeding again."

Her eyelids flickered open, and her gaze landed on his for half a moment before her eyes closed again.

Belanger cleared his throat and shifted, staring at him yet again before turning his attention back to Dani. "As I was saying, I approached, and she whirled. She still clutched the knife as though she planned to use it on me should I take another step."

"No more." Danielle mumbled, though her eyes remained closed. "Not this story."

"Hush, daughter, don't strain yourself. We need to see you well." Belanger removed his hands from her hair and stroked an errant lock off her forehead. "You'd tell me nothing about how you'd come by the knife or who your parents were or where I could find them. Do you remember? And I couldn't help but love you from the first—and determine to teach you the proper use of a knife."

Gregory ran his thumb over the knuckles on Danielle's hand. "You must have found her family, seeing how you married her mother."

The glazed look of memories left Belanger's eyes. "*Oui.* I found her mother and two little brothers, and I discovered Danielle stole my chicken because they had naught but pulse to eat and her mother was sick with fever."

"So you helped them."

Belanger's strong jaw worked back and forth. "I helped. They needed quite a bit of it."

Just as his own party had needed quite a bit of help from Danielle and Serge. He gave Dani's hand a final squeeze and released it, her eyes still closed, her breathing even and steady as though she'd fallen asleep. "Will you help us, as well? Will you take us to the coast?"

The breath stilled in his lungs as he watched the harsh man who could cart them off to prison at any time. Belanger searched Gregory's face and eyes and body, every inch of him, though he could hardly guess what Belanger looked for. Footsteps thudded the earth from somewhere in the camp and a squirrel scampered through the nearby trees, but silence lingered between them.

"*Oui.* I'll help."

Relief swept through Gregory at the simple words. "Thank y—"

"But my daughter is going home. I'll carry her tomorrow, but once we reach Abbeville, she and Serge will stay home while I take you to the coast. I'll not risk her anymore. I know not how you've planned to cross the channel, but I've a son in Saint-Valery who can ferry you across as easily as anyone else. 'Tis only a two-day walk from here."

Two days? That was all? Going up to Berck would require more than a half week of travel, and here Belanger could see them off in two days' time.

"Yes," he croaked. "It should work perfectly." Gregory glanced at Danielle, her beautiful face pale, her usually vibrant form so still. "And she'll be safe."

Which mattered more to him than he dare admit aloud.

* * *

The Englishmen.

Danielle woke with a start, pushing herself up quickly to survey the camp. The men were still there, as was her father, all up and about the camp in the dim morning light. At least he hadn't taken them to Captain Montfort in Abbeville yet. She raised herself from her bedding, ignoring the pain in her side and the throbbing in her head.

"You should be resting." Her father barreled toward her, his jaw set at a formidable angle.

"You didn't leave," she countered.

"I'll help with your bedding." He bent and scooped up the blankets with his massive arms, wadding them into a ball that would never fit into their small sacks of supplies. "Just don't aggravate your injuries."

She pressed a hand to her still-tender side. "I pushed myself too hard yesterday, but I'll not make the same mistake today. You've little need to worry."

"You've spent the past fortnight helping spies." He looked about the campsite, his gaze pausing on where Gregory, Kessler and Westerfield clustered together while Farnsworth busied himself beside the fire. "That's plenty of reason to worry. You'll not be walking today. I'll carry you until we're within a kilometer or two of home before sending you and Serge on while I take these men to the coast."

He'd been bent on taking the English to Captain Montfort, and now he'd decided to help? She gripped her father's arm, her fingers digging into the thick wool of his coat. "Did I change your mind last night?"

"Something of the sort." He slanted anther glance toward Gregory. "Now go rest by that tree yonder. I need you well, not weak and sickly."

She didn't need rest. She felt perfectly fine—well, except for the pain. But she wasn't about to walk docilely home while *Papa* led the men to safety. "I intend to see them to the coast."

Her father sighed, untold weariness behind the exhalation of breath. "Danielle, don't make things more difficult. I've already decided to involve Julien in passage across the channel rather than take the men farther up to Berck. I refuse to risk you and Serge any more than necessary."

Julien! Why hadn't she thought of him? It was perfect. "'Tis a wonderful plan, especially since we know not if the gendarmes and smugglers have set a trap for them in Berck."

"*Oui*. And Julien can keep a secret."

That he could. Her older brother might well carry the secrets of half northern France and one would never know it. "Since it's only two days' journey rather than a week's you should have no trouble with me going along."

"*Non*." The curt word rang through the camp.

"*Papa*, you've already—"

"Must you fight with every word that issues from my mouth? First you try convincing me to help a bunch of spies rather than see them imprisoned, and once I give you that, you demand to continue traveling with them. I forbid it."

She sucked in a breath through her nose, nice and long and slow. It did nothing to calm the blood burning hot through her veins. "Did you listen to nothing I said last night? They're not spies!"

Papa scowled. "Why they're here makes little difference seeing how they're English and we're at war."

"And yet you're not delivering them to Captain Montfort."

"Enough."

"It's not enough. Don't you understand?" Tears scalded the backs of her eyes, hot and mortifying. "I have to go with them, and not just to the coast, but all the way to England to ensure they get there safely. I've come too far to back away now."

Papa shifted his bulky weight from one foot to the other. "You don't need to add a trip across the channel to everything you've endured. You don't even need to add a trip *to* the channel. I promise to deliver the men safely."

But her father's promise wasn't enough. Not anymore. There had been a time when it would have sufficed. Had been a time when she'd hung on his every word and cherished them like her own sack of gold napoleons. But somewhere along this journey, things had changed. It wasn't that she didn't believe her father. She believed him as much as was possible for one person to believe another. But that trust no longer negated her own need to see the man she loved safely to his homeland.

"I have to go."

"Of all the people I envisioned claiming your heart, it was never a British aristocrat." His voice, though soft and tender, cut as sharply as the blade strapped to her ankle.

The breath stilled in her lungs, and the air grew thick around them. "How did you know?"

"You're begging for me to spare an Englishman. What other reason could there be?"

She swiped a stray tear away from her face. "I have to make the crossing with Julien. I've helped Gregory for so long I can't bear to say goodbye here when I could see him safe in his own country."

"Gregory, is it? Not Halston."

Her body turned warm at the sound of Gregory's Christian name on her father's lips. *"Oui."*

Somehow *Papa* managed to shift his burgeoning wad of blankets to one arm and held out the other for her. She needed no invitation to step inside and let his strong arm anchor her, his broad body offer shelter.

"The more you prolong your farewell, the more heartbroken you're likely to be."

She buried her face in his coat. "That doesn't change how I feel."

"Has he…"

When his voice faded, she looked up.

A muscle worked back and forth in his jaw. "Has he offered for you?"

"It's not like that between us. He's a lord."

Her father's brow furrowed, and he slanted yet another glance at Gregory. The man was going to tromp over any moment if *Papa* didn't stop staring. As though she needed Gregory Halston privy to this conversation.

"And your birth father was heir to a *seigneury*," *Papa* continued. "Perhaps if he knew—"

"Non. I want to marry a man who values me as a person, not my lineage. I might love him…I *know* I love him. But does he love me? He's never spoken such words, and I doubt he ever will. In his eyes, I'm too far beneath him to make him a good wife." Just as there'd always been some reason she wouldn't make a Frenchman a good wife. She threw knives and spent too much time in the woods. She couldn't sew, couldn't cook, couldn't do half the wifely duties she was supposed to.

Whether she fell in love with a lord or a peasant, she still wasn't good enough.

Except for her stepfather. He'd always loved her in spite of everything she did wrong. "So you see, *Papa*, I can't…can't…" Her voice cracked, and rather than try to wrench the garbled mess of words from her mouth, she pressed her face into his shoulder.

Papa's bearlike arms tightened around her, and he settled his chin atop her head, not speaking so much as a word of solace. But then, he didn't need to. The feeling of his presence and the love of someone who wasn't ashamed of her was enough…

Or at least it would be, until she said goodbye to Gregory.

Chapter Nineteen

"Halt!" Belanger's harsh whisper permeated the foggy twilight.

Gregory stilled, his heart thumping against his chest. Beside him, Farnsworth, Kessler and Westerfield all stopped in the murky gloom.

A wraithlike form appeared shrouded in mist on the empty beach ahead of them. "Gregory, you're here!"

A foul word left Belanger's mouth. "Hush, daughter, or you'll call down half the countryside."

Danielle? Gregory surveyed the stretch of sand, empty save for themselves and the woman moving toward them. She was supposed to have gone home after she and Serge broke from them last night. Clearly she hadn't obeyed her father.

Clearly he was a fool for thinking she would.

She sprinted toward them as though no musket ball had ever grazed her side, sliding to a halt when her toes were mere inches from his.

He reached out and gripped her arm, no more able to stop himself from running his eyes over her hair and face and lips than he was able to stop the war between their countries. "What are you doing here?"

"Someone had to warn Julien of your arrival. Now come, the boat's ready." She took his elbow and tugged.

Gregory tightened his hands into fists. As though she belonged on a beach at dusk helping to smuggle men across the channel rather than at home in bed. He glanced around the beach a second time. They'd once again skirted a town, this time coming out on an abandoned stretch of sandy shoreline. The mist shrouded the buildings of Saint-Valery-sur-Somme behind them, and the open bay lapped gently before them.

It seemed too easy, as though some trap lay hidden ahead. Certainly France wasn't going to let them simply board the fishing boat and be off. A pack of gendarmes or soldiers would likely come tearing across the sandy beach at any moment.

But he approached the boat without incident.

"My father and sister tell me you've coin aplenty to pay if I ferry you across the channel." A voice roughened from hours spent in the salty sea air spoke.

Gregory turned to find a shadow limping toward them, too small to be Belanger and too large to be Serge. "I'm Lord Gregory Halston. Behind me, you'll find Lord Westerfield and Lord Kessler, as well as my valet, Farnsworth. And yes, I can pay."

"Lords, are you?" With his scruffy beard, wind-chapped skin and limp, Julien Belanger could have stepped out of a children's book about pirates. "That's quite a mouthful of fancy names you got."

"Leave them alone, Julien, and take us across before someone finds us." Danielle climbed gingerly inside the little fishing vessel with its gray sails. "I didn't bring them all this way to have us discovered on the beach."

The auburn-haired man scowled at his sister. "I'm

not going anywhere with you in the boat, not when your side's all shot up."

She crossed his arms. "I already told you I'm going, just ask *Papa*."

Gregory's mouth turned dry. She was going? With them? He planted his legs in the sand. "No."

"Don't tell me you've decided to remain in France." Kessler hopped inside the boat, its fore-and-aft-rigged sails jutting into the dim sky.

"*Oui*. I thought the point of getting you safely to the coast was so you could cross the channel." Danielle frowned at him.

He tightened his grip on the sack slung over his shoulder. "I intend to go to England, and well you know it. But I refuse to endanger you any longer than necessary. You're supposed to be home right now. Abed. Healing from the injuries I caused you."

"You didn't cause me to get shot."

He turned away from her and stalked toward Belanger and Serge on the beach. The sooner they left, the sooner Danielle could return home, where she would be safe. Or perhaps she would even go inside the little cottage near the shore and rest there. Either way, she'd be better off once he departed for England—without her.

He stopped in front of Julien, Danielle, and Serge's stepfather. "You told her she could go to England? It's a needless risk, especially with her being injured."

"I agree with the lord. Danielle shouldn't cross the channel." Julien's voice was a low growl over Gregory's shoulder.

Belanger kept his gaze pinned on Gregory, as though Danielle's stubbornness was somehow his fault. "Then you try to tell her *non*."

"I will."

Serge snickered beside his father. "Have you learned nothing after spending all this time with Dani? Once she's made up her mind, no one can convince her of anything."

"Who said anything about convincing? I'll tie her up inside that cottage if necessary." Gregory jutted his chin toward the ramshackle structure, then headed back to the vessel, where Danielle now stood adjusting the sails. He jumped easily aboard, pushed past Farnsworth and stepped over a sack.

"Move, Gregory, I've yet to see to the aft sail."

He took her by the shoulders. "Danielle…"

She met his gaze, but not in her usual, defiant manner, no. He could have ordered her off the boat had she glared at him with thunderous eyes and crossed her arms over her chest. Instead, she stood with shoulders slumped and eyes wary—even a touch sad. As though she knew what he was about to say. As though she understood he was going to order her out of the boat…

And out of his life.

"What do you want?"

What did he want? He wanted to think a coherent thought, which was rather impossible when she stared at him with such sad eyes. "I, uh…"

"Just say it."

But he couldn't, because his thoughts no longer made sense. He should be thinking about getting her off the sailing vessel and keeping her safe, but she looked so lost and vulnerable, this strong woman hurt and weakened because she'd defended him from attackers. His arms ached to reach out and hold her, to offer the strength that the musket-ball wound seemed to have drained from her body.

But what good would taking her in his arms do? He'd still have to say goodbye.

Danielle shifted awkwardly from one foot to another, her gaze refusing to let him look anywhere but her somber eyes. "Did you want something from me?"

Yes. No. Perhaps. He knew not what he wanted anymore—except to kiss her one last time. Kiss her and whisper sweet words of…of what?

He had no promises of a future, no words of love to give. Could he wish her well with her life? Hope she found herself a kind French husband?

Danielle didn't need a kind man. She'd plow over a kind man like a farmer furrowing a field at springtime. She needed someone strong. Sturdy. Stubborn. Someone who would argue with her when she got fool notions in her head. Someone who would tell her to put down her knife and hold her when she needed to be held. Kiss her when she needed to be kissed. Tell her she was beautiful and perfect as she was. Someone like him.

Except it couldn't be him. He could offer her no life of happiness in England, just as she could offer him no life of happiness in France. Were they to wed and settle in France, he'd spend every day fearing being hunted down, just as he had for the past two weeks. And if they married in England, society would have no place for a commoner married to a British lord. Danielle would be shunned and his family would be disgraced.

When Danielle spoke of equality, she made it sound so easy. Everyone was equal in God's eyes, and that was that. But living that way in a world filled with hate was much more complicated than simply spouting words. He hardly had the ability to change society's strictures; nor was he willing to sacrifice his family's happiness so that he and Danielle could be together.

But even so, he hadn't the courage to wish her well in her quest for a fitting husband. He didn't want her to be successful in finding love with anyone but him.

Which meant he was likely one of the greatest cowards to ever walk the earth.

"N-no," he finally choked out. "I have nothing more to ask of you."

And he didn't. He had little business making demands on Danielle when he would no longer be part of her life.

"Nothing?" Her eyes flickered with a fragile hope, likely because he wasn't objecting to her trip to England.

"Not anymore." He turned and stepped over a fishing net, stowing his sack beneath the bench at the prow of the boat.

Danielle stood by the mast, a strand of rigging dangling absently in her hand as she stared out to sea. Part of him wanted to go to her again. A very bad part. Because, in truth, he had no right to her. He never had, and he never would.

But he'd cobble together the words to tell her goodbye after they crossed the channel.

And then he'd walk away without looking back.

Because he was a British lord. And British lords didn't allow themselves to look back at peasant girls.

Danielle stood at the prow of the boat, her eyes scanning the dark waters for England's rocky shore. Any moment now, and they should be upon the little alcove where they hid the boat whenever they visited their aunt and uncle.

Behind her, Julien manned the sails while Gregory and the others huddled beneath blankets. Sleeping?

Maybe the others, but not Gregory. The warmth of his gaze blanketed her back.

"There." She pointed toward the shadowy outcropping on the bank.

"Not yet." Julien's rusty but quiet voice carried over the boat. "Look to port."

She stilled at the sight of two thin lantern beams piercing the darkness. Excise agents? *Please, God, no. Not after we've come so close.*

"Who are they?" Gregory whispered.

She surveyed the shore, her eyes narrowing on the pattern of a flickering lantern: three long bursts of light followed by one short one. "Smugglers."

Her grandfather—the unlamented father of her natural father—had used signals such as that when he'd run his vast operation during the *Révolution*. The only question was whether the lantern signals from shore meant it was safe for the smuggling vessel to approach or whether there were excise agents in the area and the vessel needed to wait.

Julien shifted the sails, and the boat surged forward over the water, closer to shore. Did he know the signals? Was it safe to land? Or did he merely want to get Gregory and the others off his boat?

Likely the latter. The gray tinge in the eastern sky indicated dawn would be upon them shortly, and unlike smugglers, they had no second plans for where to make shore, nor did they have the food and water needed to stay afloat "fishing" all day and land the following night.

The hilly shore loomed imminently in the darkness, then sand crunched softly beneath the prow. Danielle jumped over the gunwale without thought.

'Twas a mistake. Pain lanced her side, though not

as sharp as it had been a few days earlier. Then a small splash sounded and Gregory appeared beside her, gripping the gunwale.

"I can manage," she retorted as she grabbed the boat to haul it farther onto the sand.

He stayed quiet but didn't leave his position, helping to pull the boat into the shallow alcove.

It would only take moments to conceal the small craft behind the grassy outcropping. A cave lay farther back and once the sails were down, they would push the boat inside, where previous experience told her they could leave it for weeks if need be.

"Do you always land here?" Gregory asked.

"Aye," she answered, careful to rid her voice of any French accent lest someone happen upon them. "Though we haven't come to visit Aunt Isabelle and Uncle Michel often since the peace ended."

"I still find it rather hard to believe you're related to them."

She shrugged and looked out over the water growing light in the dim illumination of dawn. Behind her, Julien and the others piled out of the boat and started dragging the craft across the sand toward the cave, leaving her and Gregory alone on the beach.

She should go help. Julien was the only other person who knew how to take down the sails, and yet, this was goodbye, was it not? She'd have no other chance to stand with Gregory again, to wish him goodbye. She drew in a breath. "Do you live far from here?"

"The marquessate is about a half hour on horseback. Longer by foot, but we'll rent horses in Hastings."

She dug the tip of her boot into the sand, the easy bond they'd shared as they traveled through France now as distant as the country itself. And it was just as well. She'd known they'd have to part. Though somehow, she'd envisioned their farewell being more passionate than this, with sincere words spoken between them rather than dull ones, possibly even a kiss they would both remember in the months and years to come.

She swallowed the lump building in her throat. "Your mother and sister will be thrilled to see Westerfield."

"Very much so, and I have you to thank for his safe return." Gregory seemed more interested in staring at the hill behind them than at her.

Then again, she was hardly any better with the way the sea kept drawing her attention. What did one tell the man she loved but would never see again? Did she wish him well for the rest of his life—without her? Did she wish him married to some perfect English debutante who would bear him a passel of dark-haired, smoky-eyed children with perfect English pedigrees?

It had all seemed so clear before. She would come to England, see Gregory safe and say goodbye. Knowing he and his party had arrived unscathed should eclipse any sorrow at leaving him, shouldn't it?

Except maybe she'd been hoping she wouldn't need to say goodbye. Maybe she'd been praying they'd get to this moment and Gregory would realize he loved her and confess his feelings. He'd say her station as a "peasant" didn't bother him any longer and promise they'd find a way to marry regardless of the war between their two countries. Then *she* could be the mother of those dark-haired children.

Foolish, immature dreams, the lot of them. "Gregory, I—"

"Will you spend a few days with your aunt?"

Her aunt. Something shattered inside her, that fragile band of hope that had clung relentlessly to the last shreds of her dreams. Gregory wanted to speak of her relatives. Not of her. Not of saying goodbye or professing his love.

She cleared her throat and spoke over the roughness that coated the inside of her mouth. "No. Julien says we'll sail on the evening tide."

"Halston, are you coming?" Kessler called over his shoulder as he and the others began the steep ascent up the hill bordering the coast.

Gregory reached out to tuck a strand of hair behind her ear. "I've business to attend—namely retrieving your money—but I'll return this afternoon to say goodbye."

"Don't." The word shot from her lips before she could think to stop it.

"I beg your pardon?"

She took a step back, her eyes suspiciously hot and wet. Oh, why had she not heeded her father's advice and made her farewells in France? "Send Farnsworth or another of your servants with the money later and say goodbye now. There's no use in prolonging this."

"But…"

She held up a hand. "We've been coming to this moment since the time we first met, no matter how many kisses or looks we've shared along the way. So let's be done. Farewell, Lord Halston."

She gave him a little curtsy. Polite, proper and a completely appropriate gesture for a peasant to make before a lord.

"You got yourself shot for me."

Her hands quivered, and she fisted them at her sides.

"*Oui*, and I'd do so again…because…because…" The words clogged in her throat. But if she didn't tell him now, when would she? It wasn't as though he'd be around for her to feel embarrassed once she spoke.

She sucked in a deep breath. "I'd take another ten musket balls for you, Gregory Halston, because I love you."

Something hard slammed into Gregory's chest. "You can't love me."

Of all the insensible things for her to do, did she not know better than to—

"I know." She flung her hands wide as though angry. With him? Why would she be angry with him? He wasn't the fool who'd gone and…and…

No, the words didn't bear thinking. He reached out and took her shoulders. "You're French. And a peasant. There can be no future for us."

She jerked away from his hold. "You think I don't understand such things? This is why I refuse to see you later. Go back to your family and marry—" she waved her hand absently in the air, her movements tight and jerky "—whoever it is you're supposed to marry. Some gentlewoman who dresses in silks and has one of those pretty little parasols to shield her complexion from the sun."

"It's not like that."

"Isn't it? Your mother probably has an entire list of perfect little wives already picked out. Women who don't know how to throw knives or sneak Englishmen past French soldiers. Women who don't know the ways of smugglers let alone have them in their family lineage. Go marry one of them."

He fully intended to.

Except he didn't want to marry anyone from his

mother's confounded list. He wanted to marry the woman in front of him.

No. Why was he thinking such thoughts again? He couldn't entertain them, not now and not ever. Too much was at stake.

"Go now, Lord Halston, and don't come back. Send a servant with my money later." Danielle's shoulders slumped, and she stared down at her feet, her eyelashes fluttering furiously. Where was her defiance? The bite underlying her words, or the stubborn set to her chin? Where was the flash in her eyes and icy stiffness in her spine?

He was destroying her, his presence slowly leaching her energy. She was right, he had to walk away. Now. Before he made an even bigger mess of everything.

And he would, except...

He pulled her into his arms. "I don't want to lose you, either." He needed this one last embrace, the feel of her body close to his, the scent of sunshine and woods and Danielle Belanger winding about him, the tender look in those wide blue eyes.

He lowered his lips to hers, tangy with the taste of the sea. She stilled but didn't jerk away as he'd half expected. So he pulled her closer, as though if he held on to her tightly enough, he might not lose her. If only kissing her could melt away their struggles and hardships. Could somehow abolish the difference between peasant and aristocrat, English and French. Could eradicate the war that raged between their countries and the prejudice that divided their countrymen.

"Ahem."

Gregory raised his head, breaking his lips from Danielle's.

"We're waiting." Kessler gestured to Westerfield

and Farnsworth, standing partway up the hill as they watched him and Danielle. Gregory's gaze skittered over the beach, where Julien also stood watching, arms crossed and face dark.

Yet, even with everyone looking on, his arms refused to release Danielle.

She pressed her face into the curve of his neck. "*Adieu*, Gregory. I shall remember you forever." Then she took his forearms gently in her hands and unwrapped them from about her.

All he could do was stand and watch as she headed to her brother, her back straight and stride long.

A bony hand landed on his shoulder, its grip far stronger than when he'd first rescued Kessler nearly three weeks prior. "She's an admirable woman, Halston. Even I can see that. But you're doing the right thing by leaving."

"Yes, quite," he muttered.

Except, as he turned to tread up the slope, his actions didn't feel right.

Chapter Twenty

"Easy on the sails, Danielle. I don't want to have to mend them before we return tonight."

Danielle scowled at her brother but stepped back from the mast, leaving him to deal with the aft sail. So perhaps her movements were a little jerky as she handled the thick fabric, but at least she was busying herself rather than standing on the beach watching Gregory walk up the hill like some lovesick dunce.

He was leaving her. Fine. Best to get on with her duties.

"You should have never fallen in love with him," Julien spoke from the other side of the boat.

She slammed her hand down on the gunwale and glared. "I didn't do it a'purpose!"

He snorted.

"Just you wait. One day love will strike you, and you'll be just as heartsick as I."

"Love doesn't strike a cripple," he spit.

Her gaze drifted down to his left leg, the injury from the war invisible beneath his trousers. "You're not crippled, you merely have a limp."

He didn't even bother to look at her.

"Besides it's not as though you can pick when you fall in love."

Julien leaned over the gunwale and glared. "There's where you're wrong. Because if I happened upon some rich, beautiful heiress along the British coast, I'd have no trouble returning her to safety rather than falling in love with her."

The arrogant lout. His words came easily, but in truth, he hadn't any idea what he would do in her situation. "What if you had to care for her for three weeks before you could return her home? What if she looked at you with eyes the color of the foggy sea and admired you despite your limp and kissed you as though…"

She looked up at the top of the hill where the break in the brown winter grass indicated the path Gregory had trod.

He wasn't standing there looking back at her. Of course he wasn't. He had to take Westerfield home and assure his family of everyone's safety, collect her money and find a servant to deliver it. He didn't have time or reason to stand atop the hill watching her, especially not when they'd already said their goodbyes.

A sob welled in her chest. She wrapped one arm about her middle and pressed her fist to her mouth.

"Aw, Dani. I didn't mean it like that." Julien came around the boat and settled an arm about her shoulder. "You'll be fine. Some French *garçon* will take a fancy to you here soon, and you—"

"There's no French *garçon* for me." She smeared a tear across her cheek. "I've spent five years looking for one. None of them ever understood me or valued me. None of them ever cared for me like Gregory."

"He doesn't care for you, Dani, not truly. If he did, he'd not have let you go today."

"He does." He had to care for her, had to love her. Had to feel something inside his heart for her. "But he can't marry me."

Julien's grip tightened about her shoulder. "He's a lord. He can do whatever he wants. He just doesn't care for you enough to make the sacrifices marrying you would require."

The sob came then, loud and unhindered. Julien spoke truth. She'd known it since she first realized she loved Gregory. Since before then. Since he'd followed her that night and held her on the rock while they'd listened to the river rushing past. If Gregory wanted to marry her badly enough, he could find a way. He simply didn't want to.

Tears streamed down her face while another sob racked her body. Julien pressed her face into his shoulder, similar to how she'd stood with Gregory not a quarter hour ago. Except Julien smelled of the sea rather than the land, and he didn't hold himself so rigidly proper. And his comfort couldn't begin to fill the gaping hole inside her.

"'Twas right strong of you to tell Halston to leave as you did. Not many a woman could manage that." Julien smoothed her hair down her back. "You wouldn't be happy with a man such as him, not for long. You deserve someone who will fight for you, not run when things get difficult." He patted her back and pushed her gently away. "There now, go on into the cave and lay down. You'll feel better after some sleep."

She nodded numbly and stumbled off toward the cave. Pulling the blankets into a tangle around her, she lay down, but sleep didn't help. She couldn't even close her eyes without her mind filling with memories of Gregory sitting atop the rock, coaxing Clyde into moving or learning to impale a rabbit on a spit for roasting. And when sleep finally claimed her, the dreams only worsened. She woke to find Julien lying beside her asleep, the boat pulled up into the opening of the cave so no one would find it.

She stood, and her stomach twisted with hunger while her eyes blurred with another bout of tears. She felt in her pocket for some of the English coin Julien had given her and then left the cave to start up the hill. A quick trip into town should yield not only meat pies but also a distraction.

Because she desperately needed something to take her mind off Gregory Halston.

She loved him. Gregory dug his heels into his mount, urging the beast faster over the road as if doing so would leave his troubled thoughts behind. He had other things to be doing, like getting money for Danielle and Julien, visiting with his mother and sister to rehash the events of the past two months in France, seeing to the myriad matters of business that had surely piled up in his absence and making arrangements to leave for London on the morrow.

Yet here he was, having been home for less than a quarter hour before calling for a mount and racing across the countryside to the home of Michel and Isabelle Belanger.

He had to see Lady Isabelle for himself. Because if a duke's daughter could be happy married to a peasant, then why not a marquess's son?

No. It was too much to hope for, too much to think of. There would be no happiness for him if he married Danielle and stayed in England.

But how could he find happiness and contentment in his life without Danielle?

There's no difference between servant and master, peasant and lord, at least not to God. Danielle's voice came back to him, proud and defiant as she'd flung the words at Kessler.

He had to see Isabelle Belanger. Had to hear from her own lips whether she minded the sacrifices she'd made so that she could marry the man she loved.

It seemed half of England had known Lady Isabelle's parents, the Duc and Duchesse de La Rouchecauld. When she'd arrived from England a decade ago, having been the only member of her immediate family to escape the peasant revolts and the Terror of the French Revolution, the entire ton had been shocked to learn she'd married a peasant. Even destitute and just off the boat from France, Isabelle de La Rouchecauld could have chosen from any number of suitors looking to marry into one of the most powerful and ancient families of France.

He'd been at Cambridge at the time but remembered coming home on holiday to hear his mother fuming about the way the horrid revolution in France had destroyed the House of La Rouchecauld and convinced their only living daughter to wed a peasant. Even worse, the Belangers had decided to settle near Hastings. "Practically on our doorstep," as Mother had put it, her tone full of disgust.

In those days, no one in England had known of Michel Belanger's talent for furniture making or his mind for business. A decade later, the man's wooden masterpieces were the most coveted in the country, but he was still in trade—a vulgar thing as far as his mother and the rest of the ton were concerned.

Gregory turned his horse up the twisting drive that led to the Belanger estate. It wasn't nearly as large as his own family's lands, but just as impressive given the wealth had been earned rather than inherited. He swung off his horse in front of the modest country home and charged up the stairs.

When the door opened, he presented his card.

The footman raised an eyebrow but showed him to the parlor before slipping silently from the room.

Midmorning sun poured through east-facing windows that overlooked brown winter grass, bare trees and a small pond. The landscape was simple and yet elegant, just as the room he stood in was decorated with stylish but not ornate furniture and drapes. Gregory paced the room from one side to the other. Belanger could well afford a more expensively appointed room and lavish grounds, but then, perhaps his conservativeness with his funds was part of the reason he had so many.

The door opened and a woman entered inside. She needed no introduction. The perfectly straight way she held her back, the relaxed yet regal slant to her shoulders, the slight tilt to her chin—she'd undoubtedly been raised as the daughter of a duke.

Her beauty was the stuff of legends, with high cheekbones and a narrow chin, a complexion like the finest porcelain, and hair so dark it reflected the light from the window. He'd thought Danielle was beautiful, and she was, but compared to this woman, Danielle's beauty looked like a wild-grown iris while Isabelle Belanger was the finest, most cultured rose. Her gown might not be made of the most expensive fabric money could buy, but with looks such as hers, she hardly needed yards of exquisite silk.

Which was likely why the ton had been so aghast

when she'd escaped from France married to a commoner. Had she been fat and sour faced, no one of consequence would have cared a whit.

"Hello." She offered a formal curtsy. "I'm Mrs. Isabelle Belanger. I believe you're an acquaintance of my husband?"

"I am his man of business, yes."

"I have sent James to notify him of your arrival. He should be with us shortly."

"I came to see you."

She tilted her head slightly, the gesture both polished and stately. "So I was informed. Whatever for?"

Indeed. He rubbed the back of his neck. Here he'd raced all the way across Hastings to meet with this woman, and suddenly his brain couldn't seem to unscramble his tangle of thoughts. So he started with the most basic words he could manage. "I met your niece Danielle in France."

Stray pebbles skittered beneath Danielle's feet as she wound her way down the hillside to the beach. She blinked into the overly bright winter sun and tucked the extra meat pies she'd purchased under her arm. The English might not make *soupe à l'oignon*, *saumon fumé*, or *moules à la crème*, but their meat pies were among the best.

"Julien," she called, stepping into the alcove. She'd dallied rather long in town, looking into storefronts and stopping by the confectionary. Her brother should have long been awake, but he didn't appear in the entrance to the cave.

"Julien," she called again, then stilled. Where was the boat? Had her brother pulled it farther inside? By himself?

Her pulse thrumming against her neck, she bent to place her meat pies on the ground and retrieve her knife from her ankle. Her fingers touched the cool leather of the hilt as the cock of a pistol resonated through the air.

"Move and I'll kill you."

She looked up into the austere faces of two men. Two unmistakably British men.

The man with the gun moved forward. "I told you there'd be more than one."

More than one? Did that mean they'd already found Julien? *Please, God, let him have escaped.*

But the prayer seemed futile. Her heart knew the answer before her mind formed the words. They must have captured Julien and the boat.

Her fingers hovered only a hand's span away from her knife. Unfortunately the dark-eyed man with the pistol kept his gaze riveted to her hand. If she attempted to grab the knife and throw it at his neck, he'd have a musket ball lodged in her head before the knife ever left her hand—and that would still leave the second man to contend with.

"Stand, wench. And slowly."

She carefully rose to her feet. "I didn't do anything."

The man smirked. "You're here, aren't you? That's enough."

She met his gaze. "I'm here on behalf of the Marquess of Westerfield."

"Lord Westerfield? That's a nice tale there." He laughed and then gestured to the man in the blue coat standing weaponless. "Take her knife, then search her to make sure she's not hiding more."

"I only have the one. I swear it."

"Sorry, wench, you'll forgive me if I don't accept the word of a smuggler."

"I'm not a smuggler!" Panic rose in her chest, and her heartbeat thrummed in her ears.

"A spy, then. Perhaps we'll see a hanging before the week is out."

"I'm neither. I told you I'm here on behalf of the Marquess of Westerfield." She took a step forward, imploring him to believe her.

He kept his gun steady while his gaze raked over her. "And what, exactly, would the Marquess of Westerfield want with the likes of you?"

"He employed me to…to…" She clamped her mouth shut as the horror of her situation swept through. How was she to answer? By claiming she'd just come from France? The mention of her country would condemn her to be hung for spying before sunset.

"Your story fails you rather quickly. Hal, search her."

"My pleasure." The other man strode forward, a wicked gleam in his eyes and a tight smile on his lips.

She started to back away, but 'twas futile when the first man still held his gun on her.

Chapter Twenty-One

"You met Danielle?" Lady Isabelle's dark eyes widened, and she gestured to a chair. "Perhaps you'd better sit down, Lord Gregory. I'll ring for tea. It seems you've quite the story."

"I can't stay. I just…" Gregory ran a hand through his hair and stalked to the window before turning back to face her. "Why'd you do it?"

"I beg your pardon?"

His hands slicked with sweat and itched inside his gloves. "Why'd you marry your husband? French or not, you could have come to England and chosen any of two dozen men from the ton. Men of wealth and position—part of the society you were raised in. Yet you married a commoner."

She straightened, a defiant gesture that would have caused him to blubber some apology at offending her had he not become accustomed to such actions with Danielle. "You probably think me weak or half-mad for marrying a peasant. But look me in the eyes, Lord Gregory Halston, and tell me, have you ever had anything that mattered ripped away from you? I'm not talking about the natural death of your father or lamenting some childhood friend who's fallen on hard times. I'm speaking of *everything*. Your house. Your servants. Your wealth. Your lands. Your parents, siblings, friends. Your very position in the world and your trust in your countrymen. All of it torn away in a night."

Her voice shook, and a sickening sensation crept through Gregory's gut. Perhaps he ought not have asked. The French Revolution would have been terrible for someone of her station, and he'd never intended to dredge up painful memories.

"Lady Isabelle, there's no need to continue. I meant not—"

"Imagine, if you will, what might happen if all your brother's tenants join with half the poor of Hastings and march on your house." The words shot like little arrows, sharp and determined, from her mouth. "If they pounded down your door and flooded inside, stealing everything they could and smashing that which they couldn't take. Imagine your parents and brother being brutally killed, their heads paraded on pikes through the village, their bodies…their bodies…" She pressed a hand to her mouth while moisture welled in her eyes.

He'd never imagined such a thing, no. He fished around in his pocket for his handkerchief and approached. "I'm sorry. I didn't intend to upset you. I merely wondered…"

He clamped his lips shut. Why had he even asked? He hadn't needed her words so much as he needed to see her happy and content—which she'd been until he brought up her past.

The chamber door swung open. "Lord Gregory, I'm glad to hear of your return. I trust…" Michel Belanger's gaze riveted on his wife.

"Isabelle?" Rather than offer his own handkerchief,

he strode toward her and wrapped her in his arms. "Is something wrong, *mon amour*?"

She only sobbed harder.

Belanger turned furious eyes on Gregory. "What did you do to my wife?"

Lady Isabelle shook her head, still burrowed in his chest. "N-nothing. It's not him. He came to ask about Danielle. And I was just explaining…" She drew in another deep, shuddering breath.

"Danielle? As in my niece?"

She nodded and sniffled. "Lord Gregory and Danielle apparently met in France. I assume they came to know each other rather well."

Michel Belanger glowered at Gregory over his wife's head. "I heard a rumor you'd gone to France for your brother, but I assumed it to be just that—a rumor. Only a fool would attempt such a thing with Napoleon preparing to invade."

And only a fool would fall in love with a common woman from Napoleon's country. "Yes, well, as it turns out, I happened upon Danielle and Serge quite by accident, but they proved invaluable on our journey. We arrived at dawn on Julien's fishing boat."

Jaw hard, Belanger set his wife aside and took a step toward Gregory. "That's information you had best keep to yourself. If anything happens to Julien or—"

"He loves her." Lady Isabelle pressed the handkerchief to the corner of her eye and gently wiped away the last of her tears.

"What was that?" Belanger turned back toward his wife, his brow marred with confusion.

"Lord Gregory, he loves our Danielle. That's why he's here. He wanted to ask me about why I married you, and if I regret it."

Gregory swallowed tightly. The time for claiming his feelings were just some passing infatuation or fancy had passed. Perhaps he shouldn't love Danielle. Perhaps he had every reason imaginable not to love her.

But love her he did.

Then again, knowing the truth in his heart and admitting it aloud were two different things. Surely Lady Isabelle understood the impossibilities that faced him if he decided to wed Danielle.

"I…I can't care for Danielle that way." His voice sounded weak and shaky, even to his own ears.

"So you're going to act like that, are you?" Lady Isabelle laughed derisively. "You're all the same, every last one of you English aristocrats. You look at me as though I'm poor for marrying the man I love and turning my back on the ton, but you don't understand that I'm rich in the ways that matter most. I never finished what I was saying before my husband entered. Allow me to do so before you take your leave."

Gregory's gut twisted again—a reaction that Isabelle Belanger seemed quite adept at provoking.

"Everything I'd ever known, the entire world I'd grown up in was torn away from me in a matter of days. My own servants stole from me and my sister, the only other member of my immediate family to survive that first terrible night, and we became paupers living in a forgotten cottage on our aunt's decimated estate. I found work as a seamstress while Marie stayed and tended the house. We worked for four years to earn passage to England, and still, Marie was caught and taken to the…the…" She sucked in a heavy breath, her eyes welling with tears anew.

"Hush now, Isabelle. You don't have to share this story." Belanger reached out to take her hand.

"I do. He needs to hear it." She drew her shoulders back into her elegant, regal pose. "Imagine all of that, live through that, find a way to survive that. And I guarantee you, *Lord* Gregory Halston, that if a person finds you after all you've lost and offers you help— offers you food and water. Offers you life once more… you will not look down on him or her for who their parents are. Nor will you criticize the size of their house or number of their barns."

She met his gaze, her eyes wet with moisture yet somehow strong and undefeatable. "You will see them as your equal. Because that's who they are. You think money, silks, carriages and lands make you valuable and equal to others with similar holdings? You're wrong. What makes you equal to a person is your heart. Look at a person like my niece and what's inside her heart. I'd wager, Lord Gregory, that hers will surpass the hearts of most young women you'll find in the ton."

The jagged words lodged like shards of glass, barbed and biting, in his chest. Lady Isabelle was right. Here he thought himself different, better, commendable for giving Danielle a chance when Kessler had belittled her from the start.

He'd listened to her verses about equality and importance before God. He'd even ignored Westerfield and Kessler's warnings about how close he was growing to Danielle.

But he wasn't any better than Kessler or the rest of the ton—not if he was prepared to walk away from Danielle for his own pride.

"God forgive me. I don't deserve her. I've never deserved her. And I'm a fool for not understanding sooner." He raised his chin and met Lady Isabelle's eyes. "If you'll excuse me, I've a rather urgent matter to attend to."

One that had already waited far too long.

"Come back and release me!" Danielle rattled the shackles that chained her arms to the wall above her head. "You've no right to hold me here—I've done nothing!"

No footsteps echoed and no lantern flickered in the deserted corridor beyond her prison cell, just like no footsteps or lantern or guard had appeared the last twenty times she'd called.

"Help!" she shouted again from her undignified position on the floor. "Please, someone, anyone. I'm not a smuggler. I didn't spy!"

Her words bounced off the bare stone walls and straw-covered floor, but no one came. No one could likely even hear. 'Twas probably part of the reason they'd imprisoned her in the lowest, darkest level of the house of corrections. They planned to forget she existed.

Either that or leave her there without food and water until they hanged her.

Perhaps if she could free herself, somehow find a way to loosen her hands from the shackles or the shackles from the wall, she could use them to bludgeon the guards when they came for her. She twisted her wrists inside the unforgiving metal bands above. They bit into her flesh, causing a thin stream of blood to trail down her arm, but they didn't slacken or allow her hands to slip in the slightest. She got up onto her knees and attempted to turn toward the damp stone wall. The chains that held her twisted in the process, and she gave them a good, hard yank.

The bolts anchoring the chains didn't budge.

She pulled again, the shackle on her left wrist dug fiercely into her flesh, producing yet another stream of blood. She yelped, then fell against the wall. 'Twas no use. Her side hurt from the strain her writhing put on her wound, and the bands weren't about to give.

It was probably just as well. Fighting the excise men and then the prison guards earlier had done little but get her face cuffed, her stomach bludgeoned and her arms chained above her head. Now she had to use the privy—or rather, the foul bucket over in the corner— but had no means of doing so.

"Come back! I need to be unchained."

And she needed to know where Julien was. Both the excise men and the guards had been silent about him when she'd demanded answers, and she'd not seen him when the guards led her past the filled cells upstairs.

Was he chained down here as she was?

If so, would he not have heard her cries and answered? The small barred window in the cell door allowed at least some sound to carry. It also allowed the only bit of light she had, which flickered through the ghastly bars from the lantern across the corridor.

She raised herself onto her knees, trying to get a better view of the corridor through the window. Why did no one come? Where were the guards?

Where was Gregory?

She pressed her eyes shut against the hot flood of moisture that rushed through them at the mere thought of his name. Would he come for her? Did he know she'd been imprisoned? If so, did he care enough to help?

The hard set to his eyes when she'd declared her love for him that morning swam through her mind. He'd washed his hands of her, then turned his back and walked away. *Oui*, she'd told him to send one of his servants back to the beach with her money, but the servant would probably see the cave absent of people and the boat and assume they'd returned to France early.

With Julien having disappeared and Gregory thinking she'd already left for France, who would help her?

"God, did I do something wrong? Why am I here? I was only trying to help. Only trying to treat men the way You would have me treat them, even if they were English."

She stared up into the darkness, at the eerie play of shadows across the cracked stone ceiling of her cell. But no heavenly answer drifted down from above.

To think she'd been worried about being thrust into a French prison, had even felt bad for what Westerfield and Kessler endured in her country. Now she suffered the same fate they had previously known. Was that why she was here? Some strange sort of justice that resulted from the hate-filled broken world in which they lived? First Westerfield and Kessler were wrongly imprisoned, now her?

She leaned back against the cold stone and shivered. That would make sense had she turned her back on Gregory and refused to nurse Westerfield, had she left them as she'd first planned to after learning all of France thought them spies.

But she hadn't turned her back on them. She'd helped.

And for what?

To end up rejected by the man she loved, rotting in the depths of some foul British dungeon for a crime she hadn't committed?

A tear slipped down her cheek, and she hadn't even the ability to brush it away.

Was it just this morning she'd dreamed of marrying Gregory? Had hoped he'd confess his love when she'd told him of hers? The idea seemed laughable now. Gregory wasn't coming. No one was coming. Westerfield and Kessler had languished in their dungeon for over a year. Would she languish just as long? Or would the excise men take her before a magistrate and see her hanged long before the year was out?

"Help!" she called one more time into the darkness, her voice weaker and quieter than when she'd first started shouting many hours ago.

Like all the other times, no one came.

Gregory ducked his head against the salty winter wind coming off the sea as his horse raced over the road toward the hills lining the shore. His saddlebags held six thousand pound notes—the four thousand he'd promised Danielle, the one thousand he'd promised Julien plus an extra thousand for…

Well, he didn't precisely know, but Danielle and her family deserved it nonetheless.

He'd offer her every last note. He prayed she'd take none of it and agree to marry him. Or maybe she'd take all of it and still agree to marry him, sending the monies back to France with her brother.

As long as she became his wife. Then the two of them could sneak back across the channel to France, where they could live…but no, France wouldn't make a good home for him and his English accent. He'd be arrested as a spy within a week and end up in one of those forgotten dungeon cells, if not beneath the guillotine's blade. And Danielle would probably be accused of treason with him.

Perhaps they could marry here and board a ship to America. Yes, America might work. They weren't so picky about titles and such there, were they? And even if it was shocking for a lord to marry a peasant, no one needed to know that he was a lord, or that Danielle wasn't a lady. Yes, that would work splendidly. Perhaps he'd never see his family again, but they'd be safe from the scandal of his marriage, and he'd have Danielle. He could sell off some of his investments and whisk Danielle across the ocean within a few days of their marriage.

Assuming she wanted to be his wife, that is. She may have proclaimed to love him earlier, but that wasn't quite the same as agreeing to marry him.

Nor did it guarantee she wanted to be with him forever after the way he'd left her.

He kicked the beast beneath his thighs into a harder run. What had he been thinking to leave her standing alone on the beach? To listen to her declaration of feelings and give her nothing in return?

Foolish, foolish man. Why did it take Isabelle Belanger's piercing words for his stubborn brain to finally understand what his heart had been trying to tell him for weeks?

Because he was a dunce.

Because he was practical.

Because he'd been raised to value a person's lineage over a person's actions.

Flimsy excuses, the lot of them. Perhaps he'd been taught nobility was bound to one's blood rather than one's heart, but why had he been foolish enough to believe it?

Dear God, please let her take me back.

He reined in the horse at the top of the hill overlooking the channel and tethered it to a shrub before racing down the grassy path to the strip of sand lining the beach.

"Danielle!" He hurried into the fissure in the hill and the little alcove that had shielded them earlier. What would she say when she saw him? Would delight shine in her eyes? Anger? Confusion?

Whatever her reaction, he wasn't leaving this patch of sand without her.

Except she wasn't there.

He frowned and strode closer to the cave where Julien had planned to slide his boat, but the fishing sloop with its dark sails was nowhere to be seen. Had Julien and Danielle departed early? Gregory turned toward the sea, not that he could see the English Channel with the large hill rising in front of him. He bent to study the sand. Danielle could probably make sense of the myriad footprints clumped along the wet muck, but not he. People had been here, lovely. He already knew as much from this morning.

He made his way back along the coast, rounding the grassy slope to face the sea. So she'd gone back to France without his money. Did she truly think she could evade him? He knew where she lived, and he'd stop at nothing to return to France for her, no matter how dangerous the journey might be. By the end of this week, he'd be holding Danielle—

"Halt!"

Gregory stilled at the command.

Two men rushed down the beach, the silver glint of a pistol shining in one of the men's hands. "Stop in the name of the king and place your hands atop your head."

He slowly brought his hands up as the men approached. "What is the meaning of this?"

But he needed not ask. The men were clearly excise

officers, with their dark blue coats and quick maneuverability in the mucky ground.

"You're being arrested for smuggling and spying."

He raised an eyebrow. "Am I? And by whose authority, may I ask, do you arrest Lord Gregory Halston, brother to the Marquess of Westerfield, for such dastardly activities?"

"Lord Gregory?" The man without the firearm halted, gazing into his face. "By Jove, Larry. That's Lord Gregory Halston if I ever seen 'im."

The second man's gun wavered, and Gregory pulled his hands off the top of his head. A most ridiculous position, that.

"A-apologies, my lord." The second man stuffed his gun back into his coat. "I didn't know it was you."

"I imagine not," Gregory growled.

"It's just that we found some smugglers earlier today, two of 'em. So we're watching the coast rather closely. We think there was more on the boat."

Panic flared in his chest. Not Danielle and Julien, anyone but them. "Tell me, was one of these smugglers a woman with long black hair and blue eyes?"

The man with the gun narrowed his eyes and raised the pistol ever so slightly. "Aye, you know them, then?"

"I do, indeed, seeing how the only things they smuggled were the Marquess of Westerfield, Lord Kessler, myself and my valet back onto English soil this morning. Where are they?"

"Ah…"

Gregory grabbed the man by his collar and yanked him forward. "If so much as one hair on either of their heads is harmed, I'll see to it that you spend the next year rotting in a forgotten prison cell."

"Yes, my lord," he choked.

The man without a weapon swallowed loudly and stared at the sand.

"Well, what is it?" Gregory released the first excise agent and turned to the second. "I can tell you've more to say."

"Th-they're already gone, my lord."

"Gone?" Ice slicked through Gregory's veins. "What do you mean, gone?"

Chapter Twenty-Two

Gregory burst through the wooden office door and charged forward. "Where are they?"

The governor of the house of corrections set his cup of tea down with a rattle, sloshing brown liquid across the papers spread over his desk. "Lord Gregory? What brings you here?"

"Danielle and Julien Belanger. Where have you stashed them?"

"Belanger, you say?" The man pushed to his feet and took a piece of tea-stained foolscap from his desk, surveying the handwriting scrawled across the sheet. "I've no one here by that name."

The door banged behind him as the excise men clambered inside the small, sparsely furnished office. The man who'd originally pulled the pistol on Gregory rushed to the governor's desk. "The smugglers we took today? Lord Gregory here verifies their story."

The paper slipped from the governor's hand. "They brought the Marquess of Westerfield back from France?"

"That they did." Gregory gritted his teeth together. "Now take me to them."

"Ah…" The governor's face turned a decidedly green hue. "It might be rather late for the sailor. The navy needing men the way they do, we sent him on to Portsmouth."

Fear cramped in Gregory's stomach. The British navy *did* need men, so badly they took both countrymen and enemies alike and forced them to serve in the bowels of their dreadful men-of-war. If Julien Belanger was already en route to Portsmouth, it might well be too late for him—or even Westerfield—to free Julien.

Gregory whirled and pointed a finger at the excise man standing behind him, the shorter one without the gun. "Get Julien Belanger back here and have him delivered to my brother's estate before the sun sets. Do you understand?"

The man, suddenly pale, gave a curt nod and fled out the door.

Gregory turned back to the governor. "Take me to Danielle."

"You see, Lord Gregory, she…ah, proved to be a rather difficult prisoner," the remaining excise man stuttered.

Difficult prisoner? What, precisely, did that mean?

But he could well guess. Danielle would never have allowed herself to be captured without a fight—a fight she must have lost if she was being held within these walls. And she already had a wounded side and head.

"Perhaps we ought to bring her to you, rather than have you enter the holding cells." The governor stepped away from his desk. "Make yourself comfortable in my office, and I'll see that Miss Belanger is brought to you shortly."

"I think not. Either take me to her, or I'll find her myself."

Gregory spun toward the door and strode out of the office. Three women sat waiting on a hard wooden bench while a farmer argued with one of the guards and a small line of people formed behind him. All commoners with some sort of business here. All waiting in line. All at the mercy of a guard who looked none too happy to deal with them—the same guard who had smiled at him and ushered him directly into his superior's office when Gregory had first entered the building.

Being a lord, he could barge into a prison such as this and demand the release of an innocent person, while the cobbler down the street was stuck waiting in line only to have his entreaties stymied by the bureaucrats meant to help him. Was this not what Danielle meant when she spoke of men and women being valued because of their birth rather than their actions?

Here he was using his title, birth and position in society for his own advantage while countless others had to suffer. He'd happily claim the benefits of his title a thousand times over if they would help save Danielle, but what would become of those here without his advantages? Danielle was right—there was no justice to these divisions.

He strode toward the imposing wooden door that would give him access to the internees. "Open up."

The governor rushed up behind him, rattling his keys and using his heavy girth to push aside the people waiting in the foyer. "I'll escort you, Lord Gregory. No need to rush."

The door squealed open and Gregory stepped into darkness on the other side, a foul stench rising up to greet him.

"Who you got there? Another man to add to our ranks?" A voice rose from the row of cells lining the wall.

"Mr. Gov'nor, sir, when do I go before the magistrate?"

"How much longer you going to let us rot in here?"

"Hey, that there's a dandy. What'd he do to get hisself in here?"

"Don't matter, he won't be staying. His type never do."

"Edward! Come here." The governor's voice bounced over those of the prisoners, and a hulking guard made his way down the long row of cells.

"Where are the women held?" Gregory turned toward a passage leading to the right.

"Your lady's down this way," the governor answered.

Gregory took a step forward. "But these are all men. Surely you don't house the men and women together."

"We don't have facilities for confinement in the women's section. This is only a house of corrections, not a gaol."

"Confinement?" Gregory shouted the word so loudly the prisoners fell silent.

"We put prisoners who attack guards in confinement for a few days." The guard took an already burning lantern from the wall and started down the corridor.

Gregory followed closely behind. "She attacked a guard?"

"With a knife," the governor answered. "The excise men said they searched her…"

Men had searched her? Gregory's stomach churned.

Edward stopped at the end of the corridor and unlocked another heavy wooden door that led to a dank, narrow stairway.

Behind him, the governor was rambling about why it had been necessary to search and then confine Danielle, words like "blade" and "attack" and "disrespect" filling his diatribe.

"Enough! Just take me to her."

The guard glanced over Gregory's shoulder at the governor, then cleared his throat. "This way, then."

The air on the floor above had been foul, but the stench inside the stairway grew more rancid with each descending step as the scents of human waste and sweat fought to overpower the stale, damp air. Unlike on the floor above, no dim light trickled into this part of the building from small, barred windows. If not for the lantern in the guard's hand and another single lantern mounted to the wall halfway down the filthy corridor, they would be surrounded by impenetrable blackness.

"Hello?" Danielle's voice, weak and tentative, called out. "Is anyone there? Please, unchain me."

"You chained her!" Gregory turned toward the guard, fire coursing through his blood.

The guard blanched, then pointed to the governor. "He ordered it."

The governor tugged at his collar. "It's standard treatment for prisoners who attack guards."

Gregory snatched the lantern from the guard's hand and burst ahead, following the sounds that emanated from the last door on the left.

"Dani?" He held the light up to the barred window surrounded by heavy iron. She sat on a squalid floor with her arms chained to the wall above. Dirt and tears smeared her face, while her hair fell in disarray about her shoulders and a jagged tear cut across the bodice of her dress to reveal her chemise beneath. She glanced up, fear in her eyes as they met his.

Gregory rattled the bars separating him from Danielle. "Unlock this door. Now."

"Yes, sir, Lord Gregory." The guard hastened forward, keys rattling as he shoved the correct one into the lock and turned it.

Gregory rushed inside, hanging the lantern on a wall hook before kneeling in the rotten straw to enfold Danielle in his arms.

"Gregory?" Her tear-glazed eyes moved to his. "You came? I thought..."

"Shh. Of course I came." He stroked a hand over her matted hair. "I couldn't leave you here. Just a moment, and you'll be free."

"She's a violent one, Lord Gregory," the guard spoke. "Are you certain you want me to—"

"Release her now!"

The large man crossed the room and inserted the key into the manacles on her wrist.

"Faster."

"But Lord Gregory," the governor protested from somewhere in the foul cell behind him, "she's dangerous. She had three knives on her and fought while we searched her. We can't be sure whether she's got another."

Danielle's eyes went from dazed and frightened to humiliated, and his throat tightened at the hint of what Danielle surely endured at these men's hands—of what he could have prevented had he whisked Danielle away to marry him that morn rather than left her on the beach.

"She fights like a hoyden even without a weapon," the guard offered.

"I said, unlock the shackles."

One simple click and the cruel irons released her. She sagged back against the cold, grimy stone and fumbled with the front of her dress, pressing the torn fabric tight against her chest.

"Let's get you out of here." He swooped her up in his arms.

She gasped in pain at the jostling, but he started toward the doorway where the governor stood. She needed to get out of this horrid prison before her injuries were tended.

"Wh-what about my brother?" Danielle's voice was so quiet it could barely be heard above his footsteps on the straw. Her chin trembled as she raised her eyes to the governor's. "Have you freed him yet?"

Gregory paused before the governor and glared. "Yes, tell the lady what you've done with her brother."

"He's, ah…not exactly here anymore."

Her body tensed in his hold. "What do you mean, 'not exactly here'?"

"Dani." Gregory tightened his grip on her, partly because he craved the warmth of her body against his, and partly to support her when she learned what had befallen Julien. "I have a man out searching now and will put more men on it as soon as we leave, but Julien has been taken to Portsmouth."

"Portsmouth." Her confused eyes sought his. "Why Portsmouth?"

"He's an able enough sailor, miss. The navy can use him."

Given her weakened state, Gregory half expected her to swoon from the news. But a sob tore from her chest, and she clawed at his hold, her gaze riveted to the governor.

"You impressed him into the navy? I should kill you. If Gregory can't find him, if he ends up on one of your wretched English war machines like the one that killed his twin, if—"

"Not here, Dani." He hefted her higher in his arms

and strode through the doorway and into the dank corridor lit only by the one meager lantern on the wall. Her diatribe turned from shouts to mutterings to soft sobs with each step he took farther away from the filthy cell.

Chapter Twenty-Three

"I love her." Gregory sat in the drawing room with Westerfield, staring down at his hands as though they could somehow give him the answers he sought. "I want to marry her."

"She'd make you a good wife. She'd make any man a good wife, for that matter."

Gregory's head shot up, and he eyed his brother reclining across the settee. "This is quite a different tune from what you were singing back in France. You discouraged me from getting close to her—and don't pretend you don't see the obstacles to the union. A marriage to her would ruin Lilliana's hope for a husband and your search for a new wife. Mother would be devastated and—"

"Yes, I most certainly would be devastated."

Gregory glanced toward the door, where his mother had suddenly appeared, and stood. "But I love her," he stated firmly.

"That he does." Westerfield smiled, his eyes dancing with merriment. He seemed to be enjoying this conversation a little too much.

"Don't start spouting notions of love." Mother's perfectly coiffed hair trembled as she stomped a dainty little foot into the Turkish rug beneath their feet. "A good marriage involves more than love."

"Love seems like a solid place to start. As does respect. Commitment."

"Commitment! She's French, doubtless tempestuous and full of passion. Her commitment to you will not last more than a fortnight."

"Her commitment to me has already exceeded a fortnight." Gregory drew in a breath and reached out to settle his hands on his mother's shoulders. "She saved us. Your eldest son is home and well, not because of me, but because of her. I should think you'd be upstairs thanking her, not denying us a future together."

Mother slanted her gaze around him toward Westerfield, her blue eyes brimming with moisture when they swung back up to Gregory's face. "You'll be mocked out of London for marrying a French peasant. Never invited to another ball, never—"

"I'll not be mocked out of London, because no one will know I've wed at all, let alone who my new bride is. Danielle and I will marry one evening and leave for America the next morn."

"America?" The stern lines around Mother's eyes drooped. "Certainly you don't mean to…to… Why, I've just gotten your brother back, and now you intend to sail across the ocean?"

"It's the only way to protect our family. I can wed Danielle, and it won't hurt Lilliana's chances with a husband or Westerfield's with a new wife. My marriage won't bring shame on the family, not if it's done clandestinely, and in the end, I can still build a life with the woman I love."

"That's a noble sacrifice to make for Danielle,

Halston, but it's not necessary." Westerfield raised himself to a sitting position. "Not if we spread the story of how Danielle aided Kessler and me in our escape, or the news of who her grandfather was."

"Her grandfather?" Mother's eyes narrowed on Westerfield the way a hawk's would when spotting a mouse in a field. "Who was her grandfather?"

Gregory sighed and ran a hand through his hair. "A farmer."

"A *seigneur*." Westerfield answered at the same time. "Or perhaps he was even a baron. 'The Gentleman Smuggler,' he used to be called, though I understand there was little gentlemanly about him. He ran a smuggling ring out of Calais for the first part of the French Revolution."

Gregory turned to face his brother. "A seigneur? How do you know this?"

Westerfield raised an eyebrow. "I asked."

"You…but…how? When?"

Westerfield chuckled low in his chest—which soon turned into a cough, but not even the hacking wiped the devious smile from his face. "'Who?' would be the better question, and the answer is Serge, not Danielle. That woman is too tight-lipped to reveal such a thing. The boy, on the other hand, doesn't have a reserved bone in his body."

Gregory's body felt suddenly light, as though his feet stood on clouds rather than the solid floor of the drawing room. She was a *seigneur*'s granddaughter? All this time, he'd assumed her descended solely from peasants—an assumption that she'd never once bothered to correct.

"That solves everything," he muttered to himself.

"What was that, brother?"

He beamed at Westerfield. "I can marry her and stay in England. Ha! I can marry her tomorrow if I wish it. And I think I will. Yes, yes. I'll do just that!"

"Ah, you might want to ask the lady first." The teasing smile was still plastered across Westerfield's face.

Ask the lady. That was precisely what he needed to do. He bolted for the door.

"What about dinner?" Mother called after him.

But he cared not. He was already taking the steps two at a time up to Danielle's room.

Propped against pillows, Danielle stared at the darkness outside the window. She lay on the most comfortable mattress she'd ever felt in her twenty-two years. The feathers beneath her cocooned her in a world of warmth, the bedclothes were so soft they could be cut up and used for undergarments, and one of the maids had heated a brick and tucked it down by her toes so her feet stayed warm.

A special brick solely for the purpose of warming a bed. Of all the frivolous things. Why could the English simply not wear a pair of stockings when they went to sleep?

She sighed and settled back into the pillows, pressing her eyes shut against the candlelight flickering over the opulent bedchamber.

Sleep. The mistress of the house, doctor and a maid had all commanded her to do that very thing. But her side hurt, having reopened itself during her struggle earlier; her wrists were bloody and wrapped in bandages, and her throat ached from the hours she'd shouted in the jail.

And Julien was still missing. How could she sleep

when her brother was, in all likelihood, imprisoned in the galleys of a British man-of-war?

The latch on her bedchamber door clicked, and Danielle opened her eyes to find Gregory barreling into the room.

She pushed herself up onto her elbows. "Did you find—?"

"You're not descended from a peasant."

She collapsed back into the pillows. So he didn't have news of Julien.

"Why didn't you tell me?"

"It didn't seem…significant enough to mention." She absently traced the patterned quilt atop her bedclothes. "My country doesn't recognize barons, or lords, or any of that foolishness under the consulate."

"Empire."

"I beg your pardon?"

Gregory approached the bed. "Evidently sometime while we were winding our way through northern France, your Napoleon was crowned emperor—or rather, crowned himself emperor, if the papers are to be believed.

"Oh." She bit the side of her lip. That did sound a bit like something their leader would do. She could hardly imagine Napoleon letting someone else crown him, least of all the pope. "I suppose I was a bit too occupied to be reading the news."

He smiled, a large, ridiculously silly smile. "Why didn't you tell me?"

"About Napoleon?"

"Danielle." He drew her name out until it dripped with unspoken warning, though it wasn't too convincing given the grin still covering his face. He plopped himself onto the bed beside and took her chin in his hand. "You knew your family line would matter to me."

"*Oui*, I knew," she whispered into the space between them then dropped her gaze. "That's why I didn't tell you. Because it would have mattered too much. It would have mattered more than…than…than me."

Tears beaded behind her eyelids, and she blinked furiously. One brief stay in a British house of corrections and she was suddenly tearing up at the most ludicrous things.

"Oh, Danielle. I was such a fool. You matter to me. You, all by yourself. More than anything else. I love you."

"You love me?"

"Yes, I love you." He wrapped an arm around her back and brought her against his chest, cradling her in his arms despite the door being open for any passerby to see. "I'm only sorry it took me so long to realize it. Forgive me for being so mule headed and proud."

She sniffled, pressing her face into the crook of his neck so that her hot, wet tears slid between them. "Of course I forgive you. I love you too much to do anything but."

"Marry me." He whispered the words, tender and soft, into the hair beside her ear. "Love me. Stay with me here in England. I'll be a good husband to you, I swear it. I'll not leave you again as I did this morning."

More tears rushed to the fore.

"Don't cry, love." He lifted her head from his neck and feathered soft kisses across her face to wipe away the moisture. "Just promise to marry me. I can send to the archbishop for a special license this very evening. We'll be married tomorrow if you wish it."

"I'll make you a terrible wife," she sniffled. "Your

mother despises me, and I'll not be satisfied to sit home and embroider or host dinners or…"

"You'll make me an interesting wife. And my mother will learn to love you in time. She's not a cruel woman—she just had a rather long list of eligible debutantes for me to consider, and you weren't one of them."

"And what about everyone else? Your entire country will hate me because I'm French." Not that she could cast much blame on that attitude given the way she'd hated him for being English when they'd first met.

But Gregory merely shook his head at her, that silly grin back on his face. "People will love you when they learn of how you boldly brought the Marquess of Westerfield back from France, though I think we shall have to change your surname so your parents don't get in trouble with the French law."

She wiped a stray tear from her cheek. He made staying together sound so believable. Because of their nationalities, no union between them would be without hardships, but… "I'll still throw knives. That's a skill I intend not to lose."

He squeezed her waist. "Danielle Belanger, I fell in love with you just how you are, and I want you to stay that way."

She swallowed thickly. "Yes. I'll marry you. And tomorrow sounds like a perfect day for our wedding."

"Ah, so this is where the lovebirds are."

Danielle jolted away from Gregory to find Westerfield standing in the doorway, one shoulder propped against the molding and a wicked smile on his lips.

"Leave us be." Gregory looped an arm about her shoulders and pulled her back to his side. "I was just about to kiss my lady."

He lowered his head until his lips hovered a hairbreadth away, but she shoved against his chest. Fiancée or not, she wasn't about to kiss him in front of an audience.

Westerfield's laughter echoed across the room. "Looks like you've got a little wooing to do yet before you can call her 'your lady.'"

"Dani," Gregory huffed, "you spent the past fortnight baring Westerfield to the waist and slathering plaster over his chest. Certainly you're not embarrassed to kiss your betrothed in front of him."

She peeked at Westerfield, who started laughing at her all over again. "You'd best watch yourself, Lord Westerfield. The governor gave my knives back before I left the house of corrections."

Unfortunately her words only caused him to cough and then laugh harder. And Gregory, taking advantage of the distraction, turned her face back and planted his lips atop hers before she could do naught to stop the kiss.

Not that she really wanted to stop it.

If anything, she wanted to burrow closer to Gregory, surrounding herself with the calm strength that had fortified her through the past weeks, resting in the peace that invaded her heart whenever his arms surrounded her. She settled closer against his chest and let his mouth play over hers. Not because she loved him—which she did—but because he loved her back. All of her. Even the parts of her that threw knives and blurted things best left unsaid. Even the parts that had scared off every other suitor. Even the parts of her that no sane person ought to love.

For some reason she'd never fully understand, Gregory Halston loved her despite her myriad faults. She wrapped her arms around his neck and drew in the familiar scent of him.

Tomorrow's wedding seemed far away indeed.

Epilogue

London, England
September 1806

"When you grip the knife, you need to hold the blade just so. Not too tight around the hilt, but not so loosely you can't point it accurately. Then when you throw, you—"

"Darling, don't you think Laurence is a little young to take up knife throwing?"

Danielle glanced up from little Laurence, softly nursing on her lap while his tiny eyelids fluttered with coming sleep.

Her husband stood in the door of the nursery, watching her closely.

She proudly produced the toy wooden knife she'd made for their son. "There's no such thing as too young, not with a matter so serious as this. Besides, have you felt how tightly he grips your finger? Best to start teaching him now. A grip such as that will never do."

Gregory stepped into the room, all dark hair and intense eyes and strong shoulders. She sighed just looking at him.

He plucked the toy from her hand, and her sigh turned to a scowl.

"That's what you call too loose a grip."

"Not if you intend to throw it." Which she clearly should have done, straight at her husband's mouth to wipe that ridiculously arrogant smirk off his face.

He only grinned wider, as though reading her thoughts—something he'd grown rather adept at in the twenty months they'd been married. "I believe your little charge has fallen asleep."

She looked down to find Laurence still, his eyes closed in slumber, and his cheek pressed softly against her. "I'd have noticed if I wasn't so distracted."

She lifted the ten-week-old babe up to her shoulder and patted his back.

"You do know that if you ever tire of feeding him, I'll find you a nursemaid."

She nuzzled her son's downy head. "I know that's what's done in England, but I love nursing him too much to give the task to another."

"Our neighbors must think you insane for taking the burden upon yourself."

"'Tis fitting then. Our neighbors think you insane for marrying a Frenchwoman."

"Touché." He smiled faintly and reached out to stroke some hair back from her face. "You left your hair down today."

"Not all day." The staff would have been scandalized, though she'd yet to figure out what England found quite so scandalous about a woman having hair. "I let it down when I came in here."

"Because?"

She shrugged. "I like feeding Laurence with my hair down."

"I like looking at you with your hair down." His eyes turned from their usual soft blue-gray to a dark smoke color. He bent to place a kiss on her forehead, but as he did so, his frock coat fell open to reveal a rolled-up newspaper.

"You brought me news."

He straightened. "You weren't supposed to see that quite yet."

"What's happened?"

"Our navy invaded the port at Copenhagen and destroyed the Danish fleet two weeks ago."

"The British navy, you mean." She would have teased him further about precisely whose navy it was—his— and whose navy it wasn't—hers. But the somber glint to his eyes stopped her.

"Yes. The British navy."

"That's a foolish move. Now Denmark will surely fight alongside France rather than remain neutral."

He handed her the paper, and she unrolled it to reveal a headline that stated precisely such: the once-neutral Denmark had officially allied itself with France and was joining the war. Beneath the main article, smaller pieces about France's likely invasion of Prussia sometime before the year's end filled the page.

She crumpled the paper into a ball. "Is it ever going to end between our countries?"

"It doesn't seem as though things will conclude anytime soon, no."

"I want…" What? To be free to visit her parents and siblings without being called a spy? To have Laurent back, to erase the six months Julien had been imprisoned on a British man-of-war before Westerfield and Gregory had found and freed him. To have no more fighting between their countries, hear no more insults hurled at "Frogs" when she spent a day shopping.

"Don't be sad, darling." Gregory cupped her chin, drawing it up. "I might not be able to stop the war, but we have little Laurence. We have God. We'll muddle our way through the rest of it."

She sniffled back a tear and smiled tentatively at her husband. "I know." And she did. Somewhere deep inside, she knew. The world around them might clamor for one another's blood, but she and Gregory had found a way to make peace between themselves and forge a life together despite two hostile countries.

'Twas a lesson she prayed the rest of the world would learn sometime soon.

* * * * *

Dear Reader,

I'm excited to finally get Danielle's story into your hands! When I wrote the first book in this series, *Sanctuary for a Lady*, two years ago, I never thought I'd get to continue the Belanger Family Saga and share Danielle's story with you. But here it is, the third book of the Belanger Family Saga! I hope you enjoyed reading this novel and cheering for Gregory and Danielle.

One of the things I love about the French Revolution and Napoleonic Wars is France's belief in equality. In fact, that belief was the motto of the French Revolution, *Liberty, Equality, Fraternity*. As we look back at history with our own modern mind-set, we can certainly see areas where France failed to truly provide things like liberty or equality, but France had a dream of it. In the midst of monarchial Europe, the people of France understood the importance of equality and fought several wars to keep other European countries such as England from reinstating both a king and a way of life that had been terribly hard on the French commoner.

When I wrote Danielle's story, I wanted to bring to life some of the differences in ideals between the French and English, which is why notions of equality and liberty for the commoner cause so much hardship between Gregory and Danielle. Many people think the French Revolutionary and Napoleonic Wars were solely about land, but for the French people, at least, the wars were about liberty and equality. And looking back at this period of history, a part of me wishes that the French people had triumphed.

If you enjoyed my book, I would love to hear from you. You can contact me via my website at www.naomirawlings.com or write to me at PO Box 134, Ontonagon, MI, 49953. And thank you for taking time from your busy life to read Danielle's story.

Naomi Rawlings

Questions for Discussion

1. How did the countries of France and England differ in their treatment of commoners?

2. What was Danielle and her family's greatest fear if England won the war?

3. How do you feel about Napoleon's system of secret prisons and methods for dealing with possible spies? What are some fairer punishments that Napoleon might have meted out for threats against France?

4. Do you think there are ever times when it's morally right to go against a law? Give some examples.

5. What sacrifices does Danielle make to help Gregory and his friends?

6. What sacrifices does Gregory make in order to marry Danielle?

7. What types of sacrifices have you had to make in your own life? Do you think those sacrifices were worth the ultimate good you were able to do?

8. What does Danielle initially think about Gregory's British nationality? Why does she have such hard feelings toward the British?

9. What biblical principles does Danielle use to counter this prejudice?

10. What does Gregory initially think about Danielle's position as a peasant?

11. What caused Gregory to overcome his prejudice?

12. Where do you think prejudices exist in society today? What are some ways we can all work together to eradicate such prejudices?

COMING NEXT MONTH FROM
Love Inspired® Historical

Available February 3, 2015

BIG SKY HOMECOMING
Montana Marriages
by Linda Ford

Rancher Duke Caldwell is the son of her family's enemy—and everyone knows a Caldwell cannot be trusted. But when a snowstorm strands them together, Rose Bell starts to fall for the disarmingly handsome thorn in her side.

THE ENGAGEMENT BARGAIN
Prairie Courtships
by Sherri Shackelford

Caleb McCoy can't deny the entrancing Anna Bishop the protection she requires. A pretend betrothal seems like the best option to hide her identity. Until they both wonder whether it could be a permanent solution...

SHELTERED BY THE WARRIOR
by Barbara Phinney

After townspeople destroy Rowena's home, Baron Stephen de Bretonne offers a safe haven for her and her baby. Still, Rowena wonders what the baron stands to gain—and why she finds him so captivating.

A DAUGHTER'S RETURN
Boardinghouse Betrothals
by Janet Lee Barton

Benjamin Roth is immediately drawn to the newest Heaton House boarder. Rebecca Dickerson and her daughter appear to be a lovely family, but will he still think so after he discovers her secret?

LIHCNM0115

REQUEST YOUR FREE BOOKS!

2 FREE INSPIRATIONAL NOVELS
PLUS 2
FREE
MYSTERY GIFTS

Love Inspired
HISTORICAL
INSPIRATIONAL HISTORICAL ROMANCE

YES! Please send me 2 FREE Love Inspired® Historical novels and my 2 FREE mystery gifts (gifts are worth about $10). After receiving them, if I don't wish to receive any more books, I can return the shipping statement marked "cancel." If I don't cancel, I will receive 4 brand-new novels every month and be billed just $4.74 per book in the U.S. or $5.24 per book in Canada. That's a saving of at least 21% off the cover price. It's quite a bargain! Shipping and handling is just 50¢ per book in the U.S. and 75¢ per book in Canada.* I understand that accepting the 2 free books and gifts places me under no obligation to buy anything. I can always return a shipment and cancel at any time. Even if I never buy another book, the two free books and gifts are mine to keep forever.

102/302 IDN F5CN

Name	(PLEASE PRINT)	

Address		Apt. #

City	State/Prov.	Zip/Postal Code

Signature (if under 18, a parent or guardian must sign)

Mail to the Harlequin® Reader Service:
IN U.S.A.: P.O. Box 1867, Buffalo, NY 14240-1867
IN CANADA: P.O. Box 609, Fort Erie, Ontario L2A 5X3

Want to try two free books from another series?
Call 1-800-873-8635 or visit www.ReaderService.com.

* Terms and prices subject to change without notice. Prices do not include applicable taxes. Sales tax applicable in N.Y. Canadian residents will be charged applicable taxes. Offer not valid in Quebec. This offer is limited to one order per household. Not valid for current subscribers to Love Inspired Historical books. All orders subject to credit approval. Credit or debit balances in a customer's account(s) may be offset by any other outstanding balance owed by or to the customer. Please allow 4 to 6 weeks for delivery. Offer available while quantities last.

Your Privacy—The Harlequin® Reader Service is committed to protecting your privacy. Our Privacy Policy is available online at www.ReaderService.com or upon request from the Harlequin Reader Service.

We make a portion of our mailing list available to reputable third parties that offer products we believe may interest you. If you prefer that we not exchange your name with third parties, or if you wish to clarify or modify your communication preferences, please visit us at www.ReaderService.com/consumerschoice or write to us at Harlequin Reader Service Preference Service, P.O. Box 9062, Buffalo, NY 14269. Include your complete name and address.

LIH13R

"You must find it hard to do this."

"Do what?" His voice settled her wandering mind.

"Coddle me."

"Am I doing that?" Her words came out soft and sweet, from a place within her she normally saved for family. "Seems to me all I'm doing is helping a neighbor in need."

"It's nice we can now be friendly neighbors."

This was not the time to point out that friendly neighbors did not open gates and let animals out.

Duke lowered his gaze, freeing her from its silent hold. He sipped the tea. "You're right. This is just what I needed. I'm feeling better already." He indicated he wanted to put the cup and saucer on the stool at his knees. "I haven't thanked you for rescuing me. Thank you." He smiled.

She noticed his eyes looked clearer. He was feeling better. The tea had been a good idea.

"You're welcome." She could barely pull away from his gaze. Why did he have this power over her? It had to be the brightness of those blue eyes…

LIHEXP0115

What was she doing? She had to stop this. She resolved to not be trapped by his look.

Who was he? Truly? A manipulator who said the feud was over when it obviously wasn't? A hero who'd almost drowned rescuing someone weaker than him in every way?

He was a curious mixture of strength and vulnerability. Could he be both at the same time? What was she to believe?

Was he a feuding neighbor, the arrogant son of the rich rancher?

Or a kind, noble man?

She tried to dismiss the questions. What difference did it make to her? She had only come because he'd been injured and Ma had taught all the girls to never refuse to help a sick or injured person.

Apart from that, she was Rose Bell and he, Duke Caldwell. That was all she needed to know about him.

But her fierce admonitions did not stop the churning of her thoughts.

Pick up BIG SKY HOMECOMING
by Linda Ford,
available February 2015 wherever
Love Inspired® Historical books and ebooks are sold.

Love the Love Inspired book you just read?

Your opinion matters.

Review this book on your favorite book site, review site, blog or your own social media properties and share your opinion with other readers!